The Journey

By

Tracy Carol Taylor

Prince of Pages, Inc.

Arlington, VA

Chapter 1

Prince Michael came downstairs for a snack. The sweet savor of fresh baking bread and roasting meat tantalized his senses with a sensuous allure as he descended the stone stairway to the kitchen. He smiled when he heard laughing voices. A happy kitchen servant is a generous kitchen servant. However, he stopped short of the doorway when he overheard them mention the King and his sons.

"It's King Rowland I feel sorry for, having the sons that he has," came the female cockney accent. "One son is an arrogant fool, and the other is a bookish weakling. He has no strength or spirit about him at all."

Michael peeked in and saw a middle-aged woman of endomorphic proportions chopping carrots and other vegetables for the stew.

"I feel sorry for us. Even if the King chooses his son, Prince Michael, we will still live by Prince Mark's rules. He'll take the throne from his brother, and his brother will let him have it.

He'll not protect us from Prince Mark's foolish ways."

Looking around, he saw a young maiden in her early twenties mixing eggs and flour into a bowl.

"Stop wagging your tongues, you two, and get back to work."

He watched the kitchen's matron, a rather large, heavy-set woman with black, stringy hair, slap them both for gossiping about the King's sons.

"But Alice, two sons have always boded evil. Civil war or complete conquest is the only outcome of such circumstances." Schooled Elizabeth, wiping her flour-caked hands on her apron.

Alice, the kitchen's matron, shot Elizabeth a mean and harrowing look. "Now, you just watch your tongue. If anyone hears you talk treason like that, I'll be looking for a new kitchen helper, and your head will be on the battlement with the others."

Prince Michael slowly and quietly retreated from the kitchen doorway, feeling dejected and small. He slowly returned to his room, his hunger forgotten, his eyes teary, and his senses dull to the world. He opened the door to his room, and BAM, a sudden force nailed him to the floor. Michael screamed as his head hit the floor. A deep Persian rug was his only savior from a cracked skull. Fear and panic shook him as his unknown attacker sat upon his chest. His first thought was to scream for help. He opened his mouth, but a hand covered it and muffled his sound.

Then the attacker leaned down and whispered in his ear.

"Make one sound, and I'll cut your throat."

Prince Michael recognized the voice and opened his eyes. His fear turned to embarrassment and shame.

"Sam?!"

"Your reaction time is slow, young prince. If I had been a real attacker..." Sam scolded as she helped him up.

"If you had been a real attacker, I would have called for my father's guards." Michael brushed himself off and rubbed his sore head.

"You tried, remember. Besides, they're all dead; I killed them. And now... you're dead too. Now, are you ready for your lessons, Your Highness?"

Michael sighed heavily and skulked over to his bed. "No, Sam. I am in no mood for my daily trouncing."

Sam laughed, and there was a merry twinkle in her eyes as she watched him pass her. "Has your brother been picking on you again?"

"No. For once, Mark is not the cause of my unhappiness." Michael sighed as he sat on the edge of his bed with his head in his hands.

"Then what is it, your highness." Sam sat backward in a chair and faced him.

"It's me, I'm all wrong. I cannot fight or ride horses because they frighten me ..."

Oh, no. Here we go again. Sam rolled her eyes, and she let out a heavy sigh.

"I have never made love to a woman; my father's servants pity me, and my own father is ashamed of me." Sam opened her mouth to say something, but Michael continued whining his discontent. "And please, do not try to convince me that this isn't true because we both know it is. Why can't a be a real man like you?"

Finally finished with ranting, Michael lay on his bed, his back to Sam and his eyes on the setting sun.

A real man like me, huh? If you only knew, my young prince. Sam mused to herself. "Even more reason for you to practice then." Sam stood up. "Show everyone how wrong they are. Come, my father says I should teach you hand-to-hand combat today," Sam said. She stood, folded her arms, and waited for his answer.

"Not today, Sam. Good night." He said, not moving from the bed.

"But Your Highness..."

"Good night, Sam." Michael insisted firmly.

Sam gave up and bowed to the young prince. "Good night, Your Highness. Sleep well."

She left his room, closing the door behind her. His gentle sobs pricked at her heart in mournful sympathy. She walked away in silent contemplation back to her room. Entering her room, she slipped on her arrows and fell onto her chain mail, which was spread carelessly across the floor.

"Blast it! I've got to clean my room someday." She cursed, picking up a broken arrow.

She picked up her chain mail and threw it onto her bed, and then she picked up the broken arrows and placed them on her dresser. She then picked up her sword in the corner and swung it, practicing her moves. She sighed; she wasn't in the mood for swordplay either. Her mind was still on Prince Michael. A man like me, ha, if he only knew. I'm a girl.

Laying down her sword, she looked in the mirror.

She looked awful. Her practice armor was muddy and wet. Her hair looked like a cow had licked it, and her face was smudged with sweat and dirt. She had been training pages on hand-to-hand combat styles in case the castle was invaded. Like her father would ever let that happen.

Sam bolted the door to her room and then closed the window. Sam changed her clothes from her practice armor to a simple shirt and pants. She combed her short red hair, moving the part to the right side. Then, she washes her face and hands in the basin beside her bed. Again, she looked into her mirror. Much better.

With her athletic medium frame, she made a fine-looking boy at five feet nine inches. Her blue eyes, red hair, and light cinnamon-tan skin testified to her mixed heritage of African and Irish descent. Sam sighed with delight at her flawless male persona. When she looked around her room, it was little wonder. She not only looked like a boy, but she lived like a boy, too.

One of these days, I've really got to clean my room. She sighed as she pondered all the work before her that it would take to clean her room. Hang it, I'll do it tomorrow.

She climbed out of her window and onto the roof.

The sun had almost disappeared for the day. Orange and magenta splashed the horizon, leaving just enough light to see a ghostly moon begin its rise into the evening sky. She could see most of the kingdom from her post on the roof. She could see the pages' quarters, the Knight's Lodge, and the practice court where her father drilled the soldiers. Beyond all this were the fields, the road, and the mountains. Sam breathed deeply in the evening air, enjoying the hint of evergreen. A shout of disgust and words of instruction turned Sam's attention back to the practice court.

Tonight, her father was training Prince Mark. Sam sneered at the thought of him. She didn't like him. He was conceited, arrogant, egotistical, and rude.

However, Prince Mark was the best rider and fighter in this kingdom besides her. At that thought, she had to smile because she had helped to train him. True, he was a pain in the neck, with his pompous attitude and arrogant nature, but you could teach him any physical activity in less than a week. Unfortunately, that was all he was interested in learning. He had no patience for book learning.

Prince Michael, on the other hand, was just the opposite. He was all book learning and no brawn. He wasn't brave or bold, but kind and gentle. His room was immaculately clean and full of books. Books of literature, history, science, medicine, languages, and law lined his shelves. He also had a sword and shield, which lay neatly in a corner and were never used. Since Michael wouldn't fight, he spent all his time with his teachers. He spoke four different languages fluently. He also had a complete command of math, science, and history. But he was afraid of horses, and he had no interest in learning to fight.

Sam understood how he felt, though. Michael had no interest in fighting, like she had no interest in learning to cook, sew, and raise children, like the other women. Sam chuckled to herself. If people knew she was a girl, heads would roll, especially hers. The family tradition of the first-born son becoming the King's Captain of the guards was eighteen generations old. But it wasn't her fault that her mother had died of the flu or that she was a girl instead of a boy. Sam's father made a boy of her to uphold the family tradition. He even planned for her to take a two-year journey to have a child and remain Captain of the King's guards without anyone finding out who she truly was. In fact, her father had her whole life planned.

Sam shrugged. Oh, well. What would I be anyway?

The wind blew over her shoulders and through her hair. It was a lovely warm breeze on this summer's night. Sam took a deep breath and let it out slowly. She may have to live like a boy, but life was good. Sam looked up and saw a night sky riddled with stars, like a celestial roadway into eternity. She took another deep breath, the smell of dinner tantalizing her senses. She leaned over the edge to see how Prince Mark was doing against her father when, off in the distance, her eye caught the faint shadow of a figure sneaking away from the castle.

She took a slight running start and jumped from the castle roof. She landed, safe and sound, in the stack of hay. Rolling out of the hay, she tracked down the stranger. Carefully stalking the shadowy figure, from bush to bush, until he stopped to get his bearings. That's when Sam pounced.

"Gotcha! Now, who are you and what...?" Sam demanded, and she pinned the stranger to the ground.

"Sam, please get off me," said Michael in a hushed voice.

"I'm sorry, your highness. I thought you were a prowler. What are you doing sneaking around out here?"

"I wasn't sneaking." He corrected her as he lay pinned beneath her. He couldn't push her off him, no matter how hard he tried.

"Young prince, had you walked confidently across the courtyard, I may have thought you were a page or a soldier on his way to see a lady. But you..."

"O.K. I get your point." He groaned as he lay there defeated. "Now, will you please get off me?"

"So where are you off to?" Sam stood and helped him up.

"How do you know I'm not off to meet with some young lady?" He asked, and he brushed the dirt from his cloak.

"No offense, Your Highness, but that would be like Prince Mark sneaking off to read a book." Sam chuckled.

Michael smiled, and then he laughed at the analogy. "O.K. then. I'm running away until I become the man my father wants me to be. I can't learn whatever I must learn here, or else I would have. So, the answer must be out there somewhere."

Sam couldn't argue with that. An adventure might get some life in his bones. Practically everything was done for him here at the palace, but if he got out on his own for a while.

"Alright, when do we leave?"

"We? No way. I have to do this alone."

"Right, I just supposed to look the other way while the King's youngest son leaves this kingdom to journey the world on his own, looking for his manhood. Not to mention the fact that my father would kill me and then your father would have my head for dinner."

"Alright, you can be my personal guard." He relented as he rolled his eyes at Sam's exaggeration.

"Actually, I am your personal guard." Sam crowed proudly.

"Your father has commanded that your safety is my sole responsibility."

"Your father must be very proud of you. You're my personal guard; you've won the knight's game four years in a row and are destined to replace your father as Captain of my father's Royal Guards."

"Yes, I am pretty amazing, good-looking, intelligent, strong..." boasted Sam in feigned vanity.

"I wish I were like you," stated Michael, chuckling at Sam's mock arrogance. "You have no idea what it is like being a constant source of discouragement to your father."

"Yes, I do. I'm not the son my father wanted." Sam's eyes twinkled with mischief.

"How can you say that when you are the best runner, fighter, and archer in the kingdom? How can he not be proud of you?" questioned Michael as he waved his hands excitedly in Sam's direction.

"Oh, I didn't say he wasn't proud of me. I said... that I'm not the son that he wanted. Your highness, can you keep a secret? My father will kill me if he ever finds out that I've told anyone, and if anyone else should ever find out..."

"Sam, I swear, on my honor and my father's kingdom, that your secret is safe with me." Prince Michael promised as he wondered what secret Sam held that could be so great.

"I'm not the son my father wanted because ... I'm... a girl," confessed Sam.

"Say that again." Prince Michael's shoulders dropped, and his eyes widened in stark disbelief.

"I'm a girl. My mother died of the flu when I was barely three years old. My father wanted a son to teach his trade and become the Captain of the guards as he did, as his grandfather did, and as his great-grandfather did. So, he called me Sam and dressed me as a boy," explained Sam as she looked around, ensuring no one else had heard.

"You are a girl!" Michael broke out laughing. "I do not believe you. You are lying."

"A little louder, if you please, I don't think the kitchen

maids heard you," scolded Sam, now fearing that she shouldn't have told him at all. She continued to motion for him to keep his voice down. "And no, I'm not. It's the truth."

"I'm sorry, Sam." He still laughed but lowered his tone. "But if the other guards knew that they had been trained by and beaten in the knight's game by a woman, they'd go insane. Oh, and Mark, the man of all men, was trained by a woman. Ha ha ha."

"Well, I'm glad to see you in such good spirits. You'll need to be if you're going out there," Sam said, pointing to the castle gates.

"Oh," Prince Michael suddenly remembered his plan to run away. "So where do we start?"

"The Swinton School, it's where all young men go to become soldiers. I've known lots of guys who have gone there, boys, and come back men." Sam told him.

This made sense to Michael. Boys who graduated from the Swinton School were strong, confident, and proud of who they were. They were everything that he wanted to be. Sam suggested they take only water and enough money to get to the next town. There, they would buy horses and food enough for their trip. Minutes later, two figures slip out of the courtyard and into the night.

Chapter 2

At daybreak, Sam and Michael sat down to rest. The sun was just rising over the hills, as if looking for people to greet. Gentle winds were blowing eastward, urging them along. The aroma of honeysuckle and pine tickled their noses. Sam lay in the grass and watched birds fly overhead.

"Your highness, outside the palace walls, it is unsafe for us if I keep calling you, your highness." Sam sat up to speak to him.

"Then call me Michael." He told her as he rested his back against a tree.

"Young prince, please, I wouldn't dare," scoffed Sam. She was shocked that he would even suggest that to her.

"Alright, then choose a name for me."

"Cody," Sam said without hesitation.

"Cody?" He questioned, wondering where that name had come from.

"It was my great-grandfather's name," Sam told him honestly. "Besides, you look like a Cody anyway."

"Cody. Cody." Michael tested out his new name.

"Now we've got to get out of these clothes." Sam stood up and looked around. "We're overdressed for the countryside. Peasants do travel somewhat safer than lords."

"From where shall we acquire these clothes?" asked Michael, thinking she must be mad.

"Over there. See that wash line." Sam pointed to a country hut.

"We are going to steal their clothes?!"

"No. Trade." Sam corrected him and walked over to the line. Sam chose a red shirt and a pair of trousers.

"So where do we change?" Michael asked, holding up a pair of trousers in front of him.

"Right here," Sam said, and she removed her shirt, with her back to Michael.

"Sam! Please. It's... It's." Michael quickly turned around and gave Sam his back, but his face was red, and his cheeks were flushed.

"It's the only place to change." She said matter-of-factly. Sam finished slipping into her new pants and turned towards Michael, still holding his change of clothes over his arm. "Come on, Your Highness... uh, Cody. I'll turn my back. But please change quickly before the owners come to check on their clothesline."

The thought of the owners returning for their clothes helped Michael to change more quickly. As he changed, though Sam had promised to turn her back, he still felt flushed with embarrassment. After which, Sam and Michael resumed their journey. They traveled all day, sometimes in silence and sometimes to a lively tune Sam sang. But by mid-afternoon, they were both hot and tired, broiled by the noonday sun until their clothes clung to them with sweat.

Michael was tired, and his feet dragged like he was pulling them in chains. He wasn't used to this much exercise. Sam stopped late in the afternoon to give Michael a rest. They had made good progress and should be in the next town by nightfall. Sam and Michael sat and rested in the shade of the trees. Sam lay in the grass and hummed, watching the late afternoon clouds drift by. Michael sat beside her and drank deeply from the water sacks.

"Are you ready?" Sam asked as she wiped the sweat from her face with her sleeve.

Michael nodded. So, they continued, walking in silence and wishing for rain. Just after nightfall, they came to a town. They walked into the first tavern they saw and fell into chairs, glad to rest their weary feet. Sam looked around the room. Seeing miners and farmers enjoying their evening meal and drink, she relaxed her guard. Michael rubbed his legs, trying to ease away the pain and numbness. Sam's palette was watering at the smell of roasted pig and mutton stew. A young and very amply bosomed barmaid came to see what they wanted. Although Sam was ordering, the barmaid only had eyes for Michael. After taking their order and giving them each a mug of ale, the barmaid left and returned to the kitchen. On the way, a drunken farmer grabbed her by the wrist.

"Let go of me, Sir!" She shouted.

"Oh, no, my dear. I think we should be good friends, you and I." He told her, and he pulled her closer to him.

"No, let go!" She screamed, and she struggled to free herself from him.

Michael's conscience would no longer tolerate this misdeed, and he stood up. Sam tried to stop him, but her grasp just missed his arm.

"Gentlemen, if you would be so kind as to stop molesting the young lady," warned Michael, standing before them.

The farmer and his friend looked at Michael and laughed. "What the hell did he say?" The farmer asked his friend, a miner.

The miner laughed, shrugged, and said. "I think he said to leave her alone."

"Yes, that was the message I was trying to convey.

Now, please release her." Michael demanded.

The farmer stood to face Michael as the miner held the young maid in his lap. The farmer was a big man with muscles of iron, a stern face, and dull brown hair. Before him, Michael stood a scrawny young man, tall but not a muscle to his frame. His clothes hung on him like someone was trying to dress a man of straw. A strong and confident middle-aged man faced an uncertain and afraid young boy.

"What are you going to do 'bout it if I don't?" asked the farmer sternly.

"Well... Uh..." Michael stuttered. His mind was stunned with confusion. He honestly never thought that this would turn into a fight.

The farmer pushed Michael, testing his tolerance, and slowly backing him up. Michael's mind was racing, and his heart was beating faster. The farmer pushed him hard before Michael could answer him and sent him stumbling backward into a chair and onto the floor. The farmer, the miner, and half the tavern laughed at him. Sam just shook her head, got up, and went to his side.

"This is not the way to impress a young girl." Sam helped him to stand up.

"Ow," Michael complained as he stood holding his aching side. "Well, I'd like to see you try."

"By your command." Sam grinned with a knowing smile.

Sam turned and faced the farmer. He gave a great grin; here was another challenger for the champion. However, this young man had the look of a fighter. He stood strong, sure, and unafraid; his bright red hair symbolized his spirit.

"I'd like to see you do that again." Sam challenged him.

"Little man, I'll squash you like a bug," avowed the farmer.

But Sam didn't wait for him to come to her. She went to him, punched him in his right eye, and delivered a left jab to his chin. Then, before he could shake it off, she kicked him in his left knee. The farmer doubled over in pain and surprise. Then, with her right, Sam gave him an uppercut that sent him to the floor. The miner released the barmaid and charged at Sam's back.

"Sam, look out!" shouted Michael.

Michael threw himself at the miner and pushed him away from Sam. The miner fell backward onto a table. Angrily, he got up and faced Michael. Michael stood his ground, put up his fists, and stared at the miner.

"Don't come any closer or I'll be forced to teach you a lesson." Michael squeaked.

The miner was heavyset. But one would be mistaken to call him fat and lazy. He had massive bulging arms, a large chest, and no sense of humor. He only grunted and swung his huge fists at Michael. Michael ducked under two of his punches but was caught by the third and was sent head-first into a table. While Michael's back was to him, the miner took Michael in his arms and began squeezing him in a bear hug. Sam sat on a table and, between swigs of ale, watched as Michael's face began to turn red. It's like watching a butterfly battle a bull. Then she noticed the miner's back was directly in front of the fireplace.

"Back up, Cody. Use your legs to push him backwards," instructed Sam. She waited to see if Michael could handle this challenge.

Though she had trained him in hand-to-hand combat, Michael had no strength to fight an opponent of that size. Michael pushed with all his might, backing the miner up. The miner backed up right into the hearth, where the meat and stew were cooking. Suddenly feeling the fire's intense heat, the miner howled in pain and released Michael. Before the miner could attack again, Michael grabbed a mug and hit the miner across the face with it. The miner looked hard at Michael, severely annoyed but otherwise unaffected by the blow. The miner took Michael's hand and forced the cup right into Michael's face. Michael fell to the floor, dizzy and in pain. The miner was about to hit Michael again when Sam stepped in.

"Tsk, Tsk, Tsk, pick on someone your own size." She ordered.

The miner looked her over. "You'll do." He growled with a smile. The miner swung at Sam and missed. "Hold still, will ya."

Sam knew better than to fight such a massive man head-on. So, she continued to dodge his blows until he was too tired to fight anymore. Then Sam took her chance when the miner stood still to catch his breath. She hit him across the face with a right and then again with a left. Blow after blow, she drove the miner backward and up against the bar.

However, with nowhere else to go, he blocked Sam's next blow and hit her with a solid left to the stomach. Sam fell to her knees and gasped for air. The miner grabbed her by her shoulders and gave her a head butt. Sam clutched her head in pain and tried to shake off its effects. Above her, the miner stood laughing. Sam's adrenaline and anger boiled over. She grabbed the closest chair and, with all her strength, bashed him into the wall with it. The miner dropped to the floor unconscious, followed by what was left of the chair. Then Sam walked over to Michael, who was still sitting on the floor.

"Well, not bad for your first try. I give you points for using the mug." Sam jested, and she helped him off the floor.

"Yeah, right. You look like you were having fun, though." He sneered as they returned to their table.

"Oh, that. That was fun." Sam smiled at him, and she watched him sit down. "You should watch me and my dad sometimes."

"Uh, yeah, so what prevented you from stepping in and helping me sooner?" scolded Michael as he rubbed his sore chin and lip.

"What would you have learned?"

After the fight was over, the young barmaid rushed to Michael's side. "Are you alright, young sir?" she asked him, trying to examine his wounds.

"Yes, miss. I'm fine." Michael politely refused her advances as he pushed her hands away from him.

"Thank you for your assistance, sir." She smiled.

"You're welcome." He blushed.

Sam just chuckled at Michael's innocence and asked for a room. The barmaid escorted them upstairs and gave them the last room on the right. Once inside, Sam locked the door and put a chair in front of it. Then she checked the room; it was small, with one bed, a table, chairs, a window, and a door. Michael lay sprawled on the bed. He smiled as every aching muscle in his body relaxed in comfort. The bed was good; lumpy, but good. Sam pulled up another chair and sat down opposite Michael.

"Alright, Cody, two things. One, your vocabulary has got to go. Your speech is too educated for a peasant. Just say what you mean without the elocution. Two, you're going to have to learn to move faster. You don't have the muscle it takes to fight head-on."

"Sam, I do not wish to go into this again. Is it not enough that I'm alive after my first real fight?" groaned Michael as his adrenaline waned.

"Cody, that was nothing compared to what's waiting for you at the Swinton School," Sam informed him. She was a little disgusted with him for thinking things were so easy.

"Sam, I don't think ..."

"O.K., then we'll go home," Sam announced, standing up.

"I do not want to go home. Not until I can prove to my father that I am as good as Mark." Michael was upset that Sam would end his journey before it began.

"Then get some sleep. We will buy horses tomorrow, and provided the weather stays good, we should reach Toad Lake before the end of the week." Sam took a pillow and a blanket and made her bed on the floor.

"Sam, horses don't like me." Michael yawned and stretched.

"Nonsense, you just let them push you around." She chuckled. "Sooner or later, you'll just have to learn to take command and give orders."

"Why are you sleeping on the floor when this bed is more than big enough for both of us?" He asked, looking down at her.

"Cody, you know I can't do that. Training the king's son to fight is one thing. Sleeping with the king's son is quite another," said Sam from the floor.

"Sam, I'm ordering you to come to bed with me." Michael ordered in a 'kingly' tone.

"Nice try, Cody." Sam chuckled. "Save it for the horses."

Michael gave up. *Some king I am going to make. My own guardsman won't even take orders from me.* Sighing heavily, he rolled over and went to sleep.

Chapter 3

"Where is my son Michael?!" The King roared with anger and great concern.

The castle was in terrible turmoil as guardsmen searched high and low for the King's son. Doors were opened, rooms were searched, the stables and the barns were checked, and the servants were questioned. But it had been two days since anyone had seen young Prince Michael.

"Your majesty, we have searched the entire castle, from the dungeon to the towers. Prince Michael isn't here and hasn't been seen since yesterday afternoon," reported one of the guardsmen.

"Find Thomas and bring him here!" The King ordered furiously.

"Yes, your majesty." One of the servants hurried away.

The King was worried about his son. It was not like him to disappear; maybe he was sick. Maybe Prince Mark had locked him in the hen house again with the rest of the chickens. The King remembered how frightened his son had been. It took weeks before he could sleep without candles and lanterns lighting up his room.

Michael had never been a strong boy or very social.

He always stayed by himself, and he studied constantly. He had hoped that by making Sam his personal guard, their friendship would bring him out of it and make him more social. He didn't see Michael as strong enough to be King. Then there was Mark, but making Mark king would be like allowing a hyena to watch over sheep. True, Mark was strong and confident and a good fighter, but there was more to being a good king besides being a good fighter. That's why he had chosen Michael to be King, and now he was nowhere to be found.

"Where is Thomas?" The King wondered.

Prince Mark entered the throne room, cocky and in a playful mood.

"Mark, have you seen your brother today?" The King inquired as he shifted on his throne.

"No, Father, I haven't. Have you tried looking in the pastures with the other sheep?" Prince Mark laughed. He stopped at the map table and sat on its edge.

"Did you lock him in the pantry again?" questioned the

King with an accusing tone.

"No Father. Honest, I haven't seen him all day." Prince Mark stated in his defense.

Suddenly, Thomas Bowman, Captain of the Royal Guards, entered the throne room. He was still dressed in his practice armor. He bowed to the King and his son.

"Thomas, have you seen my son Michael?" inquired the King.

"No, sire. I have not. Come to think of it, I haven't seen my son Sam either. They may be down by the lake, in the gardens. They often go there to talk and play chess." Thomas reminded the King.

"Unfortunately, not this time. My guards have already searched the gardens and report no sign of them. Find my son, Thomas," ordered the King.

"Yes, your majesty." Thomas acknowledged with a bow.

A feeling of dread filled Thomas' heart and mind as he thought about the missing prince and his daughter. This was not like Sam, not like her at all. Thomas went to his daughter's room, wondering where she could be. He opened the door and was shocked by what he saw. The room was clean. For once, all her weapons and clothes were put away. Her bed was made, and her books were on the shelf.

I don't believe it. Thomas thought in stunned silence. She's gone.

He looked around her room and found a note addressed to him on her table.

"Father, Prince Michael, and I have gone to the Swinton School to make a man out of him. Don't worry; I'll guard him with my life.

Your son,

Sam."

"I'm going to kill her," Thomas growled. He crumbled the note and threw it against the wall.

Sam and the prince had left the castle grounds. Thomas looked at his daughter's weapons rack. Her sword and two daggers were gone. He sighed. He knew his daughter could take care of herself; after all, he had raised her to do so. But the young prince. Thomas prayed that Sam could protect them both. Thomas closed the door to his daughter's room and prepared himself to tell the King that his son had run away.

Chapter 4

In the morning, Sam and Michael ate breakfast. Then, they left the Inn to buy horses at the stables. As they made their way over to the stables, the pungent stench of horse manure became overwhelming. Michael put his hand over his nose.

"Is anybody here?" Sam called out. She looked around the stables and searched for a stable hand.

"What do you want, child?" answered a large woman's voice. "Can't you see we are cleaning the stables today?"

"No kidding," squeaked Michael, still holding his nose.

"We'd like to buy two strong horses," reported Sam.

"Ere, Bart, go see what they want." The woman ordered.

A strapping young man with unkempt, shiny black hair and green eyes emerged from the stables. He had strong shoulders, a broad chest, and a tight stomach. Sam stared. Michael noticed Sam's lustful look and kicked her foot.

"Ow." Sam hissed, staring at Michael.

"What kind of horses do you need?" Bart asked as he came to stand before them.

"Traveling horses, strong and experienced," answered Sam. She snapped out of her lustful daydreams and got down to business.

"Well, come see what we have." Bart invited them with a smile and opened the gate for them.

Bart led them past the stables and out to the fields. Nice, plush grass replaced the muddy red dirt of the town street. A robust wooden fence corralled eight beautiful horses of various ages and even three new colts. Bart showed them the two best horses that they owned.

"This is Demonseed and Devilyn, our two finest horses." He said as he stroked Devilyn's nose.

Sam looked at Michael. He looked pale, like he was about to faint. "How about something less... massive," Sam suggested.

"Well, there's George and Lefty. They are six years old. But they are well-traveled."

Sam looked them over. When she was satisfied with their physical abilities, she paid him. Sam walked their horses out of town, and Michael followed. She stopped in a nearby field and tied her horse to a tree. Michael chewed his fingernails, and his heart began to race as he anticipated what was next.

"O.K., Cody, time to learn to ride," Sam stated, and she held the reins out to him.

"Can't I just ride behind you?" asked Michael, cringing like a frightened child.

"No. You wanted to learn to be a man, so have a little backbone." Sam chided as she put the horse's reins into Michael's hands.

"Sam, I can't do this." Michael shook his head with dread.

"Yes, you can, Cody. Now come here." Sam ordered firmly. "Come here!"

"Good horse. Steady boy. Now what?" Michael patted George's nose.

"First of all, stop shaking," Sam said with a slight grin. "Animals can smell fear. Now, get on the horse."

Sam showed him how to mount and dismount a horse and how to hold the reins. Michael did alright getting on, but staying on was something different. The horse reared, and Michael fell to the ground with a THUD.

"Damn," Michael complained and brushed off his hurting backside.

Sam sighed. How could someone destined to be a king be so hopeless? "Try again, Cody. You must show him who his master is."

Michael took a deep breath, remounted, and kicked the horse into a trot.

"Good." Sam congratulated him. "Now go a little faster."

Michael gave the horse another kick. The horse slowly sped up and then took off in a dead run across the open field.

"Whoa! Not so fast!" Michael shouted, clutching at the horse's mane.

The horse wasn't listening, and off it ran across the grassy fields, through a wooded meadow, and on. Michael's hands clutched the horse's neck in white-knuckle fear as he struggled to remain in the saddle. He cried out for Sam's help as branches and bushes beat him while the horse raced on.

"Sam! SAM!"

Sam untied her horse, mounted it quickly, and galloped after Michael. Michael's horse was taking him for a great ride. George raced across the countryside, through a brook of fresh water, over a hedge of bushes, and then jumped over a fallen tree, with a very terrified Michael clutching its mane and screaming for help.

"Where the hell does this horse think it's going?" Sam questioned as she raced after them.

Sam continued to race after George and Michael. Soon, she was gaining on them. She rode her horse parallel to Michael's until she was close enough to grab the reins. Sam pulled both horses to a stop. Once certain the horse was at a complete stop, Michael fell off the horse. He tried to stand but was still too shaken to have any strength in his legs. Sam watched in sympathy as she saw how much his body was shaking. Michael noticed her staring at him in pity.

"I do not care what you think! I am not getting back on that horse again! I'll walk to the Swinton School first!" He shouted.

Sam sighed and shook her head. "I'm sorry, your highness. It was my fault." Sam apologized. "I should have held the reins."

He's sixteen years old and still afraid of horses. This is going to be a very long trip. Sam took George's reins and tied them to her horse. Sam then rode south, and Michael followed her on foot. When Michael was tired, they rested. The trip took longer than riding, but they finally reached Toad Lake. Sam tied up the horses and made camp.

Michael sat on a log and watched. He watched her cut down four young trees, pound them into the ground like stakes, and tie a blanket over them to make a roof. Michael watched her track, kill, and skin two rabbits for their dinner. As he watched her, his mind questioned what he saw and what he had always known about women.

The more he thought about it, the more he thought about Sam. Maybe she was descended from Amazons. His studies had told him of a mythical warrior tribe of women in Ancient Greece. Michael knew Sam's father, a white, red-headed Englishman, but he had never met her mother. Sam's mother must have been from the Middle East, or maybe even Africa, for Sam's skin to be a light cinnamon brown. Michael fell asleep that night dreaming of the strong warrior women of Ancient Greece with Sam as their leader.

In the morning, he awoke to the smell of freshly cooked fish. He ate while Sam groomed the horses. He stared at Sam as she seemed to be talking to George. He swallowed the lump in his throat as Sam walked over to him.

"Time to try again, Cody." She told him.

Michael stood up and faced Sam. "I'm not getting back on that horse. And you can't make me."

"Look, you're not walking all the way to the Swinton School. And I'd like to get there sometime before the 1600s. Besides, you'll either learn now or you'll learn with fifty other boys watching and laughing at your mistakes. The choice is yours," scolded Sam. She folded her arms and gave him a stern look.

"What choice?" frowned Michael as he walked over to the horses. He placed a hand on George's head and spoke to him. "Ready to try again, George? This time, I lead."

The horse just whinnied at him. Michael groaned and swore under his breath that this horse was laughing at him.

"Just get on," Sam demanded impatiently.

Again, she put Michael and George through their paces, from trotting to galloping. Sam drilled him over and over until Michael was comfortable with the horse.

"No. No. No. Do it again."

"Sam, I can't," Michael complained yet again.

"Yes, you can." She encouraged, but even she was growing tired of Michael's incompetence.

Again, the horse reared and threw Michael off.

"Damn," Michael swore as he hit the ground again.

"Get back on."

"No, Sam. My posterior is killing me. Can't we stop?"

"We'll stop when you can keep your aching ass in that saddle," said Sam sternly.

"Sam, how can you treat me like this? I thought that you

were supposed to obey me," argued Michael. He wiped off the seat of his pants and retook George's reins.

"Sire, I must obey you in all things and would gladly do so. But when it comes to your training, you must obey me." Sam educated. Then she chuckled at him. "Do you give your other teachers such a hard time?"

"I like my other teachers." He retorted with a smirk.

Sam laughed and then ordered him to get back on the horse. Sam had tied George's reins to a rope and held this rope to keep George under control. But this time, Sam let the rope go limp so that Michael would get used to giving the commands with the reins and not rely on her. However, she still held the rope. Just in case the horse decided to make another run for it.

Day after day, ten hours a day, for the next four days, Sam taught Michael good horsemanship. Michael was getting better. He was no longer afraid of horses, but he still didn't like them. And the feeling was mutual; George still refused to believe Michael was his master. The horse reared, trying to throw Michael off.

"Whoa, George! Sam!" called Michael, pulling back on George's reins.

Michael hit the ground with a loud thud. Sam tried to get George under control, but it was no use. George ran. Sam let go of the reins, but the rope wound around her ankles. With a yank, Sam fell to the ground and was dragged away.

"Damn!!" cursed Sam. She tried to loosen the rope.

"Sam!" screamed Michael, as he stood dumbfounded and watched as Sam was dragged out of sight. His heart was racing, and his mind went blank. Then Lefty whinnied. Michael looked at Lefty, and Lefty looked at him. "Oh, boy." Michael feared. Michael grabbed Lefty's reins, mounted Lefty, and galloped after Sam. What the hell am I doing?

Being dragged by a horse was undoubtedly a new experience for Sam. It was like having your back scratched by a bear. However, the sharp rocks and logs made it truly unbearable. Sam cursed as her back, neck, and ears were abraded by the ground. Suddenly, George jumped over a log. Sam felt a great stab of pain as her head hit the ground. Slowly, the light of day faded into grey. Sam's head swam in pain and then went black.

Michael drove Lefty until he caught up to George and rode parallel to him, as Sam had done. Careful not to trample Sam, he grabbed George's reins. Then he pulled back as hard as he could, forcing George to stop. Michael jumped down and tied George to a tree. Then he went to see about Sam. Sam was unconscious, but she was still breathing. Her shirt was torn, and her back was bleeding. Michael untangled her legs and rolled her onto her stomach. He took out his water bag and poured its contents over Sam's back, washing the wounds clean. Once cleaned of the twigs and stones clinging to her hair and clothes, Michael lifted her onto Lefty's back and tied her hands to his neck so she wouldn't fall off. He tied George's reins to Lefty's saddle, mounted behind Sam, and rode for the nearest town.

Michael rode into the town of Abay, asked for the local healer, and took Sam there. Megan, the town's healer, was about forty years old and lived in a hut at the end of town. Michael burst into her cabin and began begging for her help. Megan, slightly annoyed at his lack of manners, followed Michael outside to where he had tied the horses. Megan looked at Sam's back.

"What happened?" She asked as she assessed the damage.

"He was... He was...He was..." stuttered Michael.

"Well, spit it out!" She hollered.

"Dragged by a horse." He finally revealed.

Megan felt for a pulse. "You're lucky he's not dead. But he's not getting any better out here. Bring him inside." Then Megan looked at Michael and doubted his scrawny frame. "On second thought, I'll get him, you get the door," Megan ordered. Megan cut Sam loose.

Megan carried Sam inside and over to the bed. She took off Sam's shirt to get a better look at Sam's wounds and then told Michael to leave.

"But I can't," complained Michael. "What about Sam? I can't leave him here."

"There is nothing you can do, and you'll only be in my way. Go on. I will take good care of him and send for you when he is well." Megan assured him as she pushed him out of the door and slammed it in his face.

Depressed, Michael wandered over to the tavern to wait. He fell into a seat at an empty table, and a twelve-year-old boy asked what he wanted to drink.

"Water." Michael sighed heavily, deeply worried about Sam's condition. When he looked up again, the boy looked at him rather strangely. "The healer said I can't have any more strong drink for a while. Do you think I would honestly order water if I could have a beer?"

The boy accepted this excuse and went to get his water. The truth was that strong drinks made Michael sick. He never could figure out why people drank such stuff. As Michael sat there with his head in his hands, another man entered the tavern. He had well-combed black hair, stood medium height, and only had one arm. He scanned the tavern and spied an empty seat next to Michael. Michael swallowed hard as the man sat down.

"Beer!" He bellowed.

"Yes, sir," answered a young voice.

The man stared at Michael. Michael tried to look confident and unafraid.

"May I enquire what you are looking at, sir?" Michael asked defiantly.

"My my, what a big vocabulary for such a little sapling. What's your name?" asked the one-armed stranger.

"Mi... Cody."

"Hello Cody, I'm Daniel. Nice to meet you, " he said with a smile. What are you drinking, and may I join you?" Before Michael could answer, the tavern boy brought over his water. "Water? Water is for children and horses. Bring this young man a beer, my treat."

"But I can't..." Michael began to explain.

"Megan said for him not to drink anymore, for a while," interrupted the boy.

"Megan is here. Great." Then Daniel leaned and whispered to Michael. "Don't worry about her; I'll take care of everything for you." Daniel winked. Michael opened his mouth to protest, but again, he was interrupted. "So, tell me, Cody, why are you here?"

"My friend and I had a riding accident. Megan is seeing to her...his wounds." Michael told him, and then saw his missing arm. "What happened to your arm?"

"My wife tore it off when she caught me with another woman." He said, looking serious. Then Daniel broke out laughing when he saw Michael's jaw drop. "No, seriously, I lost my arm in the war a few years back. It took me a long time to adjust, but I managed. I only drink half as much as I used to, now."

"You're a soldier?" questioned Michael in awe. As the king's son, he would command soldiers one day, but he had never actually talked to them before.

"Yes."

"Then you've been to the Swinton School, right?" pressed

Michael.

"Of course," answered Daniel. "Is that where you and your friend are going?"

"Yes." Michael was a little excited now.

"You're going to love it there. You'll learn everything a man should know. How to ride and fight, how to gamble and pick up women..." chuckled Daniel, remembering his days at the Swinton School.

"I thought the Swinton School was a military training school?" puzzled Michael, concerned that his information was wrong.

"It is, but there is more to life than just fighting. When you get there, look up a young lady by the name of Dorothy. She runs the ... night school." Daniel grinned slyly and gave Michael a wink.

The tavern boy brought two large mugs of beer. Daniel took one beer, greatly appreciative of something to drink. Michael followed suit.

"Come, drink with me. A toast to the Swinton School and to life's adventures," crowed Daniel.

"To the Swinton School." Michael echoed.

Michael lifted his glass, tilted his elbow, and drank it

down. Michael was surprised. It was good, soft, smooth, and cold, just what he needed on this hot day after that ride that he had. He had barely drained his glass when the feeling of nausea overtook him. Michael held his breath and fought to keep himself from throwing up. Then he thought about how the other boys would tease him if he couldn't drink what they did at Swinton, and he doubted they served water or milk with dinner.

Besides, he didn't want Daniel to think he was a 'sapling' who got sick after only one beer. So, he swallowed his nausea and his caution and ordered another drink.

After only one more drink, he began feeling warm, and his ears buzzed. Soon, Michael was so loaded that he couldn't sit up to drink. He fell out of his chair and onto the floor.

"Not used to drinking, are you, sapling. You've only had two."

"I'm... alright. I'm not a kidddlin. I can sssssssstand up on my own." Michael tried to stand up, but that made him very dizzy, so he sat back down. "Barkeep... I'll have...another." He hiccupped.

"No, you won't. A man knows when he's had enough. Come, we'll see Megan. She'll clear your head." Daniel picked

Michael up and helped him walk.

"Oh. Nagem...." muttered Michael. "She has a friend of mine there. A house dragged him ...for miles."

"A house, huh?" chuckled Daniel.

Daniel noticed that Michael didn't look well at all.

No one should be that shade of green. So, he carried him over his good shoulder to Megan's.

"Megan! Megan open up!" shouted Daniel, aggressively kicking at the door. "I have a sick sapling for you to mend."

The door opened.

"Quiet, I have a child recovering in here. Dragged by a horse, he was." Megan said. Then she saw Daniel, and a smile spread across her face. "Long time no see, Danny. How are you?" Then, she also saw who Daniel was carrying, and her smile turned into a frown. "Oh, not him again."

"You know him?" Daniel asked, and he laid him down on a bed.

"He brought him here. Oh, he smells awful. What have you been pouring down his gullet?" She asked as she checked Michael's eyes.

"Beer, same as always. It's my fault the little sapling is ill, so I'll pay his bill." Daniel handed her three coins.

"Thank you, that's mighty good of you." She said, smiling at his generosity. "Will you be in town long?"

"I'm sorry, Megan, I'm in town only for three days."

"Is that all? Hmm, in that case, maybe you would like to stay for breakfast?" She asked with a sly grin.

"What about your patients?" He asked, his smirking grin matching hers.

"They'll both sleep for a long while; just lock the door so they don't wander off."

Daniel locked the door. Then Megan took him by the hand and drew him towards her bedroom. Moments later, moans of passion and a shriek of pleasure woke Sam. Her head throbbed like cannonballs were being fired at the front of her skull from inside. But her shoulders and back hurt even worse as she tried to sit up. Another scream and voices drew her attention towards a closed door. Sam smiled.

Well, well, the doctor is out.

Sam tried sitting completely up. A loud bang against the wall caused her to groan and hold her head in her hands. She wished that they would stop banging that bed against the wall. Sam looked around and wondered where she was. Megan's home was divided into two sections. This room had many herbs lining the shelves, blankets stacked neatly on a trunk, and another bed in the far corner. The back section was obviously her sleeping quarters. Looking across the room at the other bed, Sam noticed Michael's body lying still on the bed.

Oh no, I've been out, and he's been beaten up. Sam thought, feeling guilty. If anything happens to him, I'm a dead man. She tiptoed over to his side, favoring her head with each step. To her amazement, he smelled foul of beer. She wondered what had happened to him. Maybe he felt guilty about the accident.

"Cody, Cody," whispered Sam.

"Ohhh, Sam. Stop shouting, please." Michael pleaded, and he rolled away from Sam.

Sam laughed. He's drunk. If only his father could see him now. "I'm sorry, Cody. Go back to sleep." Sam covered him up. Then she returned to her bed and drifted off to sleep.

In the morning, the sun beaming into her eyes woke her up. She yawned and tried to block the sun from her face. Hearing voices and the opening of a door, Sam turned over and feigned sleep.

"Goodbye, Danny. It was good to see you again," said

Megan happily. "Do come back the next time you come to town."

"Definitely." Daniel smiled and kissed her goodbye.

Sam watched as Megan checked on Cody, and then she closed her eyes as Megan turned her attention towards her wounds. Megan examined Sam's shoulders and her back. Sam decided to wake up. She slapped Megan's hands away from her shoulders.

"Ow." Sam protested, pretending to be angry.

"So, you are awake. You don't fool me," said Megan. She stood up and went over to her herb table. "You are a very strong young girl and lucky too. Luckily, that horse didn't break your neck. So, what do you think of Daniel?" She asked as she mixed a few herbs in a bowl and ground them into powder.

Sam smiled with a very mischievous grin. Megan laughed. Sam got up and stretched.

"Ow!" She complained, her neck and shoulders still in pain.

"I assume you dress like a boy to keep from being abused by men. Your business is yours, so I won't tell your secret. But tell me, why did you leave home?" Megan asked and handed Sam a new shirt.

Sam made up a great story about love, betrayal, and being

chased by a shamed Baron when she ran away with Cody. Megan sat and listened, then shook her head and rolled her eyes.

"Child, I haven't heard such tall tales since Sir. John Washington told us of his great feats in battle last year. Now, what about the truth?" said Megan wistfully.

"The truth is ... we did run away from home," confessed Sam.

"Why?" pressed Megan as she shook out Sam's blanket.

"Because he wanted to find his manhood, have an adventure, and have a few stories that were bigger than the other boys," Sam revealed.

"And you?" asked Megan.

"Me, I was bored," said Sam, hoping Megan bought this story.

"And are you helping him find his manhood?" Megan asked with great mirth.

"Oh No! Not me," objected Sam. "I'm just along for the adventure."

"Well, you and your friend are free to leave whenever he wakes up." She told her.

"How much do we owe you?" Sam reached into her pocket

for money.

"Your bill has been paid in full and with interest." Megan smiled in spite of herself.

"Thank you, and if you see him again...uh, Daniel. Tell him, thanks." Sam crossed the room over to Michael's bed. Sam took up a guarding position beside Michael's bed.

"You are much older than he is." Megan judged. "How old are you?"

"Twenty-one and four years his senior," said Sam. "We grew up together, though."

"And you look after him, don't you?" reasoned Megan.

"Mother made me promise." Sam lied.

Sleep overtook Sam while she waited for Michael to awaken. A tap on her shoulder woke her up. Sam suddenly remembered where they were and jumped to her feet.

"Cody! Are you alright?" questioned Sam, relieved to see him.

"Some watchdog you are." Michael teased, and he looked upon Sam with a whimsical smile.

"This coming from a drunk," countered Sam. "You never drink at home, why start now?"

"I do not know. Fear, I suppose." Michael answered

sheepishly.

"Fear?" quipped Sam.

"Fear of being called a child if I could drink more than water or milk at the Swinton School. Did you see Daniel, the man with one arm? He's a soldier and he attended the Swinton School. We talked for a long time," explained Michael.

"You drank a long time." Sam chuckled.

Michael and Sam stopped for lunch at the tavern, loaded up the horses, and headed east. About two hours later, two men on horseback rode into town. They inquired at the bar about two young boys, one with bright red hair. No one had seen them. Then, the two men came to Daniel.

"Aye, I saw a boy with bright red hair. He and his friend were at Megan's Place. The one had back injuries from a riding accident, and the other passed out from too much drinking." Daniel told them with a chuckle.

"Where is Megan's Place?" Asked one rider.

"Just at the end of town, on the left," answered Daniel.

The two riders arrived at Megan's and introduced themselves.

"I am Alex, and this is Jacob. We are looking for two young boys who are runaways. One has bright red hair. Have you seen them?" Alex inquired.

"Are they in trouble?" Megan asked as she remembered her promise to Sam.

"Not really, it's just that their fathers would like to have known that they were leaving. They have sent us to seek them out and bring them home," said Jacob.

"Their mothers are distraught," Alex added, hoping that she would choose to aid them.

He was lying, of course, but he knew that women tend to sympathize with other women, especially when worried about their children.

"The two young boys rode off towards the northeast." Megan smiled with a crocodile grin.

The two men thanked Megan for her help, mounted their horses, and rode away.

Chapter 5

"What's the matter, Sam? You haven't said a word since we left Megan's place. Is your back still hurting?" Michael asked curiously as he rode Lefty.

"No." Sam sighed. "I was just thinking."

Riding with the wind at their backs, a gust of wind playfully caused Sam's hair to stand up on her head. Michael laughed as he rode beside her.

"What's so funny?" She asked, raising an eyebrow at his good humor.

"It's your hair. When it stands up like that, you look like a carrot."

Sam shook her head and then ran her fingers through her hair to straighten it back out. "I should have dyed it black. I stick out," commented Sam. She was a bit miffed that she didn't think of it sooner.

"Wait until you develop a chest. Then you'll really stick out." He laughed.

"Cody, you're becoming wild one. Riding, drinking, and

now this; before you know it, you'll be making passes at women." Sam commented in a condescending tone.

"About women, Sam...I was wondering...." Michael maneuvered his horse to face hers.

"Oh, not on your life! All this fresh air and freedom have made you excited. However, if you wish to test your physical prowess, let's see if your fighting skills have improved. We haven't practiced since we left the palace." Sam dismounted her horse.

Michael dismounted also and drew his sword. The clanging of cold steel is the only sound that disturbs the quiet meadow. Sam had been right about Michael, though. Without the pressure or atmosphere of the palace, Michael fought much better. He fought with a playful determination against Sam. But Sam was in no mood to play. Her job was to ensure the king's son could defend himself against any attack. So, she pressed him harder. Suddenly, Michael's mood changed, and he lowered his sword.

"What's the matter, your highness? You were doing so well." Sam voiced her disappointment, and she also lowered her sword.

"Sam, you still don't understand. I'll fight if I have to, but only as a last resort. I'm not like my brother, who goes looking for fights. I'm not like you, who can at any time enjoy showing off their skill. I just don't find any good use for fighting." Michael explained. His lanky form was a testament to his inexperience with a sword.

"That didn't stop you from trying to rescue that girl in the tavern. Alright, if not for offense, what about defense? I'm not going to fight all your fights between here and school. And what happens when you get to school? They'll expect the same out of you as I do. But they won't let you quit just because you don't feel like it." Sam scolded him.

"I can take care of myself," yelled Michael, feeling the heat of Sam's indignation.

"Prove it." Sam swung her sword at Michael.

Michael blocked the blow, but he didn't swing at her. "Nice try, Sam."

He lowered his sword and surrendered to her. Their fight was interrupted by the sound of approaching horsemen. Sam stared at the approaching riders. They were identical twins. Both men were handsome mesomorphic specimens with broad chests, strong arms, soft brown sugar hair, and blue eyes. Sam had always had a secret crush on Alex. He was smart and strong, everything Michael could be if only he weren't so ... passive.

"Your majesty. Sam." Alex greeted them none too warmly. "We are under orders to take you back to the castle."

"No, not yet!" whined Michael, and he sheathed his sword. "Not until I have completed my quest."

Alex and Jacob looked at one another. Whatever the young prince was talking about, it was not their concern.

"We have been given special permission by the king to use any means necessary to bring you home, your highness." Jacob trotted his horse toward Michael.

"Please, Your Highness. If your father's enemies knew that you were outside the palace walls. Your life would be in great danger." Alex warned them. His worried brow expressed his concern for Michael's life.

"That's why I brought Sam," said Michael, standing his ground.

"Sam." Alex turned his attention towards her. "Is your father ever furious with you?"

Alex and Jacob dismount their horses. Michael moved to stand behind Sam.

"You will return to the castle immediately, Your

Highness?" Jacob demanded as he walked purposefully towards Michael.

"I will not," challenged Michael from behind Sam.

Sam raised her sword, ready to fight. Jacob drew his sword and confronted Sam. Sam struck first, but Jacob blocked the blow and went after Sam in full force. The time had come for Jacob to show his teacher what he had learned.

"Tsk, Tsk, Tsk, you're getting slow, Jacob," taunted Sam.

"Sam, this is ludicrous," growled Jacob. He blocked her blow and countered it with one of his own. "Return to the castle at once!"

"Make me." Sam smiled. She was eager to fight.

Alex and Michael stood watching as Sam and Jacob fought. Both realize that whoever wins this fight will determine whether Michael will go home. As Sam and Jacob's confrontation continued, the sun went down, and the coming darkness made it hard to see. The only witnesses to this discord were the crickets, owls, and other night denizens.

Soon, Michael began to grow impatient. Although he had complete confidence in Sam's ability to beat Jacob, he was tired of watching a match that seemed to be going nowhere. So, Michael, unnoticed by Alex, silently slipped away toward the horses. He cut the horses' reins from the tree, jumped on his horse's back, and raced towards Sam.

"Sam!" He yelled.

Sam turned, believing Michael was in trouble. That's when Jacob's sword caught her in the side and knocked her to the ground.

"Damn it!"

Sam cursed herself for allowing herself to be distracted as she looked at her bleeding side. Sam rolled to her feet and attacked Jacob with such vehemence that he lost his sword and fell to the ground.

"Keep practicing." She said, holding her sword to his throat.

Then she turned and ran for Michael. Alex tried to block their escape, but Sam kicked him in the stomach, causing him to fall to his knees. Sam's left hook sent Alex to the ground beside his brother. Sam jumped into her saddle as Michael rode past, taking off into the night with the moon as their only light.

However, neither Alex nor Jacob was willing to return to the king in defeat. Growling in discontentment as they mounted their horses, they perused them. Sam and Michael rode into the forest, hoping the trees would impede Alex and

Jacob. Michael rode ahead, and Sam looked back.

Damn, I'm good. I've trained them well. Thought Sam with a wicked grin. "Hey Cody, they're following us!"

"Well then, do something, guardsman." He commanded her.

"By your command. Keep the moon on your left, and I'll catch up to you."

Sam dropped back, stood on the horse's back, and jumped into an overhanging branch as her horse rode underneath. There, she waited until Jacob had gone past, and then she jumped into the saddle behind Alex. Pulling a dagger out of her boot, Sam cut his reins and knocked him off his horse. Holding on to the horse's mane, she then rode after Jacob. Paralleling him, she forced his horse into a tree. Jacob fell off when his horse reared to avoid hitting the tree. She winked at Jacob and then rode to catch up to Michael.

The clouds grew darker as Sam and Michael trotted on, and the wind picked up. Soon, the clouds blocked all light of the moon and the stars. Off in the distance, the heavy rumble of thunder echoed in their ears. The wind blew as if running from the storm they were now riding into. Sam blinked as a raindrop hit her eyes.

"Aw, no. Not now." Sam groaned and pulled her collar up.

"Shouldn't we stop?" Michael pulled his shoulders in closer to his body.

"Why, there's no shelter out here. Besides, the town of Lauren shouldn't be that far away." Sam dismounted her horse.

In awe of her talents, Michael watched as she climbed a tree and looked off in the distance. Somewhere to the southeast, there were lights—a lot of lights. Sam climbed down.

"There is a town off to the south, not far from here," reported Sam, wincing, as she remounted her horse.

"You're bleeding," Michael told her, and he wiped his face as the rain began to fall lightly.

"It's just a scratch," Sam assured him. She did not want him to be worried. "It looks worse than it is."

"Well then, how far is not far?" Michael asked, shivering against the cold wind.

"About two and a half miles."

"But it's going to rain." He complained, pulling his coat closer around him.

"You're right." Sam urged her horse into a steady gallop. "So, let's go."

By the time Sam and Michael reached town, their clothes clung to their bodies, drenched from saturation. They were soaked to the skin and shivering to their bones. Michael had fallen asleep in his saddle, so Sam held both reins. However, she was also starting to fall asleep. Sam rode to an inn and secured a room. Leaving Michael there, she put the horses in the stable and bought new clothes. She returned to the inn and found Michael asleep on the bed, sneezing and shivering with cold.

"Cody, take your clothes off and put these on," Sam commanded.

Without thought or hesitation, Michael did as he was told. Sam covered him with two dry, warm blankets, and then she also changed her clothes. She wrung out their clothes and left them on a chair to dry. Then she looked at her wound, which stung with pain every time she turned her body. It had stopped bleeding, but she wrapped it anyway. Sitting down on the floor, she went to sleep.

A loud clap of thunder woke her up. Weary and half-asleep, she checked on Michael. He was still shivering with cold. His skin was clammy, and he was still freezing. She had to make this room warmer. She ambled downstairs and got a large basin of water. Once back in the room, she put a three-legged stool in the basin and set it on fire. She opened the window to let the smoke out, and then she moved Michael to the floor near the fire; the emanating heat dispelled the cold and provided them a cocoon of warmth to sleep comfortably.

The sensation of falling awakened Sam with a jolt.

She stretched and noticed that the fire had gone out. So, Sam set another chair on fire. Then she went to check on Michael. He was warm and sleeping well. Sam observed him as he slept. She couldn't help thinking of Michael as a child. He seemed so much like a young babe without a father to show him how. Young Prince Michael was gentle, innocent, and tender. It was a wonder how Prince Mark and Prince Michael, who had the same parents, could be so different.

Maybe it was because, for as long as she could remember, Prince Mark got all the attention. He was always assertive, boastful, and pushy, making you give him what he wanted. On the other hand, Prince Michael would ask politely for the things he wanted and wouldn't challenge you when it wasn't given to him. In fact, young Michael had always needed a protector, especially from his brother, who was constantly picking on him. Sam turned and warmed her hands by the fire as her memories played out before her eyes.

**

"Sam! Sam! Help!" called little Michael, running from his brother.

Prince Mark had been chasing his brother with mud pies most of the afternoon. Prince Michael ran, trying to find Sam. Out of everyone at the palace, only Sam would stand up to Prince Mark. Prince Michael hid behind Sam, cowering in fear. Sam stood firm against Prince Mark and glared at him disapprovingly.

"Prince Mark, please stop torturing your little brother," ordered Sam. "Now stop it or else."

"Or else what? You can't touch me." Prince Mark challenged her. "You've been forbidden to do so. And what will you do to me if I don't?"

"Take one step more and I'll show you." Sam smiled, full of confidence.

Prince Mark liked challenging Sam's authority as much as he enjoyed teasing his brother. Smiling and gleeful, he stepped forward. Swoosh, like a rabbit in a snare, he was hauled away from the ground and left hanging suspended in the air.

"Help! Sam, you let me down, now!" shouted Prince Mark.

"You see, young prince, strong, but easily fooled." Sam laughed at him. "I'd like to let you down, your highness, but it's time for Prince Michael's lessons. I'll be back…in an hour or so."

Prince Michael skipped happily off to his lessons as Sam followed, leaving Prince Mark yelling at their backs.

"Sam! You let me down right now! Sam Bowman! I'm telling my father, the king, and he'll have you beheaded. Sam!" yelled Prince Mark angrily.

Unofficially, Sam had always been Michael's protector. Sam was at Michael's side whenever she wasn't helping her father train guardsmen. No matter the season, Michael found solace in walking around the castle gardens. He enjoyed reading and playing chess near the lake. It was here, at the lake, that Michael confided in Sam all his fears and dreams. Here, he had taught her to play chess and speak French. It was here that they had become friends.

**

Shaking her head clear of the memories, Sam wondered what her father was doing right now. Images of her father ranting and raving about the foolishness of her actions and the dangerous position in which she has put the king's son filled her head, and dread filled her soul.

"Oh, my father's going to kill me."

"No, he won't. I won't let him. This trip was my idea, remember." Michael sat up on his elbows.

"I thought you were asleep," sighed Sam as she stretched.

"Who can sleep with all this noise?" Michael commented, indicating the storm outside.

"You're not afraid, are you?" Sam yawned.

"I'm not a coward," Michael stated firmly as he completely sat up to face Sam. "I just don't like horses."

"That doesn't matter now, does it? You ride well enough. You should try to rest. We have a long ride when the weather clears up."

"I'm not tired anymore. Sam, isn't it rather dangerous to build a fire in here?"

"I had to keep us warm and to keep you from catching pneumonia." Sam looked over at the burning stool. "I won't ever be able to go home if I kill the king's son."

Michael looked at Sam by the fire's light. Her hair was getting long, and she looked like a sheepdog. He reached out to Sam, moving her hair out of her eyes, and their eyes met. Sam moved to get up but winced in pain.

"Arrrgh." She groaned and clutched her side.

Michael went to her side. He reached out to look at Sam's side, but she pushed him away.

"Please, Sam, let me see it. It wouldn't hurt so much if it were just a scratch." Michael cautioned her.

Sam was reluctant. However, she undid the last three buttons of her shirt and allowed Michael to see her bandaged side. Michael unwrapped her soggy bandage and gently pushed parts of her side, watching her reaction. Then he announced that two of her ribs were bruised but not broken. Michael took his dry shirt and cut his sleeves into a bandage using Sam's dagger. Then he wrapped her wound. Sam stared unflinchingly at the far wall as Michael put his arms around her to dress her wound.

"That should keep out infection." He announced, tossing her bloody bandages in the fire. "But I'll change the bandage in the morning."

"Thanks. Did you learn how to do this in your books?" She asked, re-buttoning her shirt.

"Yes. The study of medicine is an offshoot of biology.

You know, I don't think I've ever seen you this bashful before." He said, sitting next to her and staring into the fire.

"Most likely because the last boy to put his arms around me

was trying to pin me in combat practice," chuckled Sam.

"Has any man ever held you, without trying to kill you, I mean?" Michael inquired as he looked at her.

Sam felt a strangely warm sensation, and she was sure it wasn't because of the fire in the middle of the room.

"No. Would you like some breakfast?" Sam offered, changing the subject as she stood up.

Michael's stomach growled in strong agreement. "Yes."

As Sam closed the door behind them, the wind invaded through the window with such force that it knocked the burning chair and basin of water over and onto the floor. Sam had almost finished her second plate of pancakes, eggs, and sausage when she saw smoke coming from their room.

"Holy...! Cody, look!" Sam shouted, pointing to their room.

Michael lifted his eyes in surprise. Upon seeing the smoke, he and Sam raced up the stairs. She opened the door, and their eyes were filled with smoke. Rushing in, Sam took the blankets off the bed and started beating at the flames. The smoke troubled Sam's breathing, and her eyes watered in sympathy. The intense heat kept her at the outer edges of the blaze and induced her to sweat. Realizing Sam's efforts were in vain,

Michael ran downstairs to get more water. The fire was extinguished with the help of the innkeeper and two barmaids.

When Sam offered to pay for the damages, the innkeeper grabbed them by the collars and hauled them before the town arbiter. He charged them with the destruction of property and begged for the maximum sentence. The arbiter sentenced them with the task of rebuilding the room, painting the inn, and adding new rooms to the inn. Sam protested against so much work for destroying only one room and told him about their need to be at the Swinton School before September. But the arbiter would not hear them, and he took their weapons until their time was done.

"And don't get any ideas about leaving town or not doing the work. My guards will be watching you. And they have orders to kill if you do not comply with my wishes," warned the arbiter.

Thus sentenced, Sam and Michael cleaned, rebuilt, and painted their fire-damaged room for the next three weeks. When they had finished and the weather had cleared, the innkeeper gave them large buckets of paint for the entire inn. Sam was tired and hot from the noonday sun as they painted the inn's walls. Her hands were sweating, but her mouth was dry. Their guards gave her a questioning look whenever she came down to quench her thirst. To Sam, they looked as if they wanted her to try to escape, if naught but to spice up their boring lives. Michael, on the other hand, didn't seem to mind. He even sang as he painted.

"This is stupid." Sam sighed, and she walked back towards Michael.

"Aw, it's not that bad. Free room and board, no Mark picking on me, no sword practice, no servants asking you what you need. Just you, me, this inn, and a bucket of paint," expressed Michael joyfully.

"I'm so glad you're having a good time," Sam growled at Michael's good mood.

"Oh, Sam. Temper, Temper."

"I'm sorry, Cody. It's my fault that we're here, isn't it?"

"But Sam, is this not why we left home, to experience life?" Michael reminded her. His hands rose and fell as he painted the inn.

"If you say so, I just came along to watch," said Sam, once again taking up her paintbrush.

In two months, they had finished painting the inn. Lauren's inn stood out in the day, a brilliant white with bright blue trimmed windows. It looked so good that it drew more customers. More customers meant that the innkeeper needed more rooms. He then set Sam and Michael to work building his ten new rooms. Sam growled as she stretched. They had been working for almost three months straight now, six days a week, from sunup to sundown, with only breaks for lunch, except for Sundays. They spent Sundays locked in the cellar so they couldn't escape.

Sam wiped her face with her sleeves and rested while Michael continued to hammer nails into the wooden frame of the wall. Without thinking, Sam sat down on a plank that was holding paint. The plank flipped over, and she fell.

"Whoa!" She exclaimed in surprise.

Michael turned to see if Sam was O.K. He watched as the paint bucket sailed into the air.

"I'll get it." He said, chasing it down.

However, he only got the paint. Later, the bucket came down and landed right on his head. Sam stared wide-eyed and smiled, trying to suppress the urge to laugh. She couldn't do it and burst out laughing as Michael threw down the bucket and wiped the paint off his face.

"I am so sorry, Cody. Are you O.K.?" Sam asked, trying to

be serious and compassionate.

"Yeah, blue is my favorite color." He wiped the paint off his arms. "What's yours?"

"I like red." She said, still laughing.

"Of course, I should have known. O.K., red it is, to match your hair." He picked up a bucket of red paint.

Sam stopped laughing when she saw him pick up a bucket of paint. She turned and ran but tripped over an ax she had left carelessly on the ground. Michael dumped red paint all over her. Now it was Michael's turn to laugh at her as she wiped red paint off her arms. Sam growled playfully at Michael. She jumped up and chased him all over the yard. She finally succeeded in tackling him to the ground. Then she sat on his chest, pinned his arms beneath her, and started tickling him.

"Sam! Stop it! Get off me! Sam!" Screaming with glee, Michael was unable to control his fits of laughter.

The innkeeper came outside to see what all the noise was about. "What in the blazes is this?! You don't have enough to do, then I'll give you more!" He yelled at them. "Clean up this mess and prepare to serve dinner. You two are my new serving boys!"

It was now the beginning of October. The air grew cooler,

and the leaves displayed an array of colors, from red to orange to yellow. Five new rooms stood erect. Michael watched as Sam stood cutting planks for the walls of the five rooms yet to be finished.

"Not like that." He instructed. "Like this, it supports the wood and prevents you from cutting yourself."

Sam wiped the sweat from her face as she stood watching his example. "How can you know so much about something you've never done?"

"Sam, I'll have you know, I used to study architecture. And when the builders came to build the castles' new rooms, I watched, learned, and practiced." Michael informed her.

"You practiced," asked Sam skeptically.

"Yes, I practiced. I built my own bookshelf. I admit it is not as well-crafted as a woodsman may have made, but it works...and I built it," crowed Michael proudly.

"So, what other hidden talents do you possess?" Sam sat down on the ground and rested a spell.

"I can cook, sort of. I made those pastry tarts I gave you last year. I can play a mandolin. I can work with metal. I made a very small dagger once. But it wasn't very good. I think Dad uses it to hold down his papers." Michael revealed.

"Why didn't you say something before?" asked Sam, somewhat stunned by all of Michael's 'secret' accomplishments.

"Who would believe me? We have servants to provide music, servants who cook, and we hire builders. Why would anyone let me do these things for myself simply because I wish to try them? That's one reason why I ran away."

"Why have you never told anybody you wish to do these things? Why should they let you do anything? You are the son of a king; you should be telling them what you are going to do. Your brother does. Don't let others decide your life, or your advisors will rule your kingdom," educated Sam.

"What about you, Sam?" Michael questioned, and he sat down next to her.

"What about me?" She asked, unsure of what he was asking her.

"What do you want to do?"

"To replace my father as captain of the king's guards," recited Sam.

"No, I mean... if your father hadn't made a boy of you... or...do you like being ..." Michael was a bit unsure of how to ask her such a personal question.

"Are you asking me if I like how my life has turned out?

Yeah, I do. But if you're asking me if I have other interests, I like music. My mother played the violin and a shepherd's flute. She always said she'd teach me to play, but... I wish I had known my mother better. But she died when I was only three."

Sam leaned her head back and sniffed the air.

Something sure smelled delicious. As Sam savored the smell of the chicken, the cold wind reminded her that winter was coming. She nudged Michael, and they both returned to work. Day after day went by. The days grew shorter, and the nights became longer. Sam and Michael have finished six of the ten new rooms. As the moon had risen two hours ago, the innkeeper came to get them.

"Quitting time, boys."

The innkeeper fed them and locked them in the cellar, as he did every night. Sam and Michael collapsed onto their beds of straw and drifted into the land of dreams.

Chapter 6

Alex and Jacob were not in agreeable moods. Sam had beaten up Jacob and made him feel like a fool. And then they lost them in the woods. Since then, they had been caught in two major downpours. Alex's horse had lost a shoe, and they were both angry about the money they wasted on inns looking for Sam and Michael. They had even ridden all the way to the Swinton School and waited two months for them to show up. But they never did, and nobody among the new arrivals at the school had seen them.

Finally, they sent word back to the king about what had happened, how they had lost them, and how they had just disappeared. The king told them to return and that he would send messengers to all the towns between the castle and Swinton School to inquire about them. So, Alex and Jacob were heading back to the palace when they passed through Lauren. They stopped at Lauren's inn and asked for rooms, food, and information about two runaways. The rooms and food were gladly given to them by the innkeeper. However,

Alex is sure the innkeeper is lying about Sam and Michael, especially when he mentions Sam's red hair.

"Maybe they went to Tambrook." The innkeeper suggested. He did not want to lose his slaves just yet.

Alex and Jacob spent the night in their room, devising a plan. If they appeared to leave town and then observed the innkeeper, Alex was sure he would lead them right to Sam and Michael. After Alex and Jacob went to bed, the innkeeper went down to the cellar and woke his slaves with a kick.

"Ow. What was that for?" Sam complained, and she rubbed her sore side.

Michael yawned and stretched. "Is it morning yet?"

"What are you wanted for?" The innkeeper asked sternly.

"Wanted, I don't want anything," yawned Sam, downright miffed at being awake from a very nice dream.

"We ran away from home," enlightened Michael, sticking to Sam's original story.

"Then why are there two soldiers upstairs looking for you?" The innkeeper questioned them gruffly.

"Are they twins?" Sam surmised that Alex and Jacob must still be looking for them.

"Yes," said the innkeeper.

"Wow, I thought they'd go home by now." Sam stood up.

"Do you honestly think they would return home to my father without us?" Michael remarked, and he looked for his shoes.

"Relax," said the innkeeper, pushing her into a chair. "I've told them that you went to Tambrook. Besides, you still have work to do on my inn. So now tell me, who are they?"

"Alex and Jacob, they are ... are... bounty hunters.

We kinda left our hometown in a hurry," said Sam, hoping he would swallow the story.

"So, you are thieves. I thought so. That story about the Swinton School was a lie. Just look at you, they wouldn't take you anyway." The innkeeper reasoned as he looked at Sam. With that, the innkeeper again locked the cellar door.

"You know, Cody, I really hate him," growled Sam.

The following day, Sam and Michael went back to work. Unfortunately, they had to dig all their tools out of the snow. Last night, the snow fell, leaving the town in a blanket of white. It was a frigid day today, and Sam blew on her hands to keep them warm. She watched Michael as he bent over to dig the saws out of the snow. Sam noticed that his buttocks had molded into a tight muscle and that his legs were no longer skinny sticks attached to his feet. As he stood up, she saw that the width of his back had broadened, and his arms displayed growing biceps. His face had become fuller and was developing a jawline. His soft brown eyes and jet-black hair gave him the look of a suave young man.

It would seem that common work agrees with him. *"Congratulations, Sire, you are no longer a scrawny little runt."* Sam thought playfully.

Michael was still no ox, like his brother, but he wasn't the child she had left home with, at least not physically. Sam called to Michael, and a snowball stung her in the face. Michael laughed at her as she wiped the snow from her wet face. With a wicked grin, Sam retaliated with two snowballs of her own. Michael and Sam laughed in childlike delight as they pelted each other with snowballs.

"Aw, you throw like a girl," laughed Michael.

"Oh, funny." Sam threw a snowball into the tree above Michael's head.

"Ha! You missed." He taunted.

"Think so." Sam grinned in victory.

Sam threw another snowball into the tree, and a huge

snowdrift landed on Michael. Sam laughed as Michael climbed out of the snow.

"Hey!" Michael laughed, gathering more snow for another snowball. "I'll get you for that one."

"You and what guardsmen?" Sam playfully ducked for cover behind a tree. When things got too quiet, Sam ventured a look. "Cody?"

"Over here, Sam." He called, jumping out from behind another tree.

Sam turned, and a snowball hit her square in the face. Sam charged at Michael, pushing him to the ground. Snow seeped into and soaked their clothes as they rolled around in the snow. Sam found it more challenging to pin Michael than it used to be. In fact, it surprised her that she was the one lying flat on her back beneath him. But Sam was not about to start losing to him now. Pushing hard against him and rolling over, she had just pinned him to the ground when someone jerked her off Michael's chest. It was the innkeeper.

"At it again, are you? You're playing games instead of working?

Well, you're in luck. No work outside for you today. In fact, I have a surprise for you." He told them as he dragged them by their ears back inside the inn.

"You know I'm getting tired of being yanked around," complained Sam.

A blackbird joined two figures upon the roof of the adjacent Candle Shop; all three watched the scene down below with great interest.

"I told you that lying innkeeper would lead us to them." Alex grinned. His hunches were always correct.

"Are you sure that's them? That doesn't look like Prince Michael." Jacob was amazed at the change in Michael.

"Of course, who could mistake Sam's red hair? I'd know him anywhere."

Back inside the inn, the innkeeper gave Sam and Michael their surprise.

"Alright, boys, you can open your eyes."

Sam and Michael opened their eyes to two new shirts and pants on the table.

"New clothes? Why?" Sam asked sternly. She still didn't trust or like this innkeeper at all.

"Because I have a lot of noblemen coming and I'm

shorthanded. Besides, ugly-looking servants are bad for business." The innkeeper laughed at them. "You will take orders and clean tables. Got it?"

"Yeah." They responded, none too happily.

Sam and Michael went back to the cellar to change clothes. In the time that they had been there, Sam's hair had grown long and thick. Michael watched Sam's movements as she changed clothes. She was shapely, muscular, and lean. If she wasn't an Amazon, he didn't know what was. When he found himself gawking, he spoke.

"Doesn't it bother you to undress in front of me?"

"Not really. I've been around boys all my life. You're kinda like brothers to me. Sometimes, I even used to watch the other boys take baths." Sam admitted, nonchalantly, her back to him.

"You didn't watch me, did you?" Michael was slightly concerned with her perverted behavior.

"Of course not, you were the king's son. Besides, you were always too bashful to undress near windows." Sam slipped into her new pants and buttoned them.

"Did you ever undress in front of the others?" asked Michael, wondering if anyone else had seen as much of Sam as he had.

"Hell no." Sam chuckled. "Then they'd know I was a girl."

"Yet you undress in front of me."

"But you already know I'm a girl. Besides, if it bothers you so much, turn around," instructed Sam as she put on her new shirt. "There was a time when your eyes would be on the wall, not me."

"I guess I've grown used to your company." He smiled, and he thought about their time together.

"Speaking of growing, how old are you now?" asked Sam, sitting down to put on her boots.

"I'll be seventeen in March," Michael answered, and he removed his shirt.

"Seventeen, huh, then I'd say your hormones have overridden your modesty."

"How old are you?" He asked as he changed his pants, too.

"Twenty-one."

"Really? Then how come...your...chest hasn't fully developed?" He blushed.

Sam laughed heartily, and she looked up at him. "Wow, blunt, aren't we? I was blessed to be less developed. An underdeveloped woman is easier to hide."

"I cannot believe that in twenty-one years, nobody has ever

discovered your secret," commented Michael, now pulling his shirt over his head.

"That's because I kill whoever finds out. A secret between me and a dead man is a well-kept secret." Sam joked in mock seriousness.

"Sam?!" exclaimed Michael. He was afraid that she was telling the truth.

"Well, my father trained me well. So well, in fact, I stopped thinking of myself as a girl. However, that all changed when I turned fourteen. Now, my father gives me a week's vacation every month. As for my physical features, all my clothes are one size too big."

"And none of the other knights you helped train in wrestling, ever..." Michael hopped on one foot as he slipped into his new boots.

"I don't let them get that close to me. That's one reason why I'm the best. My secret actually pushes me to be a better fighter." Sam walked over to the mirror.

Her shirt was a perfect fit, which was a problem because her chest showed. Michael smiled. He liked the way Sam's clothes fit.

"You look good."

"Yeah, too good." Sam frowned, and she worried. "I'll trade you shirts."

Both of them took off their shirts and exchanged them. Now, Sam's shirt was loose, and Michael's was tight.

"That's better." Sam again looked into the mirror. "I'm hidden, but you're showing off muscle."

Next, it was time for a haircut. Sam took up a pair of scissors and started cutting her locks.

"Allow me." Michael offered, taking the scissors from her.

"Don't tell me. You used to watch the barbers and practice on the cat." Sam jested as she sat still for him.

Michael shook his head in mirth and began cutting her hair. When finished, he wet his hands with white wine and styled Sam's hair. Sam was impressed; it looked like she had just come from a bath. They switched places, and Sam cut Michael's hair, also wetting it with white wine.

"You are quite a handsome young man," smiled Sam as she looked at his reflection.

"Thanks, so are you."

They both laughed.

"Boys!" The innkeeper yelled from above.

"Come on ...before he has a fit," sighed Sam heavily.

The very important people that the innkeeper was expecting were from the palace. They had been sent to assist Alex and Jacob in their search. After the king had received word that their last sighting was in that area, he sent out his knights dressed as nobles, lords, and serfs to find them. When Alex and Jacob learned of their arrival, they informed them about the innkeeper. That he had Sam and Michael as servants in his establishment. Alex and Jacob didn't join them for dinner, as the innkeeper had already seen them. They waited atop the roof of the Candle shop.

"Alright, boys, about your business, mind your manners, and keep your hands out of their pockets, or I'll cut your hands off." Warned the innkeeper. His eyes were dead serious.

"If you cut our hands off, how will we finish the inn?" Sam quipped with a smug grin.

Michael laughed. The innkeeper didn't, and he slapped both of them. "None of your smart mouth. Now off you go!" He ordered as he left to see about the bar.

Sam raised her fists, ready to strike back, when Michael grabbed her wrist. "Let it go, Sam."

Sam let her arm drop. This was the first time Michael had

ever prevented her actions by taking any actions of his own. A voice calling for a waiter broke her train of thought. She and Michael went about cleaning tables and taking orders.

"Boy." called a nobleman.

"Aye sir." Michael answered, trying to sound like a peasant.

"Have you ... Well, Prince Michael." greeted a palace guardsman.

"I think you have mistaken me for someone else." The surprise in Michael's eyes betrayed him.

"Not with that vocabulary, sire." said the other.

Michael smiled and then took off running towards Sam. The two guardsmen followed him. He ran and hid behind the bar. Sam stood up, hitting both men simultaneously with a boom.

"Sam. This inn is crawling with the king's men." informed Michael.

"I know. Why do you think I'm hiding behind the bar?" She said, cautiously looking around the room.

"So, what do we do?" He asked, in a panic.

"We start a fight."

"You're kidding." Michael frowned and hoped that she was kidding.

"Best diversion is the world." She smiled brightly at the thought of a good fight.

Giving him no warning, she pushed him into the innkeeper, who was holding meat and drinks on his tray. Michael fell, causing the innkeeper to lose his tray of drinks. The drinks landed in the lap of a young Army sergeant. Michael apologized, but the soldier didn't want an apology. He wanted Michael. He chased Michael around the room.

Seeing the young prince in danger, several knights stood up to rescue him, forcing the sergeant to stop. However, the sergeant's buddies were unwilling to let this intrusion go unanswered, and they rose to defend him. The army sergeant, now free, resumed chasing Michael. Michael pushed past all of them, heading straight for Sam, and stood behind her. Sam stepped forward and hit the soldier with such a right hook that he fell backward, knocking a miner face-first into his meal.

"Excuse you." The angry miner wiped his face free of food.

"Stay out of this, groundhog." The soldier yelled at him. Then he knocked the miner's beer into his lap.

That did it. Sam just laughed and shook her head. Males were so egotistical that starting a fight was as easy as crushing nuts with rocks. Soon, the fight grew so large that the innkeeper went to get the arbiter and his men to break it up. In the meantime, Sam and Michael took the opportunity to get away.

"Quite a party, huh?" laughed Sam.

While the arbiter was at the inn trying to break up the fights, Sam broke into the arbiter's office and retrieved their weapons.

"A physician's bag, we could use this." Michael surmised, taking the bag off the shelf.

She and Michael left the arbiter's office and headed for the stables, but an old friend blocked their way.

"It's good to see you again, Sam. Your majesty, I must insist that you return to the castle with me, " the voice said.

It was James, one of the last knights she had helped train.

"Well, Jamie, your first real mission. You must be excited," teased Sam.

James was about to say something when Sam punched James in the stomach, knocking the wind out of him, and then brought her knee up to meet his face, knocking him to the ground.

"I'm sorry, James. But the young prince doesn't want to go home yet," said Sam, standing above him.

"Sam, come on," Michael called out to her.

With the arbiter at the inn, getting their swords back was easy. But getting their horses away from Alex and Jacob wasn't.

"Not you two again," Sam complained.

"Now, you really didn't think we'd return to the king without Prince Michael, did you?" Jacob sneered at her. He hated Sam for all she was putting them through.

Sam drew her sword, and so did Jacob. Each stared unwaveringly at the other. Michael and Alex just stood and watched.

"Do you ever get the feeling that we've done this before?" quipped Michael.

However, Alex wasn't about to let Michael get the upper hand again. "I am truly sorry about this, sire." Alex grabbed Prince Michael by his wrists.

Alex shackled Michael to a tree, drew his sword, and went to join Jacob. This time, Jacob attacked first. Sam, purely by reflex, blocked a vicious blow to her head. Jacob was in no mood for this again. His anger at being humiliated by Sam, being caught in the rain, and wandering around the country when he had better things to do gave him great strength. And he attacked Sam with such force that Sam's only defense was to retreat.

However, Sam knew that they were running out of time, so she challenged his blows with a harshness of her own. Blow for blow, they assaulted each other but were too evenly matched for either of them to win. Both were utterly unaware of Alex's presence until ...

"Sam! Behind you!" Michael called out in warning.

This time, keeping one eye on Jacob, she looked back and saw Alex sneaking up on her.

"Two at once? Maybe I should have taught you about fair play." Sam joked, and she shifted her position to take on both of them better.

"This is no game, Sam! The king wants his son back in the palace, now!" shouted Jacob.

"I really would like to comply with you, but I can't." Sam stared down both men and stood ready for the next blow. "There's yet more for him to learn."

"Your first duty is to the king, not the whims of his sons. You should know better, " Alex admonished.

Sam's training allowed her to fight off both Jacob and Alex. But she was running out of time. She could already hear the voices of others coming from the tavern. They would be here soon.

"Sam!" Michael hollered, still handcuffed to the tree.

"What?! I'm kinda busy here." She yelled, blocking a blow from Alex and thrusting her sword at Jacob, causing him to back up.

"Kill them!" He ordered.

"What?!" exclaimed Sam, Alex, and Jacob simultaneously.

"It's obvious that they will not let us go, nor stop pursuing us. They are only slowing us down, and the others are coming. So, kill them both." Shouted Michael. "That's an order!"

"By your command, your highness." Sam complied, surprised by Michael's logic.

Sam turned on her heels and swung her sword upward, cutting Jacob across his abdomen. Jacob fell to the ground and clutched his stomach, his red blood tainting the pure white snow.

"Jacob!"

Alex growled in anger at Sam's betrayal as he rushed at her. Sam heard him coming and fell to her knees. Alex had his sword raised to attack from above. He hadn't expected an attack from below. Alex clutched his right side as Sam pulled her dagger from his belly. A voice called Alex's name as he fell to the ground and lay wounded beside his brother. Sam looked behind her, and there stood James. She had been afraid of this; the sounds of battle had drawn the attention of the other knights. She quickly checked the wounds of her friends. If treated soon, they would live, but they'd have to return to the castle.

"I'm really sorry about this, guys. Please tell my father..." Sam began.

"Sam, time is short. Come and cut me loose!" ordered Michael.

Sam got up, freed Michael, and ran to her horse. Mounting it, she rode after Michael. Three of the knights stayed with Alex and Jacob and tended their wounds. Confused by Sam's brutal attack on fellow knights, the other twelve rode after Sam and Michael, determined not to let them escape. Sam looked back to count their pursuers and did not like what she saw.

"There are too many of them and we are too easy to follow in the snow," said Sam. "We've got to split them up."

"How?" asked Michael.

Sam looked back to make sure the others couldn't see them. Then she hopped onto Michael's horse and sent her horse off in another direction.

"Hopefully, only six will follow us. Head for those pine trees."

"How many tree tricks do you know?" Michael chuckled as he sped up.

"Stop here. Now climb into the tree without touching the ground."

"What?" Michael curiously watched Sam's movements.

"Like this." Sam stood on the horse's back and climbed into the tree. She helped Michael up and then sent the horse on its way. Sam urged Michael to stay in the middle of the tree; the less movement in the tree, the less chance of detection. Sam shushed Michael when she heard hooves and voices. They held their breath as the knights followed the hoof prints to the tree.

"We'll follow the tracks; you two search the trees here. Sam is the Captain's son; he knows all the tricks. So be careful. If you don't find them, meet us at Snyder." One knight told the others.

"Yes, sir." The other knights acknowledged.

Michael slid his finger across his throat. Sam nodded. Two were much better odds than twelve. Sam jumped from the pine and attacked the one whose back was to her. She knocked him unconscious with a blow to his head.

"Peter, you should know better than to turn you back on an

enemy." joked Sam.

"And your overconfidence shall be your downfall, Sam." said the other knight.

"Well, if it isn't the great Tom Talley." Sam greeted him with a smile. "How's my dad?"

"Furious." said Tom, without any grin at all.

"Wife and kids?" Sam asked, and her sword as she circled Tom.

"I know what you're doing, Sam. And it's not going to work." He warned.

"Are you sure?" Sam smiled as Tom drew his sword.

Sam swung her sword, backhanded, across Tom's midsection. Tom jumped back and blocked the blow. Sam was surprised but not discouraged. Sam tried several tricks, all of which Tom blocked and returned blows. Sam could block them, but Tom was much older than Sam. He was a great figure of a man who stood six feet tall. He had wavy black hair, a full-grown beard, and keen blue eyes. He had always looked like a bear to Sam, and he was a well-seasoned soldier trained by her father. This time, it was Sam who was outmatched. Twice, Sam was driven to her knees, and with Tom's last blow, he disarmed her. Sam now lay at his mercy, with his sword at her throat.

"Now, Sam, you and the young prince will return to the castle," Tom informed her sternly.

"No, we won't," said Michael, standing behind Tom.

Tom turned to face Michael, and Michael hit him with a hard right hook. Tom lay unconscious in the snow beside Sam. Michael helped Sam up, then mounted Tom and Peter's horses. Peter's horse was uneasy with the new rider and reared.

"Look, horse, I'm in no mood today," Michael growled impatiently.

Michael held on, pulled back on the reins, and made the horse obey him. The horse soon settled down. Sam was impressed.

"I'm impressed." She said, slightly surprised.

But most of all, she was cold. The sun was setting, and the night was getting colder. They had no coats, no food, and no options. They had to travel north to avoid the king's men.

Sam took the lead, and Michael fell in step right behind her. Traveling in a single file left only one set of prints, plus it shielded the second rider from the stinging winter wind. Sam was so cold; her hands were frozen to the reins. She huddled closer to the horse's back for some warmth. But it was too little horse for so much cold. If freezing to death wasn't bad enough, it had started to snow again and showed no signs of stopping.

Sam looked back at Michael. His head was down close to his horse to keep the snow out of his eyes and the sting of the wind off his face. The only good thing about this snow was that it was covering up their tracks; not even Sam could follow this trail. So, Sam and Michael rode on like this until it was too dark to see. Sam humbly thanked God when she saw the little cave. It wasn't deep, but it was enough cover for them and the horses. They took the horse's saddle blankets and covered the entrance to keep out the snow. Then, they collected enough firewood to last them the night. However, shivering with cold was not as disturbing to Michael as the silence coming from Sam.

"What's the matter, Sam? You haven't said a word since we lost the knights," asked Michael as he warmed his hands over the fire.

"I lost to Tom." She said sadly, as she stared into the fire's light. "Yes, he was trained by my father. But so was I. I'm his son."

"Daughter," corrected Michael.

"What?" Sam asked, not really hearing him.

"You said son. You're not his son; you are his daughter."

"Whatever I am, I used to believe I could beat anyone. But I can't. How am I going to protect you?" Sam asked quietly. She hugged her knees for warmth. "Maybe we should go home."

"When we began this journey, it was to find my... backbone." But now it has also become a test of your skill. Think of it: if we survive this journey, you will have more than earned the right to replace your father as captain of the king's guards." Michael tried to comfort her.

Sam shrugged. There was only one blanket left, so she gave it to Michael. Then, she curled up, hugged her knees, and lay as close as she could to the fire.

"Sam," Michael called to her. "It's too cold to conform to the rules of convention. Why not sleep over here, with me, and we'll share the blanket."

Sam said nothing as she lay shuddering. To suffer for the comfort of your king was her duty; her father had taught her so.

"Sam? Sam, come on," urged Michael, serious with concern. "You're no good to me dead from frostbite."

A shudder ran through Sam's entire body. Then Sam got up and made her way over to Michael. "O.K. But only because you ordered me too." She said, still shivering with cold.

Michael held her close to him and shared the blanket. After being in the cold for so long, it felt good to be trapped between the heat of a fire and the body heat of Sam. Michael put his arms around Sam so that they could get closer. Sam slept with her back to Michael and her head on his elbow. The warmth from Michael's body lulled her to sleep, and neither awoke until midmorning the next day.

Chapter 7

When Sam awoke, she was in pain. She was sleeping on the ground beside Michael, but without a blanket. Michael had turned over and had taken the blanket with him. She shook her head as she got up and stretched, trying to relieve the tension in her neck and shoulders. Her stomach growled a painfully empty growl. She hadn't eaten anything since yesterday morning. Wondering what there was to eat, she checked the saddlebags.

"Nothing. Good grief, what idiot would leave home without a little something in his pack? What can I hunt without a bow? How will I hunt without a bow? Blast it all." She complained.

She tended the fire, keeping it high, and then she ventured out into the snow. She was struck blind by the sun's light reflecting off the snow. She blinked until her eyes could adjust. The snow had stopped, and the earth was quiet. The air was crisp, clean, and cold. Movement to her left drew her eyes to a tree in the distance. A young buck was foraging for his breakfast, too. How Sam wished she had a bow. Instead, she would have to use her wits.

Sam dug up what huckleberries she could find and laid them beneath a tree. Then, she climbed into its branches and waited for the buck. She almost fell asleep waiting for that buck to pick up the scent of the berries. But when he did, he wandered right over and began eating. Sam pounced from the tree and clung to its throat. The buck kicked and kicked. But Sam was hungry, and this buck was breakfast. Holding its neck with her left hand, she cut its throat with the dagger in her right hand. The buck stumbled to his knees as his life drained from his neck and onto the snow.

Sam covered the blood with layers of snow, resolving not to leave any clues for the knights or other predators. She shouldered the buck and walked back to the cave. When she came in, Michael was up and tending the fire.

"I was wondering where you went." He said, seeing the buck.

Sam skinned the buck. Laying the skin aside, she cut the buck into sections. She left Michael roasting two flanks while she buried the other flanks in the snow. After cleaning the hide with snow, she made a shirt and pants. She scraped a very crude needle from one of the buck's hooves against a rock.

"I thought you didn't know how to sew," commented Michael.

"I said I don't like sewing and that I wouldn't spend my life doing it. I just need to find something to use as thread and rosin. I also need to make a bow." Sam tested the needle's ability to pass through the hide.

"Willow Reeds," suggested Michael as he turned the roasting meat.

"Willow Reeds?"

"Yeah, inside is a nice, silky string. Don't worry, it's strong. That's what makes them hard to pull up."

"So where do I find them?" Sam asked and prepared to leave.

Three hours later, Sam returned, blue and cold but with plenty of reeds. Michael split the reeds and pulled out the thread as Sam got warm and ate her lunch. By evening, Sam had made one deerskin suit, a bow, and twelve arrows.

"The poor buck was only big enough for one suit.

"If I can find another one tomorrow, we'll have enough food to get us to Gatlin Market," Sam told him.

"You must carry a map in your head. How do you know where we are?" questioned Michael.

"My father is responsible for the safety of the king's domain. He knows all the towns in England. So, he knows where the king's enemies will come from. He made me memorize all of England, so that I would know it too. Hey, at least I never get lost," chuckled Sam. "Here, try this on."

"You keep it," Michael said. He refused to take it. "You're the hunter."

Sam picked a spot near the fire but away from Michael to go to sleep.

"Are we back to the rules of convection again?" He asked, downheartedly.

"Yes," said Sam flatly.

"Why don't you trust me?" He quipped with a raised eyebrow.

"No," sighed Sam, with her back to him. "I don't trust myself."

Michael said nothing but wondered what Sam thought of him. Did she dream of him in her arms as he had done last night? He had never had a girl that close to him before. It felt...nice.

However, he was a prince and would one day marry a princess, even Sam had said so. However, the more he thought about it, the less he wanted to. A princess would be far more critical of him than Sam, and for some strange reason, Sam had always believed in him. You can do anything you want, but you must try first. A princess would be more confined to the rules of convention to try anything out of the ordinary or different and unusual. Michael fell asleep dreaming of a life without limitations, without responsibilities to the throne, and a life with Sam as his wife.

This time, Michael awoke first. He was surprised to see Sam still asleep. Deer wrestling must be a tiring sport. He gently shook her to wake her up. Instinctively, she attacked. She pushed Michael onto his back and held a dagger to his throat.

"Sam!" Michael screamed, hoping to stop her before she slit his throat.

"Blast it, don't ever do that," scolded Sam. "I could have killed you."

"If I thought that you would ever kill without thinking. I wouldn't have told you to kill Alex and Jacob. You're too disciplined for that." Michael praised her. "Now, as much as I am growing to like this position, please get off me."

"Sorry." Sam apologized, and she stood up.

Two hours later, Sam came back with another kill.

This time, she had Michael skin the deer and make clothes from it. She also taught him to make a bow and arrows. By midday, they were ready to start again. They set the horses north and rode single file. Two weeks later, they came to a frozen river. The horses grazed while Michael and Sam considered their predicament.

"Do you think it's safe enough to cross?" Sam asked, and she studied the ground.

"I don't know. That depends on how deep it is." He answered.

"Why?" She questioned, looking over the lake and wondering how deep it was.

"Because shallow bodies of water freeze more completely than deep ones. However, I think we should walk the horses across." He suggested.

They collected their horses and, with great caution, proceeded to walk across the ice. Although seemingly solid, they were haunted by cracking noises beneath their feet. But now Sam's horse grew skittish as if sensing the danger that they were in.

"Sam, if he keeps that up, we're going to fall through," warned Michael. He petted his horse to reassure it.

"Maybe he's skittish because something is wrong.

He's been O.K. until now." Sam tried to calm her horse down.

Suddenly, something moved on the far shore. She cocked her head as if listening to someone speak, and then she sniffed the air.

"Young prince," called Sam in warning.

"What's wrong, Sam?" Michael dreaded the answer.

"We've got wolves in front of us." She stared at the shore ahead of them.

Michael could hardly believe Sam was serious until he raised his hand to shield his eyes from the sun and saw why. They were wearing deerskin suits to keep themselves from freezing, but the wolves smelled the deerskin.

"We can't mount until we cross, or we'll drown. But we'll get mauled by wolves if we're on foot. So, what do we do?" asked Michael.

Sam drew her bow and strung it with an arrow. "You take

the horses. I'll see if I can't scare them away by dwindling their numbers."

She aimed at the nearest one, hoping he was the leader. The number one rule of combat is to take out the leaders, and the rest of the army will fall apart. Hopefully, that worked on wolves as well as men. She let the arrow fly. It missed its mark but sent the wolf in another direction. She let four more arrows fly, pushing the wolves back from the river's edge. Out of six arrows shot, she only managed to hit four wolves. Unfortunately, the dead were quickly replaced, and the howling of more wolves signaled reinforcements.

"Damn, this is no good." chided Sam.

"Good enough," Michael affirmed as he pulled his horse to move forward.

At least they now had room to run. Upon reaching the river's edge, they mounted the horses and made a run for it. The gallop of the horse's hoofs thundered in their ears. The howl of the pack on their trail froze their souls with fear.

Suddenly, without warning, a wolf attacked Michael's horse and began snapping at its legs. Michael kicked at the wolf. Sam drew her bow and shot the wolf through the neck. It fell dead in the snow. Michael urged his horse to go faster. The landscape rushed by him in a blur. Worrying about Sam caused him to look back. Sam was right behind him, bow in hand and ready for wolves. When he turned around, something jumped in his face and knocked him to the ground. Growling, snapping, and clawing, the wolf pinned Michael to the ground.

"Sam!!!" shouted Michael. He used his arms to keep the wolf from getting to his neck.

In a flash, Sam was by his side. She grabbed the wolf by his neck and slit its throat with her dagger. Before Sam could help Michael up, a wolf jumped at her from behind and began snapping at her throat. Michael took his sword and stabbed the wolf in the back. Sam stood up, thrusting the wolf's dead body to the ground. She and Michael stood in a circle of blood, back-to-back, swords ready.

The rest of the pack wasted no time but charged all at once. Sam and Michael swung their swords, slashing left to right to left. One wolf got past Michael's defense and pinned him to the ground. Wrestling with Sam was easier than wrestling with a wolf. Sam's body only twisted one way. This wolf seemed to be coming at him from all directions. But as all his attention was on the wolf on his chest, he didn't see the other two at his feet until they bit into his flesh.

Michael's screams brought Sam to his side. Grabbing them by their furry necks, she cut their throats. Again, neglecting to watch her back, she was jumped from behind. The wolf tore at her back and ears. Michael thrust his sword into the wolf's side and removed it from Sam's back. Sam got up and growled. She had had enough. This time, she didn't wait for the wolves to come to her; she went after them.

"Sam! Sam! What the hell are you doing?!" shouted Michael in horror and disbelief.

Sam didn't answer him. Michael stood by the horses, watching in terror and amazement at the bloodlust with which Sam cut, slashed, and gutted every wolf in the pack. When she returned, she was covered in blood; some was hers, but most of it was the wolves. She mounted her horse, favoring her bloody and wolf-chewed left arm.

"Sam? Sam? Are you alright?" asked Michael with great concern.

Sam said nothing. She only mounted her horse and took the lead. As they rode away from the woods, ten dead wolves lay silent as pools of red sank into the snow.

Chapter 8

"Are you alright?" Michael asked again after about an hour of silence.

"Yes. Are you?" Sam asked weakly.

"Yes. But I think we should wash these wounds before they become infected," suggested Michael, urging his horse to catch up to her.

Sam said nothing but kept riding. Michael positioned his horse in front of her, causing her to stop.

"Sam, we need to wash these wounds, and the horses need a rest. Besides, you killed all the wolves, and we're back on the main road. I think we can stop now." Michael told her firmly.

Sam said nothing. She only nodded, and then she dismounted. This time, Michael started the fire and melted snow for water. He wouldn't allow Sam to do anything for fear of aggravating her wounds. Sam removed her shredded deerskin shirt, paying dearly for each movement with sharp stabs of pain. Thank God, the shirt the innkeeper had given her had fared better. At least it was still in one piece, enough to cover her chest and back. Sam used the ice-cold snow to wash the blood from her left arm so she could see just how bad it was. It wasn't good. Sam's arm was covered with deep gouges.

"Aw, blast it!" She swore.

Michael came to see her. "Don't do that, you'll only make it worse." Michael whistled when he saw how bad her arm really was. "You'll have to keep that wrapped." He said and returned to the water.

Sam also removed her white shirt so that Michael could clean the wounds on her back. Once the water had thawed and was warm, Michael sat on his knees and washed the blood from her back. He winced as he saw her back. It was awfully and deeply scarred. He could see that the wolf's marks covered over the wounds made earlier from her horse-dragging accident.

She grimaced and groaned in pain as Michael cleaned the wounds. As Michael washed her back free from the caked-on and drying blood, he noticed the difference between his white hands and her light brown back.

"Sam, where was your mother from?" He asked, dipping the cloth back into the now red water.

"Tor, Egypt," Sam answered as she stared at her feet.

"Was she an Amazon?"

Sam chuckled at his fanciful idea as she felt him again place the cloth against her back. "No, but father always said that she should have been."

Her father had told her about the Amazons when he decided to make a boy out of her. It was flattering to think that this was how he saw her. Sensing that he was done with her back, Sam turned around so that he could wash her front as well. Michael had watched Sam undress before. However, her back was always towards him. He had never seen her before while she was bare-chested. The gentle movement of her breasts as she breathed was more than he could take and still be a gentleman. He swallowed hard and turned away from her.

"Um, I can't. Sam, you can do your front." He said, blushing bright red, as he handed her the wash rag.

"Sorry, I forgot." Apologized, Sam. Sam cleaned her chest, her left arm, and her face. Then she put her white shirt back on. "Ok. Now let's see about you." Sam turned to face Michael.

The water was now stained blood red as Sam washed the blood-soaked cloth in it. Sam wrung out the fabric and approached Michael, who sat waiting with his shirt off. Sam sat behind him and washed his wounds.

"See, nothing to it." Sam teased him.

"Easy for you to say, you've probably cleaned the wounds of a thousand boys. But you're my first attempt at doctoring."

"Don't worry, if our bad luck continues, you'll get plenty of practice.".

Sam knelt beside him to do his front. Michael tried to think of something else besides Sam's chest beneath her shirt, but it wasn't easy. So, he looked up at her face. Their eyes met. Sam smiled as she continued washing the blood from his chest. Michael noticed Sam's face. Yesterday, it had been smooth and untouched. But she now had three claw marks on her right cheek. Michael reached up to touch them, but he stopped himself. Sam moved to see about his leg. But Michael shunned her efforts.

"I'll do that," said Michael, bashfully.

Sam relinquished the washcloth and sat near the fire, warming her hands. Michael cleaned and wrapped his leg, then went to see about the horses. As he groomed them, he found it hard to believe he had ever been afraid of these animals. He cleared some ground for them to graze and returned to Sam. Sam had fallen asleep.

It was late in the afternoon when she finally woke up. She stretched in pain and yawned. When Sam joined him, Michael was roasting parts of the young buck for dinner.

"Why did you let me sleep so long?" She asked.

"Because you needed the rest." He answered. He turned the buck slowly to evenly cook both sides. "Don't worry; I haven't seen hide or hair of life, human or otherwise, for hours. Care for some venison?"

Sam and Michael dined on deer and then prepared to set out again. It took four weeks to trudge through the snow to get to Gatlin's Market. The scenery didn't change for four weeks, just bare trees, pine trees, snow, and two lone riders. Until one day...

"What's that noise?" asked Michael, looking around with curiosity.

"Sounds like a wagon." Sam turned in her saddle to see what was behind them.

"Out of my way." Shouted a voice over the noise of four horses and a squeaky wagon.

Sam and Michael barely avoided being hit by the wagon train as it flew past them. Following the speeding wagon, they soon came to Gatlin Market.

Gatlin Market was a seaport and thriving marketplace.

The variety of items from other countries made it a merchant's paradise. People from all over England and foreign sailors came here for work and to play.

Voices of men and women in conversation and commerce, the smell of the sea, cooking meat, and a hundred new things bombarded their senses. Markets back home, a few stalls and wagons, were nothing compared to this; even Sam found it all overwhelming. Sam stared at the enormous sails of the ships in port and wondered about life at sea. Michael watched a variety of people pack and unpack their goods. He watched as people haggled over the price of apples and peppers. He saw a young maiden with hair as red as Sam's. She winked at him as she went by. Michael continued to watch her go down the street and rode right into a man with a cart of fruit and vegetables.

"Hey!!" He shouted at Michael and shook his fists at him. "Watch where you are going!"

Sam rode up beside Michael to see what all the yelling was about.

"This is great. Can we stay here a couple of days?" asked Michael excitedly.

"Sure, why not?" She smiled. "But we'd better change clothes first. I don't like some of the looks we're getting."

Sam and Michael first went to a doctor. Though they cleaned their wounds daily, it was no substitute for good medicine and fresh bandages.

Then they went to the tailor's shop for new clothes. Both bought simple white shirts, black pants, and leather knee-length boots. Sam had chosen a shirt one size too big so that her left arm would have plenty of room. As Sam admired her new clothes in a mirror, Michael marveled at how Sam's short-cut red hair made her a fascinating boy. It was unusual to see anyone of Sam's color with such red hair.

"Come on, Sam. You look great, now let's go," urged Michael.

"You're just jealous, cause the girls like me better." Sam mocked him.

Michael snickered. He had to admit Sam played the part well. Sam was just as rowdy and full of mischief as any of the pages he remembered. He never would have guessed that she wasn't a boy if he hadn't tended her wounds.

Now dressed in clothes befitting the style of the town, Sam and Michael went exploring. Leaving their horses at the stables, they walked through the town, visiting every shop and walking among the ships in port. They walked into a clock shop that sold clocks in the shape of sea animals. The most fascinating was a starfish-shaped clock whose arms rotated every second. The fish market sold every fish you could name, of all sizes, shapes, and colors. There were two fortunetellers in town, a massage shop, several brothels, twelve taverns, eight inns, and four weapon shops.

"Let's go inside, and I'll buy you a new dagger." Sam happily suggested as they came upon The Deadly Dirk Weapon's Shop.

"No way, I'd never get you out of there. What is it with you, anyway?" He complained, disgusted with her love of violence.

"As I've said, there is nothing as exhilarating as defeating someone in fair combat, rising to a challenge, and overcoming it," explained Sam robustly.

"It is not always necessary to fight," Michael told her, and they looked in the shop window.

"If you mean whether it is better to fight for advancement or to protect one's home, then fighting should only be used to protect one's home. But I'm not talking about war, I'm talking about friendly combat and competition," conceded Sam.

"There's no such thing," retorted Michael with a chuckle.

Music drifted in the air beneath the din of the sailors and

merchants who talked, traded, and fought. The sound of flutes, violins, horns, and lutes floated on the afternoon air. The sun hung low in the western sky, lighting their path among the shops with the orange glow of evening. There was also an apothecary, a tattoo place, two money exchangers, and a lost and found shop. The crowds of people were incredible. You had to press your way through the crowds of some shops.

Sam and Michael stopped to listen to the musicians play their flutes, lutes, and drums. Sam caught two pickpockets trying to relieve her of the coins in her pockets. Sam's greatest pleasure, though, was to find a toy store. Sam's memories walked among the shelves. Part of her wished she had been given toy boats and stuffed animals instead of daggers and swords.

"I had one of these," Sam recalled sadly.

"You had a stuffed cat?" Michael wondered if she had any toys besides swords.

"My mother gave it to me. She said that it would bring me luck. I used to sleep with it all the time. It was my favorite pillow," remembered Sam as she rubbed its furry body.

As dusk arrived, they headed back towards the inn.

"Sam!" shouted a voice. "Sam Bowman!"

Sam turned to see who was calling her. Then she saw Todd, a plump, bearded young man with unkempt black hair and bright blue eyes.

"Todd Towers! What are you doing here?" She exclaimed in surprise and walked towards him.

"Working, I live here." He said, heartily shaking her hand.

"If I had known I would have visited. Gad, what's this? You're putting on weight." Sam rubbed Todd's stomach playfully.

"Who's the barnacle?" Todd pointed at Michael.

"Allow me to introduce my traveling companion, Cody...Cody Wolf." Sam announced proudly.

"Hello, Cody." Todd addressed him. Then he saw Sam's face. "What happened to you, Sam?"

"Wolf attack," replied Sam, running her fingers along her cheek.

"Wow, that's so strange. Cerca said that I'd meet two wolves today. A wolf attacked you, and he's named after one. But I am glad it turned out to be you two, instead of real ones." Todd escorted them to Finn's inn and tavern.

Finn's Inn and Tavern was the favorite hangout of all the sailors. Great big glasses of beer, excellent roast boar and beer-baked fish, beautiful barmaids, and free drinks for anyone who could beat Marvin in arm wrestling; this tavern had it all. The din of glasses, sailors' talk, and music filled their ears as Todd chose a table for four and called for drinks. Todd told Michael of the misadventures Sam, and he had as kids. Todd's father was Major William Towers, the best man in the king's army under Sam's father. She and Todd had grown up together and were the best of friends.

However, the conversation turns sour when Michael asks if Todd will take his father's place beside Sam when he becomes Captain. Todd got up to get more drinks. Sam explained the sad story to Michael, saying that Todd's father disowned him when he refused to follow in his father's footsteps. Like Sam, Todd grew up with his father, insisting that he follow in his footsteps as tradition demands. But unlike Sam, he grew to hate the Royal Guards. After a massive fight with his father, Todd left.

"This is the first time I've seen him in five years," said Sam.

"Does he know about you?" inquired Michael, wondering if Todd knew the secret.

"No. So, don't say anything."

Todd brought more drinks and challenged Sam to arm

wrestle with Marvin. Sailors laughed and placed bets as Todd and Michael pushed Sam towards Marvin. She finally relented and sat down to face Marvin. Marvin was a big Negro sailor from Africa, and he served aboard the Maralin II. Marvin laughed and said it was good to see another kinsman. Sam's arm was a twig compared to Marvin's bulging arms. But it was too late to back out now. Someone yelled begin, and although Sam gave it her best, she never had a chance. It was a short match. Sam rubbed her sore arm and thanked Marvin for the match.

"I hope you last longer with women than you do at arm wrestling," teased Todd, clapping Sam on the shoulder. "Speaking of which, are you still afraid of girls?"

"I was never afraid of girls." Sam corrected him. She quickly slapped his hand off her shoulder.

"Afraid of girls?" questioned Michael. He wanted to hear this fascinating story about Sam. "And you tease me about being afraid of horses?"

"Yeah, Sam's afraid of girls. When we were younger, he would never go near them." Todd regaled Michael with the story. "He wouldn't go with us to watch them bathe, wouldn't hold one in his arms, and I've never seen him kiss one."

Sam snorted angrily. She stood up, squared her shoulders, and walked over to one of the barmaids. She took her in her arms, held her tight, and kissed her soundly. Todd looked impressed. Michael looked sick. Cheers came from other sailors as Sam let her go and returned to her friends. The barmaid, stunned, just looked at Sam.

"Well done, I think you took her breath away," commended Todd, still looking at the barmaid.

"I always do." Sam crowed proudly. Sam wiped her mouth with the back of her hand. Michael didn't say anything. Sam saw Michael's expression. "Didn't think I had the balls to do that, did you?" Sam sat back down.

"But you don't." Michael suppressed a laugh.

Sam stared him down and shook her head, warning him not to pursue that subject now. Just then, the young barmaid came over with three large beers.

"These are on the house." She said, bending low in front of Sam and giving her ample time to gaze upon her bosom as she put their drinks down.

Sam raised an eyebrow, and the barmaid winked at her. Sam ran her fingers through her hair and returned her smile. "Thank you," said Sam, politely.

"I think she likes you." Michael teased her, and he reached for his drink.

"Well, at least this makes up for your loss to Marvin," said Todd, emptying his glass.

"Everybody loses to Marvin," scoffed Sam, lifting her glass in merriment.

"Well, I'd love to stay and chat, but I've got to get to work." Todd stood up. "It was great seeing you again, Sam."

"What do you do here, Todd?" asked Michael.

"I'm a Handyman ... and recruiter." Todd waved goodbye, and he left.

Sam asked for a room. It was luxurious compared to the other ones they'd had. It had a king-size bed, an oak chest, a large window, a giant lantern, and a bath basin. Michael lay on the bed and let his back enjoy the softness of a bed again. Sam stood, looking out the window at the town below. The night was cold; Sam shuddered and gently rubbed her arm. These bandages itch. The wind brought in air from the sea. Sam deeply breathed in the salty sea air; something about it was ... refreshing.

The town looked like the night sky, dotted with twinkling

yellow lights. Although it was very late in the evening, the town was still bustling with life, primarily sailors looking for a good time and tavern owners trying to give it to them. Sam's attention turned away from the window when Michael called her name.

"Sam?"

"Yes." She answered.

"Have you ever done that before?"

"Done what?" She looked over at Michael, lying on the bed.

"Kissed another girl, like you did tonight."

"Only once."

"When?" Michael asked as he bolted upright in surprise and with great interest.

Sam sighed and joined Michael on the bed. "Do you remember the night I won the knight's game, for the first time?"

"Do I? Your father was overjoyed. He couldn't stop smiling the whole night." Michael remembered with great mirth.

"Well, that night, some of the other squires and I did a little partying of our own. We went down to Inman's Inn. We decided to get drunk and play daggers and darts. I drank them under the table..." Sam spoke proudly.

"How many...?" Michael asked because he had never seen

Sam drunk. She was always in full control.

"Twelve." She grinned.

"And I get sick after just two." He lamented, his shoulders slumping.

"But when it came time for the kissing contest with Inman's barmaid, I refused to play. They ribbed me so badly that I took her in my arms and kissed her right then and there. And like tonight, I left her speechless. After that, they left me alone for a while. But that was the only time before tonight." Sam explained, slightly embarrassed.

"And I thought I had problems trying to be the man my father wanted me to be. I can't imagine what you must have had to endure," speculated Michael.

Chapter 9

Night settled upon Gatlin Market like a blanket, and three figures met in the shadows below the docks. Todd owed a debt to William and Macey, and tonight, they had come to collect.

"Alright, Toddy, you've done well so far. We only need two more to complete the crew. So, who are the two lucky blokes?" William rubbed his knuckles.

"What about Jason, the miller's son, and Jonathan? He's a cook," suggested Todd dryly.

"Are you kidding? They aren't big enough to feed to a guppy." Macey scolded unhappily.

"What about your two friends? I saw them in the bar tonight. I like the red-headed one, he's got balls." William stared through Todd with his glass eye.

"Oh, come on; those guys aren't seamen. Cody gets sick after only two beers. Besides, they have families who will ask questions if they disappear," pleaded Todd, not wanting to give up Sam.

"Like we care, it's either you or them. So, which will it be,"

Threatened Macey.

Todd hesitated. Sam was his best friend. He couldn't do this to him.

"You know ... your father would be glad to see you again." William reminded him with a wicked grin.

"O.K. O.K.," Surrendered Todd. The knots in his belly were beginning to get to him. His throat went dry, but his hands began to sweat.

Todd hated to betray his best friend like this, but when you owed money to William, he became your master. Besides, if Todd didn't give William what he wanted, which were able bodies for his crew, he would end up dead at the bottom of Debtor's Lake or worse. William would turn him over to his father. Todd's conscience was eating away at his soul. Choosing saps for William's crew was one thing, but handing Sam over to William was another.

"If I hand Sam over to you my debt is paid." Todd insisted sharply.

"Fair enough. If you give me Sam and his friend, you'll be free of your debt to me." William smiled, showing off his gold teeth.

William nodded to Macey, and they left Todd to do his

work. Putting on his best face, Todd returned to the inn and asked for Sam's room. Sam opened the door and let him in. Todd forced himself to be all smiles.

"Sam! Guess what?" He shouted.

"What?"

"Boss gave me the night off. Let's go play. The cards are calling," enticed Todd.

"Are you coming, Cody?" Sam got up to follow Todd.

"Only if I get to watch you kiss another maiden." Michael laughed and jumped up to join her.

"Oh, shut up." Sam pushed him out the door.

Todd took Sam and Michael to the Piranha Club, which was for real card sharks only. The place was dimly lit and filled with smoke. The smell of seawater and rotting fish assaulted their senses. Sam sat down and put her money on the table. Michael declined to join in but watched with interest as Sam took over four hundred dollars from the table.

"I've never seen anybody so lucky on their first night," complained William. He threw his cards on the table in disgust.

"Then you've never seen me with a maid and a bottle of champagne." Sam crowed, in a great and jovial mood.

"Here, have a beer." Macey laughed and offered Sam another beer.

"Naw, I've had enough for tonight," Sam refused.

William, Macey, and Todd frowned. Then Todd had an idea. "Hey Sam, do you remember the chug-a-lug game?" He smiled slyly.

"Yeah, and I remember I always beat you."

"I bet all of my money that you can't be me tonight," challenged Todd.

"Money down and bottoms up." Sam smiled, always enjoying a challenge.

Todd and Sam sat at the table, each given a tall glass of beer. Todd and Sam sat ready as the others put bets on who would win. Finally, the word GO was given. Todd and Sam both drained their glasses, but Sam put hers back on the table first.

"Damn," Todd swore, finally putting his glass down. "I want a rematch. How about you, Cody? I may not be able to beat Sam. But I'll be a sea dog's wipe if I can't at least beat you."

Michael looked at Sam. Sam nodded. "If you think you can." Sam offered him her seat.

They both knew what she meant, if he could, without

getting sick. But he didn't care; ill or not, he would try. He was tired of just watching. Michael sat down, ready to go. Macey placed two more beers on the table. Again, two glasses were drained, but Michael's glass hit the table first. Sam couldn't believe it, and she congratulated Michael. Todd only winked at William and Macey, who stood smiling in the corner.

An hour later, the party broke up. Sam, Todd, and Michael walked back to their inn. Todd staggered, Sam swayed, and Michael vomited. Suddenly, Sam's senses alerted her to the fact that they were being followed. Ever so slightly creaking floorboards, shadows moving just out of the corner of her eyes, and the anticipation of a fight sobered Sam somewhat, as her need to protect Michael kicked in.

"We're being followed," Sam said warily, looking around.

"You're drunk," replied Todd, laughing.

"I'm serious." Sam pulled out her sword.

Michael moved closer to Sam. He trusted her instincts. The attack came suddenly and from all sides. Sam slashed the air with her sword, but hit nothing. Her movements became slower and more labored. Her head was heavy and buzzed with alcohol.

"You drugged our drinks!" Sam shouted at Todd, finally

realizing what was happening.

"I had no choice. They would have killed me if I hadn't." Todd repentantly explained.

"You won't have to worry about them killing you, just me!" Sam lunged at Todd but missed.

"I'm sorry." Todd apologized sadly, and he sidestepped her attack.

A large bag came over her head, and two pairs of hands picked her up. As hard as she struggled, it was to no avail.

She lost consciousness, with the smell of a muddy bag in her nose and the thought of Michael on her mind.

Chapter 10

Sam awoke with a gallon of water in her face. Her body, believing that she was drowning, kicked upwards. Sam sat up and shook the water from her face. Michael, who was awoken in the same manner, coughed and gasped for air. Sam was relieved to see that he was still with her. However, she grew nervous as she realized that the deck was swaying. They were aboard a ship. Sam listened as the creaking timbers and the wind told her they were far at sea.

"Wake up, my dears. Time for work," said a very rough voice.

Sam looked up. An Italian seaman with a red bandanna around his head handed them mops and buckets.

"Forget it," Sam told him. She pushed the mop out of her face and stood up, trying to balance herself against the rolling of the ship's deck.

The sailor wasted no words but hit Sam in her gut. Sam dropped to the deck, gasping for air.

"Maybe you thought I was asking you. Let me tell you

again, SWAB THE DECKS!!!" He shouted.

Sam stood, glared at him, and shouted back in defiance. "Hell no!"

The Italian sailor tried to hit her again. But this time, she blocked the sailor's blow and delivered one of her own. This made him angry. He and Sam continued to exchange blows, drawing the attention of the crew, who were hungry for some excitement.

Michael was pushed aside as the other crew members wanted a better view of the fight. Their raised voices shouted taunts, cheers, and wagers as Sam fought the Italian sailor. Sam's training and her anger at being shanghaied made her more than a match for this man, who was twice as big and twice as old as she was. But the continuous rolling of the deck made it difficult.

Things only got worse when he discovered Sam was favoring her left arm. He changed his attack and came at Sam from the left. Instinctively, she blocked his blows with her left arm. The searing pain she felt only made her angrier. She grabbed a deck pin and viciously beat him into submission, teaching this man that she was not to be messed with.

The match was prematurely ended, however, with the

appearance of the Captain on deck. He yelled an order, and all hands came to attention except for the Italian sailor lying unconscious on the deck. The man Sam knew as her kidnapper appeared before them.

"Quite the little spitball, aren't you?" Captain William smiled at her. "You were right, Mr. Macey; his temper is as fiery as his hair. Tell me, boy, how does a sugar boy like you come by such red hair?"

Sam faced William, squared her shoulders with pride, and answered his question.

"My mother was a black Englishwoman and an extraordinary musician. My father was a white highland Englishman and soldier with bright red hair." Sam told him defiantly, with a thick Scottish accent.

"Interesting combination. Well, now, then, spitball. Welcome to the Shark's Eye. I'm Captain William, and this is my first mate, Mr. Macey. You are now part of my crew, and if you wish to remain part of my crew and not seafood, you will perform your duties to my satisfaction," informed William, looking from Sam to Michael and back to Sam.

Sam looked around and out to sea. She searched in every direction for land and found none. Captain William noticed her actions.

"We are four days out to sea and five months from France. So, unless you want to swim home, little spitball...." William laughed again.

Then he looked down at the deck to see what was by his feet. It was the Italian sailor who was still unconscious.

"Will someone get this sleeping sack of fish guts off my deck and throw it in the brig?" He ordered as he kicked the Italian sailor.

Sam and Michael had no choice. Michael began mopping the decks as Sam rewrapped her arm. With the continuous rolling of the deck, it took them six hours to clean the decks, and night had fallen by the time they were done. Their bunks were one above the other, in a room with two other sailors. The beds were rough and lumpy, and straw scratched her already badly abused back. She rolled over and looked down on Michael. He lay with his hands behind his head, blankly staring up at the bottom of Sam's bunk.

Sam hated the smell of stale air and unwashed pirates. But being rocked to sleep by the ship's swaying wasn't so bad once you got used to it. The sound of the sea as the ship cut through it resounded in her ears.

"So how did you like your first day at sea, spitball?" asked the sailor in the top bunk opposite Sam's bed.

"Is that to be my name, Spitball?" Sam asked, unmoving from her bunk.

"It's a good a name for a pirate," replied the sailor in the bottom bunk.

"Is that what this is...a pirate ship?" Michael asked, feeling strangely excited.

"Spices, rum, and gold, my boy. By the way, that's Deadeye and I'm Bang Shot, gunner's first mate."

"Charmed," said Sam sarcastically. "I'm Sam, and he's Cody."

For the next five months, Sam and Michael spent their days running stern and aft, learning how to raise and lower the sails, tie knots, raise the anchor, and load the cannons.

Their meals aboard the ship were a new experience for Sam and Michael. You had to catch your food before you could eat it. Michael and Sam were always the center of fun as the other sailors watched them get used to dinner at sea. Michael raised his glass to drink, but the ship lurched and spilled the drink into Shoeless' lap. Shoeless was lurid, ruff, and scarred from years at sea. He was big and strong, as all Norsemen were known to be. His eyes were as black as coal, and his skin was pale and clammy; when angry, he was downright ugly.

"Why don't you watch what you're doing, runt?" Shoeless yelled, and he stood up.

"I'm sorry," said Michael, and he tried to clean up the mess.

"Yeah, you're going to be," threatened Shoeless.

Sam got up and stood between Shoeless and Michael. "Sit down and shut up, you lumbering oaf. He said he was sorry. So just finish your dinner or it will join his beer."

"You know, you're always defending him. It's time that he learned to defend himself. Hold him." Shoeless ordered, pushing Sam out of his way.

"Come here, Guppy." Shoeless lumbered toward Michael.

Michael backed up. He didn't want to fight.

"Let go of me!" Sam struggled to free herself from the two sailors who held her tightly by the arms. "Hey, watch the arm!"

Michael looked at Sam and stumbled over Pee-Wee, a Roman dwarf with tar-black hair. Pee-Wee pushed Michael towards Shoeless.

"He's over there, runt," said Pee-Wee.

Shoeless punched Michael in the stomach. Michael doubled over in pain. Another punch, and Shoeless sent

Michael to the floor. Michael wiped his bleeding lip as Shoeless stood laughing. Michael stood, faced Shoeless, and put up his fists. A year ago, Michael would have been no match for Shoeless. However, a year of hard labor had chiseled size and muscle into Michael; he was now Shoeless' equal.

"Come on, Cody! You can beat him." Sam coached. "Just watch his left."

Sam and the others cheered them on, placing wagers and shouting instructions. Sam was surprised at Michael's success. He was still standing and even gave Shoeless a few hits he wouldn't soon forget. While all attention was on Shoeless and Michael, Sam took this opportunity to break free. She brought her fists down into her captors' groins and butted their heads together.

When Pee-Wee saw what she had done, he grabbed her. She hip-tossed him into a table. Noticing another fight, the crew broke into two groups. Some watched Shoeless and Michael, knowing better than to interrupt one of Shoeless' fights.

Others took the chance to get into a fight with Sam, and she was more than willing to oblige. Sam jabbed one sailor in the stomach, and she punched another in the face. One she right hit in the jaw, another she struck to the side, and then a back kick for Pee-Wee, who tried to jump her from behind. The mess hall was now ablaze with shouts, fighting sailors, and broken furniture.

"This is the most fun I've had since we left home. How are you doing, Cody?" Sam asked while ramming one sailor's head into a wall.

"About as well as expected," shouted Michael, ducking a blow to the head.

"You're still standing. That's better than expected." She butted the heads of two more sailors and kicked a third in the stomach.

"I had a good teacher." Michael chuckled and blocked another blow.

"Want me to finish him for you?" Sam turned to face Michael.

"No. I can do it." He stated, not taking his eyes off Shoeless.

"O.K.," Sam relented and turned to face another attacker, who was trying to sneak up on her with a chair.

However, all the fighting stopped when a gunshot was fired.

"BANG!!!"

"What the hell is this?!" Captain William bellowed.

Everyone still conscious stopped what he was doing and came to attention. The room became silent.

"Who started this fight?!" He demanded, looking around the room at the broken furniture and fourteen unconscious sailors.

No one said anything or even moved.

"If I don't find out who started this fight, there will be double duty at half rations...for everybody!" He threatened.

Sam looked around. Every finger in the room was pointed at her and Michael.

"Spitball, I should have known." He growled. "Take them to the brig."

"Let go of me!" Two big sailors grabbed Sam. It took four guys to haul her down the stairs and throw her into the brig.

"One, two, three." They counted.

"Whoa!" Sam hit the floor with a heavy thud.

"Are you okay, Sam?" Michael asked as he helped her up.

"Yeah." Sam dusted herself off and looked around the brig. "I hate this place." Sam sneered.

"How's your arm?" He asked as he pointed to it.

"It's fine." She flexed her arm and fingers. "Your face is bleeding. Are you alright?" She asked him.

"It only hurts when I laugh." He said, touching his sore cheek.

"Well, Happy Birthday." Sam joked, leaning against the bars.

"Ha. Ha. Ow." Michael laughed, remembering that it was indeed his birthday.

In time, Sam and Michael made many friends by always volunteering for night watch. Sam found it was the only time that she and Michael could talk. At night, the ship quietly sailed over the ocean. The sound of the waves against the hull of the ship, the flapping of the sails against the wind, the smell of the sea, and the wind in her hair, Sam felt that she could get used to life at sea. Michael was a quick study at navigation, while Sam earned the crew's respect as a gunner. After sinking three French ships and two Spanish Galleons, they even changed her name from Spitball to Redshot. Michael earned the name TwoStar because, given any two constellations, he could tell you where you were. In time, the cold winter air changed to cool spring breezes.

Good weather had favored them all the way to France, but now, at the journey's end, nature raged. The skies were dark and full of black clouds. The sky flashed as lightning traveled from the sky and reached into the sea. The wind blew hard as if trying to push them back to England. The ship was tossed back and forth against the waves. Thunder roared, drowning out the captain's shouts to lower the sails. Men rushed from stem to stern, trying to secure the ship and save the cargo, but the sea would not be denied her prize. The waves beat the ship unceasingly, finally cracking the ship's hull. The waves rushed in, claiming cargo and crew indiscriminately. Captain William and Mr. Macey were at the helm, valiantly trying to keep the ship on course and under control. Each time the waves reached over the sides and onto the decks, one less man was on board. Sam secured the cannons the best she could, but she couldn't care less what happened to them. Her mind was on Michael, and she prayed he was still aboard.

The sky flashed, and Sam looked up. The rain stung at her face as it fell. She could hardly hear the shouts of the others over the sound of her own beating heart. Her ears strained, weeding out the voices that were not Michael's.

"Sam!" shouted a familiar voice.

"Cody, I'm glad to see you." She took his hand with gladness.

Their joyful reunion was cut short by dread as a lightning bolt hit the ship's deck, setting it on fire. Sam and Michael rushed to extinguish the fire before it reached the gunpowder. It was no good trying to put the fire out. So, they rushed to put the kegs of gunpowder into the sea and away from the fire. Sam and Michael fought against the wind, rain, and tossing of the ship to get the kegs of powder into the sea.

However, the sea wanted everything but the powder. A flash of lightning and a clap of thunder shouted at Sam, *Hey, look around.* When Sam did, she realized she and Michael were the only two left on board. An eerie sensation crawled over Sam. They were utterly alone. Amidst the raging sea, the furious, bone-chilling wind, and the lightning's fiery fingers, Sam felt a strange silence, and time seemed to stand still. Sam's somber contemplation was broken as Michael grabbed her by the arm. He pulled her towards the mast.

"Stay here," Michael shouted above the din of the sea.

"What are you doing?" Sam asked. She clung to the mast and watched Michael cut a rope from the sails.

"I read it in a book once. The ship's captain tied himself to the mast, thus enabling him to listen to the Siren's songs without losing himself or his ship to the sea witches." He explained as he threw the rope around them.

"That is the dumbest thing I've ever heard of," hollered Sam over the din of the storm.

Nevertheless, Michael tied themselves to the mast. All night long, for what seemed to be an eternity. The ship continued to roll. Sam had been too busy to be sick. But tied to the mast, her mind was on nothing else but her stomach. She stole quick glances at Michael. He didn't look too good either; his pale white skin was a light greenish yellow.

As time passed, night became day, and the sea calmed. Once again, the ship gently swayed to the rhythm of the sea. As dawn crept up over the horizon, the ship had run aground. It rested on its side, with a gaping hole in its belly. Small crustaceans and other curious beach dwellers came to see the new wreckage.

Unaware of the world, Sam dreamed.

**

She and Michael were riding horses that became giant eagles. They were flying over land, villages, and towns. She saw people farming, soldiers marching, and woodsmen cutting down trees. As they flew over the ocean, Sam looked down and saw her father's face in the sea. He was furious. The skies became dark, and the winds blew hard. A funnel of water that became a hand as it reached up from the sea grabbed Sam. Sam sank into the sea within a whirlwind of water. Sam choked as water filled her lungs. Sam looked up and saw Michael still flying overhead, his hand stretched for hers.

"Sam! Reach for me!" He shouted.

She reached up to grab his hand but was only pulled further away from him.

**

Sam woke up screaming and gasping for air.

Chapter 11

"Michael!" Sam screamed and sat bolt upright.

"Who's Michael?" asked Michael, standing beside her.

"What?" Sam was still dazed and slightly confused. Then Sam remembered everything.

"This is the thanks I get for saving her life." Michael laughed in Spanish. "She's dreaming about another man."

Other voices, laughing, were in the background. Sam wondered what Michael was telling them. Although he had tried teaching her Spanish, she had not learned it. Sam gave Michael a puzzled look. He leaned down and whispered in her ear.

"They found us, tended our wounds, and they know you're a girl. I told them you were my half-sister, with the same father, and different mothers. Got it?"

Sam nodded and looked at her left arm. It had been freshly rewrapped. Sam wiggled her fingers. Good, still responding. Her legs were still a bit shaky, though, as she tried to stand.

"Where are we?" She asked.

"Bilboa, Spain," informed Michael, and helped her to walk.

Michael helped her to the kitchen table. Sam examined her surroundings as she waited. The kitchen's aroma was spicy. There were onions, peppers, and baking bread, but that was all she recognized. A middle-aged, heavy-set woman was preparing a meal and giving orders to a slimmer young girl who was setting the table—obviously, her daughter. The woman's three sons chattered with their father while waiting for dinner.

Different country, same rules. Sam huffed.

"Sam, this is Senior Garza," Michael introduced, pointing to the gentleman and his family. "His wife Anna Maria, his daughter Rosa, and their three sons Pedro, Fernando, and Edwardo."

Sam nodded a greeting to each one. "Buenos Dias." Sam smiled brightly.

"Buenos Noches." Michael corrected her. "You've been asleep most of the day."

"Buenos Nochas y ... Gracias por ...usted ...assistance." Sam stuttered, greatly embarrassed by her terrible pronunciation.

"Nice try," chuckled Pedro in perfect English. "Allow me to

teach you more while you are here."

Sam watched as Michael talked with their hosts like he was one of them. Rosa was the oldest, about twenty, Sam thought. Pedro, Fernando, and Edwardo came in that order, with Pedro being the oldest at about eighteen. Fernando and Edwardo, she guessed to be about twelve and eight. She wished she could understand what they were saying. She hated being left out of the fun. She tugged at Michael's elbow to get his attention.

"What's going on?"

"Well, I've been telling them about our journey, and we've been invited to join their festival celebrations tonight. It is the Cinco de Mayo festival. There will be music, food, games, and a parade." Michael's explanation was cut short by the arrival of dinner. "Gracias, Señora," Michael gladly accepted his plate.

"What is it?" whispered Sam.

"If my studies were accurate, this is a tortilla. It's a kind of bread made from cornmeal. This is a taco filled with meat, lettuce, cheese, tomatoes, and peppers. And this is chicken; you've eaten chicken before. Go on, try it." Michael encouraged her.

"You are correct, Miguel. My mother is the best cook in

Spain. She once won a blue ribbon for her spicy chicken fajitas. Try it, Sam, but be very careful. It may be hotter than you're used to," commented Pedro.

Sam decided it was best not to insult the host, so she tried the enchilada. It was good, but it was also very spicy. Sam reached for a drink to wash down the spicy aftertaste. Michael, Rosa, and Pedro chuckled at Sam as she tried to relieve her tongue from the searing spices.

"Mucho calor, eh, Sam?" teased Edwardo.

"Well, Sam. How is it?" Michael was greatly amused by watching her eat.

"Bueno. It's got a bite." She answered in between drinks.

"Maybe you should stick with the chicken and rice," suggested Michael with a mischievous grin.

After dinner, Anna Maria and Rosa cleaned up while the younger boys made masks, and something called a piñata. Piñatas were made of paper and were filled with candy and toys. Senior Garza played on his guitar, practicing for his part in the Mariachi band. He gave Michael a guitar as well and asked him to join him. Sam smiled as she listened to Michael play. He had told her that he could play a mandolin. But this was the first time that she had ever heard him play. Pedro had a shiny silver trumpet. Sam had heard horns before, but never one like this. This trumpet's notes were high and playful.

Today, Pedro was old enough to join his father in the band. So, as Pedro practiced his scales, Senior Garza taught Michael two tunes they would play tonight. When everyone was ready, faces were painted, and costumes were put on. Rosa helped Sam put on a black satin dress with gold embroidery. As Rosa helped Sam put on the dress, she noticed the hideous scars on Sam's body.

"Where did you receive such wounds, señorita?" Rosa asked in English.

"Cody didn't tell you? We were attacked by wolves about a year ago. For a while, I thought I was going to lose my arm. But it has healed quite nicely." Sam explained. "You can hardly tell except for the scars."

"Well, long sleeves will cover the scars. And the silk lace will not irritate them," offered Rosa.

"This feels so weird on me." Sam looked at the dress.

"You act like you've never worn a dress before." Rosa giggled at her.

"I haven't," confessed Sam.

"Are you serious? This is the first dress you've ever worn?" asked Rosa incredulously.

"Being a poor farmer's daughter, I don't dance much. Besides, women's clothes aren't made for the work I do." Half-truths aren't exactly lies.

Rosa looked at Sam strangely but decided not to ask. After looking Sam over one last time, Rosa announced...

"There. Now you are ready."

Rose guided Sam over to the mirror. Sam couldn't believe what she saw.

"My lord, is that really me?" She gasped at her image.

"Yes, you are very pretty. You should let your hair grow longer." Rosa smiled at her handiwork.

When Sam emerged from Rosa's room, neither Michael nor Pedro could believe their eyes. Sam was exquisite. Michael stared as he looked Sam over. Her hair was still cut short and styled like a boy's, but the shape of her body was made more pronounced by her dress. Michael could never have imagined Sam like this.

"Well, what do you think?" Sam turned around in front of him so Michael could see all of her.

"I...I...I think you look great," replied Michael softly.

"Usted es una muchacha muy Hermosa, Sam." Pedro kissed her hand.

Sam helped Rosa and her mother carry food trays to the town's center. The town square was decorated with colorful streamers, banners, and lanterns. Sam and Michael marveled at the people and their lavish costumes. Michael found the people in the large, oversized heads most amusing. On the other hand, Sam was amazed by the two people on ten-foot stilts as they walked by. They definitely had the strategic advantage of advancing danger. Having men on stilts dressed as clowns was an excellent incognito security measure.

Pedro, his father, and Michael were joined by five others, each with a lute or trumpet. As the music played, people shouted, danced, and sang. The girls smiled and laughed around the food table as they watched the boys prance and tried to impress them with their dancing skills. One by one, the girls joined the boys and celebrated the night in dance.

Michael enjoyed playing in the Mariachi Band. Never before had he ever been able to express himself. For the first time in his life, he felt free. Truly free, free to do anything. He had been dead before. He knew that now. The warm touch of the summer's wind blew through his hair, and he smiled as he looked at Sam. She was so beautiful; it was a shame that she was standing alone.

Then, Michael watched as a young man approached Sam and asked her to dance. He felt relief when Sam refused but grew annoyed as the young man leaned in and whispered in Sam's ear. Sam whispered something back. Then, the young man took Sam by the hand and led her to a less crowded location. They hadn't gone far; Michael could still see them.

However, he had mixed emotions when he saw the young man put his arms around Sam. They moved slowly to a very fast rhythm. It was evident that he was only trying to teach Sam to dance, but Michael found it hard to watch them and play at the same time. Michael had to smile; he found it hard to be mad when Sam was having a good time.

"Edwardo! Venga, come here, please. Can you tell me what they are saying?" asked Sam in desperation.

"Sure, señorita. They want to know your name, where you are from, why your hair is so red, and whether you would like to dance with them," explained Edwardo, proud of his new role as interpreter.

When the band stopped playing, Michael went looking for Sam. He found her surrounded by boys. They all asked about her past, her home in England, and her bright red hair. Sam wasn't shy about answering their questions. She was a great storyteller, although little of it was true. Michael had to laugh when he saw little Edwardo acting as her interpreter. Michael politely interrupted them.

"Sam, Senior Garza, and his family are leaving. I think that you and Edwardo should say goodbye to your new friends. We must leave tomorrow, remember." He said firmly.

Sam took the hint and excused herself. She smiled brightly at them as she bid them goodbye. "Adios amigos y buenos nochas. Edwardo, muchas gracias."

"No problema, señorita. Mucho gusto." Edwardo waved goodbye as he ran off to catch up with his family.

"You look like you enjoyed yourself," said Michael, leaning against a wall.

"I did. I had a great time. I've never danced before." Sam stood beside him.

"Oh, that's right. I forgot. You wouldn't dance back home, would you?" He remembered.

"I always wanted to. It looked like fun. But I couldn't." She sighed heavily. "My duty is not to have fun. It is to protect you."

Michael watched as several children ran past, laughing and chasing one another. Then he turned his attention back to Sam. She was radiant in that dress.

You may never get another chance. Whispered a thought.

"Sam, would...Um...would you like to dance...with me?" Michael asked as he bowed to her.

Sam also bowed. "It would be my pleasure."

"Sam, girls curtsy. Like this." Michael corrected.

"Not in these shoes. It was bad enough just learning to dance. I honestly don't know how girls can wear these things and keep their balance," complained Sam mockingly.

Michael laughed. He knew well that Sam had excellent balance. "Sam, you learned to walk a rope, didn't you?"

"Well, yeah, but...." Sam began.

"Then you can learn to wear heels, it is all balance." Michael grinned at her.

Michael took Sam in his arms, his left arm around her waist, and her right hand in his. Sam let her left arm gently rest on his shoulder. Michael searched through his memory of all the dances that he knew. Which one should he teach her? On a warm night like this, only a waltz came to mind.

"One, two, three, one, two, three."

Michael counted, trying to keep Sam in step. Both laughed as Sam tripped over Michael's feet. Michael found it amazing that Sam was so excellent in some things yet so clumsy at others.

"Sam, you're trying to lead," scolded Michael.

"I'm sorry, I don't follow well." She apologized. "I was trained to be a leader."

"Just let it go and follow me. See, it's not so bad once you get the hang of it."

As they danced, Sam realized she was beginning to feel warm inside. Waltzing with Michael was...intoxicating. It was almost like drinking champagne, light and sweet. Michael's eyes were so shiny and black, like looking at two stars in the night sky. Sam shook off the dizzying effect. After all, she was his guardsman. This was not the time to get all girly and go ga ga. She forced herself to change the mood.

"Do you want me to show you the new dance I've learned tonight?" She strongly suggested.

"Okay," relented Michael, not really wanting this to end.

Sam put her left arm around Michael's waist and held him close. Taking his right hand in hers, she began to hum. Bum,

Ba Dum, Da Dum Dum Dum, Bum, Ba Dum, Da Dum, Dum, Dum. Michael laughed.

"Sam, that's a tango. Allow me."

Michael led, and Sam followed. Back and forth, they tangoed. Sam laughed as Michael hummed the tune. Michael spun, caught her in his arms, and sat her on his knee. Sam stood up when she realized that Michael was looking at her strangely. This wasn't working, and she still felt ...peculiar. Sam walked to the well, looked inside, and sat on the edge. Michael pursued her.

Sam heard a trumpet going through its scales somewhere off in the distance. The sound of laughter drifted in the air. The air was warm and light. Michael stood in front of Sam and stared at her. Sam looked into Michael's eyes. She was perplexed by what she saw. She remembered a boy who was lanky and afraid, but the boy who stood before her was now strong and confident.

On this journey, he had overcome his fears, ridden a horse, drank beer, been in fistfights, and had made a pass at her. Now, he was just like all the other boys. However, for some strange reason, this made Sam sad. She kind of missed that skinny little kid. Or maybe it was just her imagination. Michael noticed

Sam's blank stare.

"Sam? Sam? Sam, where are you?" He called to her.

"I'm sorry. I was just thinking about a scrawny little boy that I used to know." Sam gave him a small smile.

"I've changed, haven't I?" Michael embraced her.

"I'll say." Sam raised an eyebrow as she looked him over.

"Sam."

Sam looked up, and her eyes met his. The world seemed to disappear as Sam looked into those shiny black eyes. Michael drew her closer to him and gently kissed her lips. Sam had fought many battles before, but never one like this. Half of her told her to stop, while the other half told her to go on and never let it end.

"What am I doing? He's the king's son. We shouldn't do this. So why am I not stopping it? ... Because I don't want to."

Michael's strong arms held her in a gentle embrace, one she could have easily broken if she had wanted to. It pleased Michael that she hadn't rejected him.

"You see, beneath that rough and "manly" exterior is a woman whose desire is as strong as yours. Maybe if you can fulfill her desires, she will give up being a man and become your wife. You must be out of your mind. She would never do such

a thing. Besides, you must wed a princess, remember...".

Suddenly, Sam broke the embrace. She looked at Michael, then hit the wall with her fists, using the pain to drive away the fuzzy feelings.

"Sam!" Michael called out, concerned by her actions. "What are you doing?"

"No, this is wrong. I shouldn't have done that. Please forgive me, young prince." Sam apologized hastily.

Sam bowed before Michael as a guardsman would before a king. Confused and sad, Michael watched Sam walk off toward Senior Garza's house.

Chapter 12

The following day, Michael awoke to the sounds of cheering. He looked out of the window. The sun's bright rays enlightened the world, telling him that last night had disappeared into a dream. He stretched as another cheer invaded his ears.

"It's got to be Sam," sighed Michael, wondering what was happening outside.

He got dressed and ran outside. Michael rolled his eyes and shook his head. Sam was back to being Sam. She was wearing black satin pants and a white cotton shirt two sizes too big, which hung down to her knees. Michael watched as she and a young man named Richey fought a duel. From the other boys' conversations, he gathered that they were amazed by this girl's ability to learn fencing. Richey was teaching her to fence, and she was learning fast.

"No, Sam. You are overzealous and overextended. In that stance, I can easily defeat you." Richey explained in English with a heavy accent.

"Once again, please." Sam requested, and she returned to the beginning stance.

When Sam saw Michael, she waved and called him over. "Cody, come join us. This is great. It's better than fighting two-handed. The blade is easier to control and responds faster to your wrist movements."

"I don't think so. Getting stabbed just isn't what I consider fun." He joked.

Sam smiled. Some things never changed. Every day for the next two weeks, Sam and Richey sparred. Her desire to learn and her previous battle skills made her more than a match for Richey. She became so good that one morning, Richey introduced her to his teacher, Senior Relyea. In the courtyard, he tested what Sam had learned from Richey. He was impressed by Sam's ability and challenged her to a real duel to test the full extent of her skills. It was then that he decided to take her on as a student.

A two-day rest became a month-long training lesson. Every morning, Sam practiced with Senior Relyea. And every afternoon, she tried teaching Michael what she had learned. But he refused to learn, instead immersing himself in Spanish history. Finally, fed up with Sam's explanations of different ways to kill a man, Michael took her to his room and picked up his guitar.

"Sam, for once, allow me to teach you something; something ... more constructive. Something that your mother would have approved of." Michael pulled up a chair for her to sit in.

Sam laid down her rapier and sat listening to Michael play his guitar. Then Michael gave Sam his guitar and began teaching her the scales. Sam had a good ear and nimble fingers. He taught her to play the scales and then a few chords. It made Michael's heart soar that Sam could pick up playing a musical instrument as easily as she picked up a sword. Maybe he could teach her to be gentle as much as she taught him to be strong.

The next morning, Sam was the same as she ever was, eager to fight and ready to learn.

"You fight well, Señorita. Who taught you to fight?" Senior Relyea inquired as he tried to bring his sword down upon her head.

"My father was an Army soldier." Sam blocked Senior Relyea's blow and delivered one of her own.

"Buen, but Sam, calm down. You waste too much energy.

Your movement should be done lightly, quickly, and steadily."

"Si, Senior," acknowledged Sam.

She had just reassumed the starting stance when hoof beats were heard. Sam turned to see who it was and saw three Spanish soldiers riding up into the courtyard. They stopped when they came upon the gathering of students.

They said, "Sam Redshot, Cody TwoStar, you are under arrest by the authority of His Majesty, King of Spain."

Sam and Michael looked at each other.

"Say nothing." She whispered to Michael. Then she walked forward and stood to face the soldiers. "I think you have the wrong person."

"I think not. There are not many people in Spain with Redshot's red hair, senior. You will come quietly, or we will use force." The soldier told her.

"This is your companion, TwoStar?" asked another soldier.

"I don't know him; he's just another student here. Cody and I were separated in the storm that sank our ship." Sam lied skillfully. Sam was grateful that the other students had decided to say nothing. "I'll come peacefully." Sam gave her sword to Michael. "Do nothing, just follow me."

"Sam, we should run. There are only three." Michael

urged. He was apprehensive about what was going to happen.

"That would prove us guilty and only get our hosts in trouble. My red hair is my curse. Don't worry. What could happen?" She smiled at him and turned to leave.

Sam looked around curiously as she stood before the Spanish Judge in the accused's box. To the left and right of her were four rows, each of which was a seat for the jury, and behind her was an open court for spectators to watch the trial and throw accusations at her. In front of her were the judge's seat and two Spanish guards. Sam got worried as none of them looked happy. She didn't understand a word of what was going on, but she knew it would be bad for her either way. Suddenly, the judge spoke, and thank god, he spoke to her in English.

"Sam Redshot, you are hereby found guilty of piracy and are sentenced to death. Have you anything to say?"

"I'm not guilty," Sam told him, and she tried to explain. "I was shanghaied."

"Then you did not sink three Spanish galleons," accused the judge.

"Not of my own free will."

"You did not murder their captains in cold blood?" The judge continued as he read from the list of her charges.

"No." Sam's eyes widened in alarm. "That was Captain William."

"You did not, upon the 18th of May of last year, fire upon the town of Royal."

"NO!" Sam insisted, and she slammed her hands down upon the stand. "That was before I joined the crew!"

"You did not kill 83 men and dishonor seven women."

"NO! Look, I wasn't even there when that happened. As I said, I was shanghaied this past winter. The ship never made it to port, it sank in a storm, and all hands were lost, all but...but me."

"Not all hands," said a voice from the door.

Sam turned and saw Captain William standing in chains.

"Good to see you again, Royal Redshot." Captain William greeted her with a great grin.

"Changing my name again, Captain." Sam glared at him with hatred.

"Only for my first mate." He smiled. His gold teeth were as shiny as ever, although he looked a little worse for wear.

"He's lying," sneered Sam. "I wasn't your first mate. Macey was."

"Speaking of first mates, where's your buddy TwoStar?"

Captain William questioned, and his eyes narrowed on her.

"Probably talking to Macey and Davy Jones, cursing the day we met you," Sam growled back.

"Enough!" The judge shouted and struck his gavel for silence. "You are both sentenced to death by beheading. Take them away."

"You couldn't die alone, could you?" complained Sam, with loathing, as the guards chained Sam's hands and feet. "How did you find me?"

"Redheads are rare here, Samantha. But gold is universal," revealed Captain William.

"How did you...?"

Captain William and Sam were dragged away in chains. Families of the dead had gathered to see those responsible for the destruction of the town Royal get their heads detached from their bodies. The roar of the angry crowd filled Sam's ears. Shouts of death and curses followed Sam as she was pushed through the streets. An angry mob was an angry mob, no matter what country you were in or what language they spoke. William and Sam were taunted, kicked, and spat upon as they were forced through the crowd and up the stairs to the executioner's block.

"Ladies, first," smiled William. Sam growled but was relieved when they took William first. "Sam! Have you ever seen a man's head severed from his body?"

"Yes, I have, and the ones I like, I use as sword stands." Sam hollered, in bravado.

"That's what I like about you, Redshot. You're a real spitball to the end." William laughed at her.

William stopped laughing as they forced him to kneel. They placed his head on the block and tied his hands to its base. Sam stood, shaking with dread, and watched the executioner's ax fall. She looked away when Williams's head rolled off the platform. Hands grabbed Sam and forced her to kneel at the block. Sam's stomach was in knots. Her mind was racing, and her heart was in her throat.

"God, please see Michael home safely." Sam prayed earnestly.

Sam's chin hurt against the coarse wooden block, and her hands were tied beneath her. It made her sick to think William's head had rested here only a few moments ago. Sam couldn't see him, but she heard him inhale with air as the executioner raised his ax. She took a deep breath, closed her eyes, and prepared herself for the executioner's blow.

Oh my God, I'm going to die.

"Sam!" shouted a familiar voice.

She opened her eyes and saw Michael racing towards her on a flaming wagon. Michael drove straight through the crowd. The crowd dispersed, running every which way, trying to get away from the fiery wagon. Michael stood up, aimed a crossbow, and fired. The executioner yelled and clutched his throat as he tried to remove the arrow. Michael fired four more arrows at the surrounding guards, causing them to flee the platform, as he drove the flaming wagon into the platform. Landing in front of Sam and using the executioner's ax, he cut Sam free.

"God, am I glad to see you." Sam beamed, and she jumped up.

"I'm glad to see that you haven't lost your head." He snickered.

Hearing footsteps behind him, Sam turned and swung the ax upward, blunt side forward, knocking the guard off the platform. He then punched out another guard and picked up his sword.

"Sam! Come on, this wagon is going to blow." Michael grabbed her by the wrist.

They jumped off the platform and ran. Three seconds later, the wagon exploded, taking the platform with it. Wood and flames flew everywhere. People shouted, trying to get out of the way of the flying debris. Soldiers scrambled into action; some put out the fire, others captured the fleeing prisoners.

"After them!" Sam heard someone shout.

Sam and Michael jumped two guards, took their horses, and raced away from the gathering and into the woods. They wove their horses in, out, and around the trees, trying to lose their followers.

"Here we go again," Michael called out. "Know any more tree tricks?"

"Not really. But we could try...."

Just then, an arrow flew past her head and embedded itself in a tree. Sam looked behind her and saw about fifteen horsemen with crossbows.

"Oh no." Sam's heart sank, and she urged her horse to go faster. "Cody, don't look now, but we're dead."

Michael looked behind him. "Now what, guardsman?" Michael kicked his horse for more speed.

Sam's heart gladdened when she saw the barn. "That way, ride for the barn." She ordered and turned her horse to the right. "You close the door after me and lock them inside."

"But you'll be trapped as well." He pointed out.

Another arrow and another flew past them. Sam whipped her horse with the reins, making him move faster, and another arrow grazed her right arm, just missing her.

"Just do as I say before we end up shish kabobs.

Don't worry, what could happen?" She smiled.

"The last time you said that, you nearly lost your head." He chuckled and climbed down off his horse.

Sam took Michael's horse with her, and Michael hid behind a bush.

"We've got them now. We'll trap them inside." Michael heard one say.

Three soldiers jumped off their horses and prepared to close the barn door while the others followed Sam inside. Michael stayed hidden until they did. His foot broke a branch when he got up to see if all was clear. He swore at himself for being so clumsy.

"Go see what that was," ordered a soldier.

"Come on out, whoever you are," said the other.

Michael pulled a dagger out of his boot. He waited until the soldier was standing above him. Then, with quickness,

Michael stood up and thrust the dagger into the soldier's chest. When the other soldiers heard their comrade fall, they rushed to him. Michael used the fallen soldier's crossbow to get one of them. However, the third soldier jumped on him. They struggled. Michael managed to gain the advantage and broke the soldier's neck. Michael wiped his brow and got up to see about Sam.

As he listened at the barn door, Michael heard voices shouting and horses whinnying. Walking around the barn, he noticed a small window in its roof.

"I hope Sam wasn't planning to jump from there," Michael said to himself. As he said it, a figure jumped out of the window. "Sam!"

"Look out below!" She called.

Michael positioned himself to catch her. She landed in his arms, and her velocity forced them both to the ground. Michael smiled at her. Sam rolled out of his arms and stood up.

"You shouldn't have done that. I could have killed you." Sam brushed herself off.

"You could have been killed, jumping from that height!" Michael scolded her and again looked up at the roof.

"Not really, the roof back home is higher." Sam mounted a

horse.

At the sound of soldiers trying to escape the barn, Michael and Sam galloped their horses into the woods.

Chapter 13

Sam and Michael spent most of the day riding north, at full speed, to escape the Spanish soldiers by crossing onto French soil. Towards dusk, they had to stop to rest the horses and take shelter for the night.

"Head for that farmhouse," instructed Sam.

Sam took the horses while Michael negotiated a price for sleeping in the barn with the owner. As they settled in for the night, the rain hitting the roof told them they had just missed receiving another bath.

"Looks like we're stuck here for a while," Sam commented, and she collected straw for their beds.

"Well, don't start a fire in here. Okay?" He snickered. He tied the horses in a stall and gave them oats to eat.

"What's the matter? I thought you liked construction." Sam teased him. But then she spoke more seriously. "Cody."

"Yes, Sam." He responded as he brushed down the horses.

"Thank you for saving my life."

"You're welcome." He turned to watch her gather straws.

"But you shouldn't have risked your life to save mine?" continued Sam as she fashioned their beds.

"Why not?"

"You are destined to become a king. I am to protect you at all costs, even at the cost of my own life. That is my duty, not yours."

Michael stopped feeding the horses and looked at Sam's back. "Sam, you are my best friend." He told her softly. "To give my life for you is…"

"It's an unnecessary waste," chided Sam. "Your life is more important than mine."

"Not to me. Sam, if anything ever happened to you … I'd die."

"No, you wouldn't," interrupted Sam harshly.

"Yes, I would. You are my only friend. I would die of loneliness." He stated sadly, and he stroked his horse's mane.

Sam lightened up and gave him a smile. "I must admit, I was surprised when I saw you come charging towards me on that flaming wagon and the way you dealt with those soldiers…I knew you could do it. You fight well." She came and stood face to face with him.

"You were in trouble. I had to do something." Michael

gladly accepted Sam's praise.

"If something like that had happened two years ago, I would be dead by now. Someday, you will make a fine king, strong as well as smart. I know you will." She said, going back to collecting straw for her bed.

"If something like this had happened two years ago, I would have died trying to save you. I would never let anyone kill you, Sam. I would miss you too much." Michael assured her softly. He reached out to touch Sam's shoulder.

"Cody." Sam pulled away from him.

"No, Sam. Please listen. Ever since I was a child, you've been my protector and companion. But over time, you became more than that to me. You became a confidant. I am a prince, the son of a king, and yet you were the only one who ever took the time to listen to me. You patiently listened to me when I told you about my lessons, and you never told me to go away when I complained to you about my life. And despite your reservations, you allowed me to leave home to find my manhood..."

"That was the biggest mistake that I have ever made in my life. God, how did we end up in Europe?" Sam grumbled and ran her fingers through her short hair.

"It wasn't your fault, we were shanghaied..." He reminded her.

"Yes, it is. I never should have agreed to let you leave, and I never should have challenged Alex and Jacob. I should be helping them, not fighting them. And I swear, if I ever see Todd again, I'll kill him!" ranted Sam, and she kicked at their straw beds.

"Sam, if we hadn't taken this journey, I'd still be a little boy hiding from life instead of living it. Now, I can ride horses. I've been a pirate and sailed the sea. I've faced a pack of hungry wolves and survived. But best of all, I was part of a Mariachi band. Sam, I'm having the time of my life. And there is one more thing; I now know ... how much I love you." Michael took hold of Sam's waist and pulled her into his arms.

"Uh, jeez, Cody, you don't mean that." She pulled away from him.

"No, Sam, I do mean it. I didn't realize it until you were sentenced to death. No more would we play chess by the river, have our "man to man" talks outsmart Mark, or..." Michael made Sam face him.

Sam hip-tossed Michael into the bed of hay. Michael groaned with pain as he landed with a thud against the ground.

"Cody, you wouldn't be telling me this if I hadn't told you I was a girl! So, don't get mushy on me! We still have a long ride to Paris. Now get some sleep." Sam shouted at him. She was perplexed. Not only by his feelings but by her own. Why was this getting so complicated?

"But Sam..." He pleaded with her.

"Shush. Sleep." Sam ordered, and she walked away.

Michael let it go and rolled slowly over on his side.

Sam hoped that she hadn't hurt his feelings too much, so she checked on the horses. What he was feeling was perfectly natural, so she didn't blame him. But that he should feel this way about her was unnerving and seemed unnatural. Sam refused to think about it as she went outside and collected rainwater for the horses to drink. Michael was already asleep, tired from the ride. Sam lay down three feet from Michael and went to sleep.

It rained all through the night, but by morning, it had stopped. Leaving behind it fresh watered grass and the scent of wet oak trees. Michael and Sam rode out into the new day. Not being chased by soldiers wanting your head gave Sam time to look around and enjoy the French countryside. The trees lightly shaded them from the sun as it shone down on the world. The sound of birds overhead and small animals scampering made a ride through the country quite pleasant. It was two more days before they saw a sign saying 200 kilometers to Bordeaux.

They rode all day silently, stopping only at night to make camp. Michael built a big fire to dispel the cold of the night while Sam hunted with the crossbow. However, she could only catch two rabbits and a couple of pheasants.

"You did better when jumping on them from the trees." He teased her. Michael sat, turning the pheasants as they slowly roasted over the fire. "Sam."

"Hmm," acknowledged Sam. She was busy skinning the rabbits.

"Tell me about your mother."

Sam stopped skinning the rabbit and let her mind wander back through her memories.

"She died when I was very young. I can hardly remember what she looked like. I can remember her holding me as she rocked me to sleep. I remember the song she used to sing to me every night. I remember that she used to take me hunting. She and I would go into the woods and sit listening to all the animals. My mother taught me to track, hunt, and cook animals for food. She used to tell me stories about great jungles, big cats, and birds full of colors like the rainbow..." Sam's long-forgotten memories flowed to the surface.

"...I remember the high pitches of the wooden flute she used to play and the jigs that she and father would play on their violins. She always told me that someday she would teach me to play, but ... she never got the chance." She said with a sad smile.

"Your mother sounds like a most extraordinary woman," chuckled Michael, ensuring he didn't burn their food. "If she taught you to hunt, that would explain you. The people of Africa are known for their physical strength and hunting capabilities. When did she die?"

"She died when I was about three or four. I think Father was more upset than I was. He wouldn't do anything for a long time but stare at his father's sword. For a while, I was afraid that he was going to kill himself. Then one night he got drunk and brought home another woman. He told her that he wanted a son. But he just couldn't bring himself to do it. The memory of my mother was still with him. The next day, he told me I was no longer a girl and began my training to become Captain of the guards. The rest you know. Come to think of it, my mother never really put me in girls' clothes. We always wore animal skins when we went hunting. So, keeping my gender a secret was never a problem." Sam explained.

"What do you think you would have become if your father had had a son?" Michael asked.

"I probably would have become an ewe," chuckled Sam.

"An ewe?" Michael's face was flushed with confusion.

"I would have spent my youth in my father's house learning to cook, sew, and clean. Then I would have been married off and spent my life performing these same tasks for my husband and raising his children; never dreaming of or wanting an adventure and never looking beyond my own home." Sam contemplated, and she went back to skinning the rabbits.

"Not you. With the mother you had, you were born to be a lioness. The one who eats sheep." Michael tested the pheasants to see if they were fully cooked.

"You think so." Sam laughed, and she put the rabbit on a spit.

"I know so. Even on your father's side, a temper and the lust for adventure is the curse of the redheaded." He laughed.

Sam laughed as she ran her fingers through her great red hair.

Chapter 14

On the road to Montauban, it began to rain. Dark clouds swam overhead, and their only light was the sporadic flashes of lightning. Up ahead, Michael saw a coach and six white horses traveling the same road. Upon the door was the coat of arms of the family de Letourneau. Michael saw the coach set upon by eight highwaymen. Carrying crossbows and swords, they killed the guards and robbed the coach. Michael kicked his horse into a full gallop. Sam called to him to see what was wrong. She drew her sword when she saw the coach and charged after Michael.

Michael killed two with his crossbow and a third with a dagger. Two of the highwaymen fled when they realized they were being attacked. The other three realized they outnumbered Sam and Michael and decided to fight. One highwayman rode his horse straight at her. She ducked his blow and stabbed his horse's hind legs with her sword. His horse reared and threw the robber to the ground. Sam jumped from her horse and thrust her sword through him before he could get up. The second charged at her back, his sword raised to strike. Sam dropped onto her knees and thrust her sword upwards through her attacker's body. The look of surprise from an attack from below was his last expression before he dropped dead to the ground. Sam used the rain to wash and clean her sword. Then she sloshed her way through the mud toward the coach.

She opened the door, and a dagger shot out at her.

Instinctively, Sam moved, blocking her chest with her arm.

"If you want my money so badly, take it and this too." A voice hollered.

Sam clutched her right arm and backed away from the coach. She withdrew the dagger from her arm and threw it to the ground. Michael withdrew his sword from his assailant's body and went to see what was wrong.

"What is the matter, Sam?" He worried.

"She stabbed me!" shouted Sam in disbelief.

Michael looked at her bleeding right arm. "You keep this up and you won't have any arms left to fight with." Michael joked. He then called out to the coach's owner. "Lady du Letourneau, it's me, Prince Michael Rowland of England. It is safe for you to come out now."

"Prince Michael!" Lady Letourneau was happy at a familiar voice. She stepped out of the carriage into the rain and stared at Michael.

"Good evening, your highness. My, my, you sure have grown." She curtsied before Michael.

"It is good to see you again as well." Michael gently kissed her hand.

Thunder rumbled, lightning flashed, and the rain continued to fall.

"I think it would be better if we continued this conversation inside," urged Michael. Lady De Letourneau agreed and stepped inside the coach. Michael followed. "Sam!" Michael called from the window. "Clean up this mess, will you?"

Sam said nothing as she looked at her arm. It wasn't bad; it would heal quicker than a wolf bite. She shook her head and went about collecting the dead bodies of Lady Letourneau's guardsmen and putting them on their horses. Between sneezes, she tied them on their horses, tied their horses' reins to the back of the coach, then climbed into the driver's seat and prepared the coach's horses to leave.

Michael and Lady de Letourneau continued their

conversation inside the coach, somewhat warmer and out of the rain.

"May I ask what Your Majesty is doing so far from home?" questioned Lady Letourneau with great curiosity.

"Sam and I just decided to leave the palace for a while." Michael neatly folded his hands in a princely manner.

"Sam?" questioned Lady Letourneau, unfamiliar with that name.

"Yes, the poor … boy you accidentally mistook for a robber." Michael leaned out of the window and called to her. "Sam!"

"Yes, Your Highness," Sam answered from the driver's seat, soaking wet.

"That is my guardsman and companion, Sam Bowman," introduced Prince Michael.

"Only one guardsman?" worried Lady Letourneau. "Isn't that …unsafe?"

"One attracts less attention. Besides, he's the best of my father's guards and quite proficient with a blade." Michael assured her. "It seems that all is ready. Shall we leave?"

Lady Du Letourneau nodded.

"Sam, let's go!" urged Michael.

"Yes, Sire. Um, sire, where are we going?" Sam called

down from the driver's seat.

"The Letourneaus live in Nimes." He told her.

"Nimes! That's three days off." She complained.

"Then you had better get going," Michael said in a princely tone.

Blast it. Sam grumbled and wiped the rain out of her eyes. "Yes, sire. Hiya!"

Sam snapped the whip and set the horses in motion, driving them hard and fast.

"Your Highness, it would be my honor if you would join us for dinner. My daughters would be delighted to see you again," Lady Letourneau said as Michael sat down.

"I am hardly dressed for dinner, milady." Michael waved down at his clothes.

"Not a problem. I will send my servants out for you." Lady Letourneau offered with gladness.

With that settled, Lady Letourneau asked him more questions about his journey. Towards evening, the rain stopped. Poor Sam was drenched to the skin and envied Michael and Milady, who were dry and inside. Sam thanked God for Michael's benevolence when he suggested they stop at an inn for the night. Sam and Lady du Letourneau disagreed with Sam's arrangements for her guardsmen.

"Milady, I'm not dragging those dead men all the way back to Nimes," Sam informed her firmly.

Michael finally settled the matter by assuring her that Sam was right. Sam put the horses in the stables, bought dry clothes, and was obliged to see to Lady Letourneau's needs before she could turn in for the night.

When she finally came to their room, Michael greeted her, "What's the matter, Sam? You look pitiful."

"I had forgotten about ladies of court and how rigid the rules of convention are," Sam whined.

"Sam, we've been gone so long that we've forgotten or broken most of the rules of convention. Get some sleep, Sam. I'll take first watch." Michael suggested warmly.

"I can't let you do that, sire." Sam collapsed onto the floor but sat cross-legged in a guard's position.

"Sam, a guardsman never sits or lies down in the presence of his king, unless instructed to do so." Michael reminded her with a smile.

"Ugh, have I broken that many rules? At this point, I'm too tired to care. You can behead me later if you wish. I'm sure my father would be most happy to assist you." Sam said in between yawns.

"I would, but then who would drive?" jested Michael. "Go on, get some rest. I'll need you to be rested tomorrow. Good night, Sam."

Michael gave Sam a pillow and then covered her with a blanket. Stepping over her, he sat on the bed, looking out his window at the night sky. The rain continued to fall.

In the morning, Sam hitched all of Lady Letourneau's horses, even her dead guardsmen's horses, to the carriage. She loaded Lady Letourneau's things and then Lady Letourneau. Michael followed her, and Sam climbed into the driver's seat. She envied Michael yesterday, only because it was raining. She did not envy him today. Lady Letourneau never seemed to shut up.

Michael was much relieved when Sam pulled the coach to a stop before the Letourneau Estate. Sam jumped from the driver's seat, opened the door, and helped Lady Letourneau out. Lady Letourneau escorted them into her home and sent the servants out for new clothes for Michael and Sam. Then, she accompanied them to their rooms so that they could bathe and change clothes. After that, she left to see about dinner. Sam joined Michael in his room and locked the door.

"I say we split now," warned Sam.

"Sam, you know that's not polite. Besides, I'm starving. We haven't eaten in ten hours. Anyway, now I can let my father know I'm alright before we continue." Michael pulled off his shirt.

"Continue? What do you mean by continue? I was only supposed to escort you to the Swinton School. A European tour wasn't in the plan." Sam argued, and she turned her back as he removed his pants.

"Sam, really, I will spend the rest of my life in that castle. Right now, I want to see all those places I've studied about all my life." He informed her. "Please, Sam. Besides, are you really ready to return to the rules of convention?"

Sam hated to admit it, but he had a point. "As you wish, your majesty." Sam laughed as she made a funny curtsy.

"Don't start with me, Sam," warned Michael playfully.

Michael retired to the bathroom and closed the door, but only halfway. Sam heard water splashing and then a sigh.

"Oh, Sam, this is divine," Michael called from his bath.

"You know those girls aren't going to let you have a moment's peace," Sam told him from the doorway.

"Funny, isn't it. Two years ago, they wouldn't even look at me except for the fact that I'm a prince. Now..."

"Now they'll want you for more than just your money." Sam chuckled and shook her head.

"Sam!" He threw a bar of soap at her. Sam caught it with her right hand. "Not too wounded, I see," Michael commented on Sam's dexterity.

"I heal fast." She tossed the soap back to him.

"Well, go and get dressed for dinner," urged Michael. "It is very ill-mannered to be late."

"Alright, I'm going."

She bowed before Michael and then went to her room. There, laid out on her bed, was a brand new, bright blue French 1st Lieutenant's uniform. Very nice. Sam closed the curtains to her room and locked the doors. She locked the bathroom door, disrobed, and stepped into the bath.

"Ahhh, the young prince was right. This feels good. A hot bath was every so much better than taking baths that coincided with the annual rainfall." She thought blissfully.

Minutes later, she emerged from her room in her new uniform. Michael was waiting for her in the hall.

"You look really good. That uniform suits you very well,"

complimented Michael.

"Always has, always will." Sam beamed proudly.

"Just like your father?" Michael grinned and shook his head at Sam's false modesty. "Although I think I like your hair better when parted on the left." He commented as he studied her.

Sam went back into her room and picked up a comb. Seconds later, she reentered the hall, her hair parted on the left side.

"Better?"

"Much. Are you ready?"

Sam took a deep breath and prepared to face the Letourneau's and their four daughters again. Then she remembered something.

"Heck, why am I worried? You're the one that they're fawning over. I'm just the hired help."

Michael sighed and smiled weakly.

"What's the matter?" asked Sam as they walked down the hall.

"Now that we are back among people who know me, I am once again bound by the rules of convention." He complained. "I wish that it were just you and me again."

"Just two guys traveling the open road." Sam raised an

eyebrow at him.

Then Michael remembered Sam was supposed to be a boy. "Don't worry, Sam, I'll remember." He promised.

As they descended the stairs, Lady Letourneau met and escorted them to the living room. She asked them to be seated and sent a servant to find her husband.

"I am sorry that he's not here to greet you, Your Highness. He was out hunting today, and he got caught in the rain. He will be down in a moment." She explained, gently waving her fan.

"Your Highness, having you in my home is a great honor and a privilege." Gushed Lord Letourneau as he entered the room. "My home is at your disposal."

No sooner had Lord Letourneau entered than a clatter of female voices came nearer the living room.

"Prepare yourself, Cody." Whispered Sam. "Those are his daughters, and you are not the skinny, little runt you used to be."

These words were barely out of her mouth when four elegant young ladies appeared at the door. The Eldest was Lisa, a beautiful young lady of eighteen. Then there was Terry, sixteen, and the twins, Allissa and Vanessa, both fourteen. The girls curtsied low before entering, each gliding quickly across the floor with all the grace and style their breeding demanded. Sam shook her head in disgust. Such she might have been if fate had not forced her father to make a boy of her.

Sheep one and all. Sam grimaced.

"Now, girls, please let him be. They have had a long journey, " their mother admonished them.

"Prince Michael, how are you traveling without a coach and guards?" Allissa asked.

"By horseback, Sam and I manage to get a round quite well. And with his excellent bowmanship, we are never without food," explained Michael politely.

"So, Sam, did you earn that uniform, or was it given to you?" Asked a disgruntled voice.

A young man, about twenty, stood leaning against the doorway. He was about five foot eleven inches tall, with black hair and blue eyes. His stance was strong and defiant, and every part of him screamed upper-class breeding.

"Peter!" Shouted his father. "Do not insult our guests. Your Majesty, my son Peter." Lord Letourneau frowned as he introduced his eldest son. "Peter, this is His Highness Prince

Michael Rowland and his guardsman Sam Bowman."

Peter bowed before Prince Michael, and Sam answered his question.

"Peter, I assure you that I have earned this rank with every mark on my body." Sam glared at him with a smirk.

Michael cleared his throat and smiled. Well, that was ... sort of the truth.

"What happened to your face, and why is your hair so red?" asked a small voice from behind Peter.

"And this is my other disrespectful son, Thomas," continued Lord Letourneau.

Out from behind Peter came a little boy about eight years old. He looked like a smaller version of his brother. He, too, had black hair and blue eyes, but his stature was more playful than his brother's.

"My father's name is Thomas, too." Sam kneeled to talk to Tom. "My hair is red because of my father, a white, highland Englishman. As for my scars, I received them in a wolf attack."

"Wolves attacked you? How did you ever manage to escape?" Terry asked with great interest.

"Sam charged at them, killing every one of them in my defense." Michael proudly smiled.

"How many?" Tom asked eagerly.

"Ten," Michael answered and held up his hands.

"Ten, unlikely, they would have torn you to shreds," challenged Peter, who tried not to show how interested he was in the story.

"Who says they didn't?" Sam rolled up her left sleeve and showed Thomas her arm. Although her arm had completely healed, great scars could still be seen. Thomas was impressed, and he whistled. "But I can't take the credit for killing all of them. The young prince also killed four, saving my arm and my life."

"If you are that good with a blade, then you should go to the fencing tournament tomorrow." Peter dared her.

"Fencing?" Sam's eyes perked up with great interest.

"Sam, don't even think about it," warned Michael. "What about your arms?"

"Both are perfectly fine. I told you I heal fast. Besides, Milady only scratched me with her blade."

"Mother, you stabbed him?" Vanessa spoke up for the first time.

"Your mother mistook Sam for a highwayman," explained Michael.

"You were attacked? Are you alright?" Her husband asked.

"I'm fine. But if Prince Michael hadn't come along when he did..." stated Lady Letourneau, with great emotion and securing much sympathy.

The family clamor over Lady Letourneau continued. Her father and Peter promised better protection, and her daughters expressed worry and relief about her safe return.

With their attention now off her, Sam had time to look around at the Letourneau's home. The rooms of this French home were as lavishly done, if not more so, than the ones at home. Two red velvet sofas, upon one of which they were currently sitting, a piano, two full-bodied male statues, two bust works of someone's head, draperies, curtains, and a table and four chairs, most likely for card games. Sam's observations and the family chatter ended when a servant announced that dinner was ready.

The Letourneau girls had taken all the seats near and across from Michael. So, Sam was forced to sit near the end of the table with Tom and Peter. She didn't care, anything to be away from those giggly girls.

Sheep rise and revolt. Sam stifled a laugh and quietly ate dinner.

However, she was not to eat in peace. Tom asked her all sorts of questions. On the other hand, Peter just sat and glared at her from across the table. Sam looked up at the table at Michael. Though he was the perfect guest, Sam could see he was uncomfortable. Then Sam looked over at Vanessa. Vanessa sat quietly, eating her dinner. She only asked one or two questions and then just seemed to get lost. Sam wondered if Vanessa was always left out, being the youngest of the girls.

Although Vanessa was less aggressive than her sisters, she was by no means the dullest. Her eyes seemed to hold a certain fire, like she knew something no one else knew. Sam smiled as Vanessa reminded her of a young adventurer waiting for her first adventure—a little sheep just waiting to become a wolf, like Sam.

After suffering through dinner, Michael and Sam suffered through family hour, which wasn't so bad for Sam since she had beaten Peter and Lord Letourneau out of about two hundred and fifty francs while playing poker.

"Well, of all the... You win again, Sam," announced Lord Letourneau, and he reshuffled the cards.

"I think you're palming the cards," Peter complained.

"That's enough, Peter," warned his father.

Sam just gave Peter a mischievous look and a smirk. Lord Letourneau called it a night and sent his children to bed before he and his wife also retired. Sam followed Michael to his room.

"Where are you going?" asked Michael.

"With you," said Sam.

"Damn, the rules of convention." Michael chuckled cheerfully.

"Don't be insane, it's because of the rules of convention. A guardsman is at his sire's side at ALL times," reminded Sam.

"Back to the floor?"

"Chair." Sam pointed.

"Pillow and Blanket?" He handed them to her.

"Please." Sam took them and placed them into the chair. "You know, I think Lisa likes you."

"How can you say that? They all like me; I'm a prince, " Michael said with profound dread.

"No, I mean she really likes you. You didn't see the look in her eyes this evening?"

"How could I? I was too busy trying to keep her hands out of my lap." He chuckled.

"So that's why you looked so strange." Sam laughed, and she moved a chair to the middle of the room.

As Michael dressed for bed, Sam made her bed on the chair. From this position, she could keep an eye on Michael, the window, and the door. Sam kept on her uniform and pulled the blanket up over her lap.

"Good night, Sam."

"Good night, your highness."

Michael was beginning to hate being called that, especially by Sam. After all they had been through, he wished she would just call him Cody. She hadn't even called him Cody once since this morning. He missed her. He lay his head on his pillow and stared up at the ceiling.

"Sam?"

"Yes, your highness."

"Won't you call me Cody, if you won't call me Michael?" He requested softly.

"Not while we're around people who know you," said Sam. After we leave here, when we are alone, I will call you Cody again."

Michael smiled. Sam sat in the chair with her eyes closed and hummed to herself. Michael lay in bed listening to her.

"What are you humming?"

"A lullaby my mother used to sing to me. I'll stop if it

bothers you."

"No, no. In fact, please sing it for me." requested Michael.

Sam laughed and shook her head. "Oh no, no, no. I can't sing."

"Please, Sam." He begged, full of curiosity about the tune.

"Alright. Go to sleep, my little lamb. Sail to dreamland, my little Sam. Lay down your head and close your eyes. Let go of all your questions and ask no more whys. Go to sleep, my little dear. Do not cry; I am right here. Dream, Sweet Dreams, full of delights. Sleep well, sleep fast, sleep long, sleep tight." Sam sang softly.

By the rhythm of his breathing, Sam could tell that Michael was asleep, and she settled down for the night. Michael was so enthralled with Sam's song that he could hear it in his dreams...

**

Michael opened his eyes and recognized his room back at the castle. He got up from his bed and walked down the halls. Though nothing had changed that he could remember, something was distinctly different. He went to Sam's room, but she wasn't there.

"Sam?"

He went into his son's room. A twelve-year-old boy with bright red hair was sound asleep. Michael covered him up and kissed him good night. He then went to his daughter's room. The light was still on. When he went in, he saw Sam sitting in a rocking chair, gently rocking their baby girl to sleep.

"Go to sleep, my little lamb. Sail to dreamland, my little Sam..."

"Sam," whispered Michael as Sam lay her daughter down to sleep.

Michael took Sam in his arms and kissed her. Sam gently and quietly hip-tossed Michael to the floor and sat on his chest. She leaned down to kiss him, but a hand covered his mouth instead.

**

Michael woke up, startled. Sam was crouched by Michael's side with her hand over his mouth.

"What's wrong?" He asked in a muffled voice.

"Someone is coming." She whispered.

Both sat and listened as the floorboards creaked and the door was unlocked. The door opened.

"Try not to kill them, whoever it is," Michael begged.

"Aw, just one. Please," teased Sam.

"Sam, stop that."

A figure stepped in, closed the door, and tiptoed over to the bed. Sam's keen eyes recognized the intruder. Sam kept low and stealthily crept over to the lantern on the table.

"Your highness," She whispered. "Are you asleep?"

"No, Lisa, he isn't?" Sam lit the lamp.

"Sam! Your Highness, I...I..." Lisa blushed at being caught.

"Do you need something, Lisa?" Michael tried to look serious.

"Ah ... yes." She said, ashamed to look him in the eye. "I need to speak to you in private."

"What about?" Michael hoped that Sam wouldn't leave.

Lisa looked at Sam, hoping that she would. Sam didn't move. "He's perfectly safe with me," said Lisa, hoping Sam would take the hint.

"But is he perfectly safe from you?" Thought Sam playfully.

Michael could see that Lisa wouldn't leave, so he nodded to Sam. Sam bowed to Michael and went outside onto the balcony. It had stopped raining, and the clouds had parted, revealing a beautiful night of stars. Sam relished the smell of the rain-wet trees.

When Sam turned around, she saw Michael backing away as Lisa advanced on him. She suppressed an urge to laugh as she watched this scene. When she saw Michael coming her way, Sam stepped out of the way. The balcony window swung open, and Michael closed it, shutting Lisa inside.

"Well, don't stand there laughing. Do something." Michael pleaded.

Sam just laughed. Michael pushed on the window to keep Lisa inside, and Lisa pushed on the window, trying to get outside.

"Well, it's not like wrestling deer or wolves, is it?" joked Sam.

"Don't be too sure," chuckled Michael. "She's strong."

"Step aside, sire. Let a real man handle this." Sam's manner was arrogant and cocky.

"What are you going to do?" Michael wondered, worried about just what Sam would do.

"Just you watch."

"You're not going to kiss her, are you?" He laughed.

"Oh, I'm going to do more than that," leered Sam.

"Sam, don't."

Michael moved to stop her, but it was too late. Sam

opened the window, and Lisa fell into Sam's arms.

"His Highness is... tired. But I'm not. If you care to play with me?" Sam suggested. She gently but firmly escorted Lisa back into the room.

"Let go of me, sir. I think I should leave now." Lisa pulled away from Sam.

"Must you?" Sam grabbed her by the wrist and pulled her closer. "We could...."

Sam whispered in her ear. Lisa gasped and slapped Sam's face. She collected her robe and left Michael's room.

"Ow. That stung." Sam rubbed her face.

"Are you alright?" asked Michael, laughing.

"That really hurt."

"You act like that's the first time you've ever been slapped."

"I must admit. I've never made a pass at a Lady before, only barmaids. But I always leave them speechless." Sam pretended that her pride was bruised.

"You're lucky she didn't punch you in the arm." snickered Michael. "What did you say to her anyway?"

"Just the usual stuff." Sam shrugged.

"No wonder she slapped you. Here, let me see. Oh, you'll be fine, you big baby."

Michael pushed Sam. Sam pushed him back. Michael picked up a pillow and whacked her with it. Sam snatched the pillow from him and whacked him with it. Michael picked up another pillow, and the pillow fight began. Laughing and whacking, they pounded on each other until Michael stopped it.

"Shush, Sam, people are trying to sleep."

Sam threw her pillow at him and retired to her chair. Michael made up his bed and lay down to sleep.

Chapter 15

Early the next morning, there was a pounding at their door. Sam got up to open the door. When she did, Peter hit her with a right hook.

"Sam!" called Michael as he watched his guardsman fall to the floor.

"That was for my sister! I saw her come out of this room last night, and she was distraught. What did you do to her?!" Peter shouted angrily.

"Nothing." Sam stood up and faced off against him. "I will allow you that one junior. But don't push me, it's too…"

Sam didn't finish. Peter tried to hit her again, but Sam blocked the punch and hip-tossed him to the floor.

"Peter, don't. Nothing happened, you have my word." Michael rushed over to help him up.

"Your highness, please allow me to take out the trash." Sam sneered, and she hit her left hand with a fist.

"Trash! I'll show you."

Peter took another swing at her. Sam blocked it and

punched Peter in the stomach. He backed up, holding his stomach and coughing for air.

"Sam, stop it and I mean now!" Michael ordered angrily.

Sam looked at Michael. He wasn't joking. Sam stood at parade rest before Michael. Peter regained his composure, pulled a glove from his pocket, and slapped Sam. Sam rubbed her cheek, and her temper flared. In the hallway, two little feet ran down the hall.

As he left, Peter instructed Sam to "Choose your weapon and meet me on the back lawn in five minutes."

"Sam, don't do this," Michael begged as he watched her look for her sword.

"Don't worry, I won't kill him...until he asks me to." Sam tied on her saber.

"Sam..."

"Your highness, he's been trying to pick a fight with me ever since we came here." Interrupted Sam. "I don't know what his problem is, but...."

"Sam, must you always concede to a fight?" scolded Michael.

"I didn't start this. Besides, I like fighting, remember." She smiled playfully.

"Sam, it's just a misunderstanding. I can't have you fighting our host's son just for fun."

"Cody...Sire, I promise I won't hurt him. But sometimes a man must fight to stand up for his principles. He believes I have dishonored his sister, and he is willing to fight and die for her honor. Frankly, I admire his loyalty."

"But Sam, talking could straighten this whole thing out."

"What do words matter when a lady's reputation is on the line. Will mere words cover her shame? Nay, only the blood of the offender will do." theatricalized Sam.

"Sam, stop being silly." Michael snapped, following Sam out of the room and down the stairs. "This is stupid."

"So are most wars. But this is how they usually start. With some people, honor is everything, and they are more than willing to die for it." Sam explained as they walked onto the lawn to meet Peter.

"Sam, I forbid you to fight him." Michael grabbed Sam's right arm and forced her to stop.

Sam stopped and looked at Michael. You forbid me? That's a first. "Cody, I have to. He slapped me. The challenge has been given and must be answered." Sam calmly and gently removed Michael's hand from her arm.

"Sam ..." Michael softly called her name as his eyes pleaded with her to stop this.

"Gee, it's cold out here." Sam quickly changed the subject.

It was not long before Peter came out wearing his father's sword. "Are you ready to pay for my sister's dishonor?"

"There was no dishonor, Sam and I were just pillow-fighting." Michael insisted.

"Pillow fighting? You expect me to believe that. My sister leaves your room very upset, I hear laughing, and you expect me to believe that nothing happened?!" hollered Peter.

"Yes. Believe me, Peter, it's the truth," maintained Michael.

"Let's get this over with, it's cold out here," said Sam, impatiently.

"Are you in a hurry to die, villain?" inquired Peter.

"Oh, that his brain was as sharp as his tongue." Sam laughed at him.

"En guard." Peter pulled his sword out of his scabbard.

Sam and Peter prepared to fight. Michael stood aside and watched as the duel began. Peter lunged at Sam, but Sam blocked him and thrust his legs at him.

"You think you can come here, take my command, and my sister and whatever else you want. Well, think again, I don't care if you are the king's guardsman, I will have my revenge." Peter divulged angrily.

"What the hell are you babbling about?" Sam defended herself from a very fierce attack.

Tired of retreating, Sam pressed harder on her attack. Back and forth, they parried and thrust until Lord Letourneau emerged with Vanessa, Lisa, and Tommy right behind him.

"Stop this at once!" commanded Lord Letourneau.

Peter's attention was distracted, and he didn't block Sam's lunge. Sam cut his upper arm just below his shoulder. Sam stopped when she saw Lord Letourneau. Peter clutched his arm as it lightly bled.

"What is going on here?" Lord Letourneau demanded gruffly.

"Just practicing for today's tournament." Sam lied nonchalantly.

"Don't cover for my son, sir. Peter, why were you fighting our guests?" Lord Letourneau questioned his son.

"To cover the shame of my sister with his blood." Peter pointed his sword at Sam.

"Stop being so dramatic and answer my question," scolded Lord Letourneau.

"I saw Lisa leave the prince's room last night, and she looked very upset. Then, later, I heard laughing. What was I to think?" Peter asked.

"Lisa, is this true?" asked her father sternly. Lisa didn't answer. "What were you doing in his room that late at night?"

Sam stepped in. "Pillow fighting. The young prince asked her if she wanted to join us in a game. However, she declined. She said it was improper for a girl her age to be alone with two men late at night. The laughter your son overheard was ours as we fought. Your daughter returned to her room. Sir, you needn't worry about her virtue. She is a good girl. You have raised her well." Sam explained most solemnly and sincerely.

"Is this true, daughter?" asked her father.

Unsure of what to say, Lisa just nodded.

"Well then, no harm was done." He said, clearing his throat. "And honor is satisfied. Now, Your Highness, would you care for some breakfast?"

Lord Letourneau walked back towards the house, his children in tow. Sam and Michael walked behind them, well out of earshot. Sam let out a sigh and wiped her forehead.

"You're good," complimented Michael.

"What is lying, but flattery and embellishment?" chuckled

Sam. "Come on, I'm hungry."

After breakfast, Sam and Michael retired to the library. Michael was delighted to be among books once again.

"Here, Sam, read this; I think you'll find it... interesting." He said, tossing a book at her.

"Taming of the Shrew by William Shakespeare." Sam read the cover and looked the book over.

Intrigued, Sam sat on the brown velvet sofa and began reading. Minutes later, there was a knock at the door.

"Come in," called Michael.

When the door opened, Lisa curtsied, entered the room, and shut the door behind her. Sam looked up from her book to see who it was, then returned to her reading. Michael left off looking for a book and went to see her.

"Hello, Lisa. Is everything O.K.?" He inquired.

"Yes, I just came to thank you for covering for me and to apologize for my behavior last night." She apologized bashfully.

"I should apologize also for allowing Sam to tease you like that. I assure you, he meant no harm. He's just incorrigible." Michael spoke agreeably.

"I hardly think I'm manipulating you," Sam commented

from the corner, still reading.

"Aren't you?" smirked Michael as he raised an eyebrow at Sam.

Sam just stared at him and raised an eyebrow back at him. "Well, let's hope you become as tame as she and grow up to be the man your father wants you to be."

Sam and Michael just stared at each other for a while, and then Michael remembered Lisa.

"Lisa, if I may ask, what's the matter with Peter? I believe he was actually trying to kill Sam," Michael said.

"You must forgive him, your highness. He was passed over for promotion. A promotion that he worked very hard for and..." Lisa revealed.

"Then he should marry the Captain's daughter as I did." Sam chuckled from the corner.

"You did?" Lisa asked in astonishment.

"He did not. He's teasing you again. Pay no attention to him." Michael gave Sam a "behave or else" look.

"Anyway, I'd better go. Thanks again." She curtsied.

"Bye," said Sam.

"Sam," snapped Michael. "Goodbye, Lisa." Michael gently kissed her hand.

An hour later, there was another knock at the door. This time, Sam got up and opened the door. It was Vanessa.

"Hello...Vanessa, right," stated Sam.

"Yes." Vanessa strolled into the room.

"What do you want?" Sam asked, none too politely.

"Sam," warned Michael. "Be nice."

"What can I do for you, milady?" rephrased Sam.

"I want to speak to you in private." Vanessa addressed Sam but then looked at Michael.

Michael smiled and got up to leave. "It's your turn." He whispered, grinning at Sam.

Sam pretended to kick Michael as he closed the door. Sam sighed and then fell into a chair.

"You two must be excellent friends for you to treat the prince in such a manner," Vanessa plainly stated as she watched Sam plop down into the chair.

"We grew up together. I've been his protector all his life," said Sam. "But it is true; he does let me get away with a lot. Please, sit down. What's on your mind?"

"Does he know you're a girl?" Vanessa asked, point blank, as she gracefully sat down opposite Sam.

"What makes you...?" questioned Sam with great surprise.

"Well, you have no Adam's apple, mustache, or beard. One of your age shouldn't be so... baby-faced. You should pencil one in and wear higher collars. The wolf marks help, though. It gives you a stern look," enlightened Vanessa.

"Well, I'll be..." Sam stroked her chin. "I have been meaning to grow one. I just haven't gotten around to it yet. And yes, the prince knows."

"Let me guess. He's a prince, you're a commoner, and you're running away together," fantasized Vanessa as she elegantly crossed her legs.

"Ha-Ha-Ha, nothing so fanciful. We were shanghaied while we were staying in Gatlin's market. I am his real guardsman, though. My father needed a boy to carry on our family's tradition. He got me instead. No one knows that but you and Prince Michael." Sam revealed, flabbergasted, that her secret had been discovered. "Please don't ever tell anyone."

"So why didn't your father just take another wife?" Vanessa leaned forward and listened to Sam's story.

"You know, I truly have no idea. I always thought that it was because of my mother's memory. Fortunately, we've both adjusted. I actually like living this way. I get to do so much more than one would think a woman is capable of. My father and I may make our mistakes, but we have no regrets," Sam said.

"I wish I could. I want to live how I want, do whatever I want, have no one judge me, and never be sorry for anything. I want to travel the world, see and learn, and have a man who would risk his life for me and fulfill my every desire. Speaking of which, do you and the prince ever...?" Vanessa gave Sam a very sly look.

"No! We don't," interrupted Sam, not at all liking the direction of this conversation.

"Why not?" Vanessa grinned coyly.

"Because it would make things very difficult when he becomes king, and I am to be his Captain of the Guard. As a man, I could not explain having his child." Sam crossed her arms and eyed Vanessa.

Vanessa nodded. She could see how that might be a problem. However, with a very mischievous look, she asked...

"But, ah...all problems aside, if you could...would you?"

Sam thought about it. She thought about sleeping by his side in a cold cave and their night of dancing in Spain. She had greatly enjoyed dancing with him in Spain. The more she thought about it, the more troubled she grew. She was supposed to be a boy, raised to be a fighter and someday Captain of the King's Guards. How could she entertain such thoughts? She would never be able to know any man. Besides, he was her charge, but more than that, she considered him a close friend and nothing else. Still, there was that nagging little, mischievous voice.

But what if you were a woman, not a guardsman, and he was a peasant, destined to be nobody? Would you?

"If he were not destined to become king...maybe I...would...consider it," Sam confessed, and she shrugged.

Vanessa's eyes sparkled with laughter as she smiled. "I wonder how I would look in my brother's uniform?" She pondered as she rose to leave. "Don't worry, Sam. I promise that your secret is safe with me. And though you are to be a Guardsman, I don't see anything wrong with you "mingling" with him."

"My father would not agree with you," chuckled Sam as she ran her fingers through her bright red hair.

"But your father isn't here," reminded Vanessa, closing the door behind her.

In two days, Sam and Michael resumed their journey.

Lord Letourneau gave them two of his finest horses and two packhorses. This time, they left with enough food, water, and clothes to last a month. As they rode through the French countryside, Michael told Sam about all he had learned about France from his tutors. However, Sam wasn't listening. She was thoroughly engrossed in As You Like It by William Shakespeare. Lord Letourneau gave it to her as a present for Peter's poor behavior. Her horse ambled on behind Michael's as she read.

The weather was uncommonly good for a change. Warm winds wrapped around them as they made their way East. Trees rustled, and grass bowed as the wind blew. The sun overshadowed them with its rays and led them on as they traveled northeast. The weather remained suitable for the next four weeks as they made their way into Switzerland.

Chapter 16

Sam and Michael traveled to the northern tip of Italy. They refilled their water sacks in a courtyard fountain. In town, they enjoyed the hospitality of a little inn called the Vino Rouge. They dined on bread, goat cheese, fresh fruits, and wine. After dinner, they went to the map shop to purchase a map of Europe. Sam kept insisting that they return home, but Michael refused.

In three months, she and Michael finally reached Austria. It was well into the evening when Sam and Michael rode into Vienna. Michael was excited to be in Vienna, Austria, home to and classroom of music's finest and most famous musicians. Sam was tired and just wanted to get some sleep.

"Sam, how can you not be excited. Your mother was a musician." Michael bubbled with enthusiasm.

"I'm too tired to care. I'll be excited tomorrow after a good night's sleep." She yawned as she stretched. "Oh, and do me a favor. Don't tell anyone who you are. I can't bear to sit through another social dinner like the one at the Letourneau's."

"Agreed, we'll just be two boys out on the town. First class though, sons of lords, no more leaving like peasants." He spoke.

"Done, now where is the best hotel in all of Austria?" She asked, with a grand and sweeping hand gesture.

Today was Wednesday. Sam and Michael changed their clothes and went out for dinner. As Sam adored the Filet Minion, Michael savored the lobster. After dinner, Sam talked Michael into going to a men's club for a couple of rounds of poker to replenish their pockets, or so she said.

The men's club was very different from the taverns she had visited. Things were tranquil in the men's club. The atmosphere was very upper-class. The rooms were exceptionally well-lit, warm, and comfortable. No one said a word in the reading room. The only noise here was the rustle of pages being turned. The poker room had a little more life.

The day's important topics, reviews of shows, and male gossip, things unfit for ladylike ears, were openly discussed. Sam introduced herself to the gentlemen at the table. She introduced Michael as Cody and then sat down for a friendly game. By the time Sam and Michael left, Sam had over 1200 Schillings in her pockets. Then Sam and Michael followed two young women on their way to a concert by Cornelius Canis. After that, Michael dragged Sam to a Shakespearian play.

"Trust me; you'll enjoy this. If I had to write about our travels, it would be like this play." Michael beamed as they walked side by side.

"Why don't you?" asked Sam.

"Why don't I what? Write about our travels? I don't know. I thought you didn't want anyone to know that you were a girl?" He ribbed her.

"Well, leave that part out. But someday you will be able to tell your grandchildren about your adventures."

"Not a bad idea. Maybe I will."

The following day, Michael had a surprise for Sam.

"I hate surprises." She groaned as Michael led her down the street.

"Come on Sam. You love this one. I promise." Implored Michael.

Michael took her to Mr. Chang, a master violinist. Michael had enrolled her in his class, and lessons began today.

"No, No, No. We have no time for this." She argued.

"Of course, we do. Besides, you're a fighter like your father.

Now I want to see if you can be a musician like your mother."

"Cody...I ... can't." She said gruffly, refusing to give in to girlish tears.

"Go on, Sam. For everything that you've given me and the one thing your mother never lived to teach you." Insisted Michael with a great smile.

"Thanks." Whispered Sam, and she gently punched Michael in the shoulder.

"Go on." Michael pushed her into the classroom. "You don't want to be late on your first day."

So, every afternoon, Sam studied violin and cello under Mr. Chang. And every evening, she and Michael would play duets in the park. Her violin and his mandolin would always attract many eager listeners as the orange sun set into the evening sky. Sam and Michael enjoyed Vienna. Michael taught Sam to speak Austrian. He also taught her history and art in their spare time.

Sam noticed Michael's confidence and easy manner. Life away from the castle suited him well. He was no longer jumpy, nervous, or afraid. Sam had to smile as she watched him try to sketch the front of the Museum of Art. She had never known him to be so happy. Then suddenly, she realized that Michael's body may have changed as he grew older, but his simple manner had not. He was still kind, gentle, and patient.

"What am I teaching him to fight for? I am his guardsman. I can protect him. Still, he needs to know how to fight. Suppose something should happen to you. But won't that ruin him? It hasn't changed him so far. In fact, the only one that has changed is you."

Sam shook her head clear of such thoughts. There is no room for doubt. You have a job to do, regardless of personal feelings. And don't you forget it. Sam decided that she was worrying needlessly and let the matter drop. Michael noticed a blank stare on Sam's face.

"Sam. What are you thinking about?"

"Nothing important." She said, shaking the last of the thoughts out of her head. "Are you done?" Michael showed Sam the picture, and Sam hid a smile. "Not bad. What is it supposed to be?"

"It's...Sam." He laughed. "You are incorrigible."

"And you are easy prey. Come on, it's time for dinner. I'll race you to Julian's, the last one there pays for dinner." Sam challenged.

"O.K. Go!" Michael cheated, and he took off running before he said Go.

Sam looked at her cards, placed a bet, and waited for her opponent to decide which cards he would play. She looked out the window over his shoulder and stared at the night. At the sound of a boisterous damn, she turned at looked across the room at Michael's table. Sam smiled. The boy was learning; that was his third winning hand. Sam studied her cards again, and then she felt a strange sensation; the back of her neck tingled. Suddenly, Alex and Jacob walked in. They surveyed the room and then discreetly questioned each patron about Sam and Michael.

"Of course, I have, the red head, anyway. I've lost over 1000 Schillings to him in the past three weeks. He's over there," informed Mr. Chesney, one of the club's patrons.

Alex and Jacob smiled and walked over to Sam's table. Sam had just won another hand. A hand landed on her shoulder as she reached out to rake in her winnings. Sam looked up, and her eyes grew wide with recognition.

"Hello, Sam," said Jacob with a big frown. "Leaving England was a no-no."

"Hello, Jacob," Sam responded. "Nice to see you up and about again. No hard feelings…I hope?"

Jacob, none too gently, hauled Sam out of her seat and placed manacles on her hands. "No way are you getting away from me this time. Where's Prince Michael, and why aren't you with him?"

"He's… He's behind you?" She smiled as Michael walked towards them.

"Really, Sam. Not even you…" sneered Jacob.

"But I am." Michael chuckled.

As Jacob turned around, Michael hit him with a hard right. Sam caught Jacob as he fell into her arms.

"Get his keys." She ordered.

"What for?" He asked as he searched Jacob's pockets.

"For these." Sam showed him her wrists.

"Why didn't you tell me that you liked jewelry?" He quipped.

"Oh, very funny. Ha-Ha." She mumbled. "Behind you!"

Michael quickly turned and faced Alex. And an amused smile covered his face. "Hi."

Then with quickness, Michael grabbed Alex by the shoulders and gave him a head butt. Alex stumbled, but he was still standing. Michael had to sit down, though.

"Good grief, Sam. I don't know how you do that." Michael rubbed his forehead in pain.

"Have I taught you nothing? You do it like this." Sam stepped over Michael and approached Alex, who was stunned.

Sam grabbed Alex and butted his head against hers. Alex fell against a table, completely knocking it over, as he fell to the floor.

"Ow. I must be losing my touch. That hurt." Sam complained as she shook her head to clear her vision.

Michael used Jacob's keys to free Sam. Then, Sam used the manacles to bind Alex and Jacob to the table. Sam apologized for the disturbance as she scooped up her winnings, and then she and Michael left. They paid their bill at the inn, collected their belongings, and left town. They had just cleared the edges of town and were about to enter the forest when Sam suddenly pulled her horse to a stop.

"Cody, why are we running from Alex and Jacob? You said only to Austria." Sam reminded angrily.

"I've changed my mind," Michael told her, still driving his horse forward. "I'd like to see Romania, too."

"You act like you don't ever want to go home." Sam raced

after Michael to catch up.

"I don't. Let Mark become king. Let him worry about the kingdom, responsibilities, and rules. I just want to have some fun for a change." Michael urged his horse to go faster.

"I think you've had enough fun." Admonished Sam. "It's time to go home."

"Then you'll have to catch me first." Challenged Michael, kicking his horse into a faster pace.

"Oh, no you don't!" Sam raced after him.

Michael headed into the woods, jumped from his horse, and hid among the trees. Sam followed him into the woods. Sam grew very cautious when she found his horse without him on it.

"Cody!" She called out as she looked among the tree branches, hoping to spot him.

Sam searched the area. She knew he hadn't gone far but couldn't see him. Maybe she was too good a teacher. She couldn't hear him either. Sam turned when she heard a rustling of leaves. Suddenly, a figure jumped from the trees and knocked Sam from her horse. She fell to the ground and wrestled with her attacker; she lost. Michael pinned her arms beneath him and sat on her stomach.

"Cody, get off me!" She yelled, angry that she had lost.

"Do you yield?" He demanded.

"No!" Sam struggled and kicked, but nothing she tried could free her from his hold. Getting tired and getting nowhere, she yielded.

"That's the first time I've ever beaten you," said Michael, still sitting on her stomach.

"Yeah, well, it will also be the last. I must admit, though, I've taught you well," crowed Sam, still wiggling, trying to get free.

"Oh, your modesty is overwhelming." He smiled down at her.

"Would you care to get off me?!" Sam shouted. She hated being at Michael's mercy and was so glad her father wasn't here to see this. He'd disown her.

"Not so easy to shake me off anymore, is it?" Michael crowded with great pride.

"Oh, I can still get you off. Trust me. But it's getting dark, we'd better make camp," snarled Sam, still angry that she had lost to him.

However, Michael didn't move. He just stared at her. "Your eyes are so beautiful." He said softly.

"Aw, now don't start that again." Sam groaned.

"What is your problem, Sam? Why do you refuse to believe that I have feelings for you?"

"Because I was raised as a boy, I know all about their feelings for girls. Boys have no idea what the true concept of love is. They only feel lust. Now get off me."

"Make me," challenged Michael.

Sam just smiled and thrust her two forefingers into the bottom of his pants. Michael nervously jumped up just enough for Sam to use her legs to toss him over her head and onto the ground. Sam jumped onto his back and pinned his arms behind him.

"That's what we call a Nedder." She explained, keeping his face close to the ground.

"Why?" asked Michael, struggling to get up.

"Let's just say it's named after the stable boy who started it." Sam smiled wickedly.

"So that's why all the horses are so jumpy," reasoned Michael.

"Not all of them, just yours." Sam helped him to stand up.

Michael set up the tents and started a fire. Sam went hunting. She caught a pheasant, but the chicken was lacking compared to the filet mignon. The night was warm, and the breeze was light. Sam was amazed at the abundance of stars in the heavens, like gemstones in a black river. The crickets chirped, the owls asked who, and other animals sang their odes to the night. Sam found it hard to sleep, but Michael didn't. Sam swatted a mosquito and gently scratched the bite.

"Ow, blasted bugs."

But within minutes, Sam was asleep too.

"It seems that Mr. Chang was right about the legend of the Griffin. Now the Chiou clan will be defeated," spoke Nuygen.

"Are you sure they will not awaken before we get them to China?" asked Tseng.

"Do not worry, Tseng. The dose that I gave them will keep them out for days."

Chapter 17

Sam awoke to the sensation of being very cold. She tried to draw her knees up for warmth but found their path blocked. Fear gripped her when she realized that she was in a wooden box. She began kicking against the walls and pushing the lid to get it open. The noise of someone knocking woke Michael, who found that he was also in a wooden box when he tried to stretch. He also began banging on the lid of his box. All this knocking alerted the two Asian kidnappers that their cargo was awake. They stopped their wagon, pulled the wooden crates out of the back, and opened the lids. Sam jumped out, ready for a fight. Michael just sat up, yawned, stretched, and asked...

"Where are we?"

"I don't know, but we've been shanghaied again," Sam told him, not taking an eye off their captors.

Michael looked around at the snow-covered land and his two Asian captors.

"Not again. Sam, this really is becoming intolerable," complained Michael. "Brrrrrrr. I'm freezing."

"Please, Griffin...." Tseng said with a low bow to Sam. "Forgive us for this mode of travel, but if we are to get you safely to your destination, it must be this way."

Sam turned and looked at the wagon. "Coffins! You carried us here in Coffins!" exclaimed Sam.

"An effective mode of travel, no one bothers the dead," Nuygen explained, coming to stand beside his companion.

"Who are you?" questioned Sam, slightly annoyed.

"I am Tseng Ngo, and this is Chen Nuygen."

"Where are we going?" asked Michael, slapping his sides to keep warm.

"To see Master Yom," enlightened Ngo.

"Who?" Sam blew on her hands to warm them up.

"Master Yom is one of the Emperor's shoguns. He rules the northwest quadrant," explained Michael.

"You are well learned, for an escort of the Griffin," praised Ngo.

"Escort? He thinks that I am escorting you." Michael snickered, slightly amused.

"Why do you keep calling me the Griffin?" asked Sam, not amused at all.

"The Griffin is two different animals made into one.

It has the strength of a lion and the swiftness of an eagle. You are obviously of two tribes made one. Therefore, you must be the Griffin." Enlightened Ngo.

"That's you alright, Sam." Michael tucked his hands under his arms to keep them warm.

"Legend says that the great Griffin was once shogun of the western half of the Emperor's kingdom. But he was betrayed by his brother, who wanted to rule all, and was cast out of China. His brother's reign of terror would end only when the Griffin returned to reclaim his throne. You must enter the Black Dragon tournament and defeat all its champions to win back our kingdom for the Yom clan," explained Chen.

"In other words, you need me to fight for the Yom clan to regain its control over half of China," Sam summarized.

"Yes." They said.

"Why should I?" Sam folded her arms.

"Because it is your destiny. We have waited centuries for your return. Mr. Chang said you were the one," insisted Ngo.

"Besides, you will gain the right to wed Master Yom's eldest daughter, Lien," added Chen.

Michael stifled a laugh.

"Mr. Chang," growled Sam, remembering her teacher's

great interest in her.

"He said you were a great warrior. He said that you saved his life," informed Chen.

"There were only five, and they were drunk." Sam cursed herself again for letting Michael out of the castle that night, so long ago.

"He also said that you were very modest," added Ngo.

"Just what else did he say?" Sam wondered just what her old teacher had told them.

"But come, time grows short. We must be on our way," warned Chen. "We must get you back to Master Yom's before Master Chiou's spies find us."

Sam didn't move. She stood and thought about it. "Oh hell, anything to get out of this snow." She finally conceded.

Sam and Michael climbed back into the wagon but refused to get back into the coffins. Each was given a yak fur to keep warm. From the back of the wagon, Sam and Michael looked at the toothpick-like trees against the white of the snow, a view that did not change for the next eight days. She and Michael sat and huddled for warmth in the back of the wagon as it rolled along the road to China. Suddenly, one morning, the wagon stopped. Michael woke up Sam.

"Sam, listen." He urged.

The sounds of swords clanging and voices shouting filtered through the wagon's walls. The sounds of battle stirred up Sam's interest in a good fight. Sam jumped out of the back of the wagon, and Michael followed her.

Sam and Michael's Asian drivers had gotten out to help a fellow coach who seemed to be under attack.

"That's a coach?" Sam wondered, in awe, about its design.

"In China and Japan, coaches are square wooden boxes with staves. Depending on the weight of the coach, there are anywhere between four and ten servants who carry the coach on their shoulders." Michael enlightened her.

"On their shoulders? That would require extreme strength," gasped Sam, in awe at such strength.

"Yes and no. The weight is distributed evenly among the servants so that it doesn't overwhelm the individual," said Michael.

A young girl's shout for help ended the lesson. Sam and Michael rushed to help their Asian drivers defend her. However, Sam and Michael were unfamiliar with these new fighting styles, and they were easily defeated. Only Tseng's interference saved them from being killed.

"Thanks," Sam said as she stood up and wiped the snow off her.

"Please, Griffin, you must not endanger yourself," warned Chen.

"The Griffin," repeated one of the intruders.

With this knowledge, he decided it was better to withdraw and return to tell his master than to complete his mission. He jumped onto a horse and rode away. As Sam, Michael, Tseng, and Chen stood talking, another intruder, who was thought to be dead, rose and thrust a sword at the young girl.

"Look out."

Sam pushed her aside and stepped in front of the assassin's blade. Sam felt a strange heat as the blade went through her body. It was a very unusual sensation, cold steel against warm blood. Sam could hear people calling her, but they sounded so far away. Sam looked down and saw her red blood color, the white snow. She clutched her stomach and fell.

"*So, this is what happened to Alex and Jacob when I cut them.*"

"Sam!" Michael yelled as Sam fell into his arms. "Damn it Sam, don't you die on me!"

Sam coughed up blood, and tears rolled nonstop from the

corners of her eyes. Sam looked up at Michael, but her gaze went right through him.

"Come on, Sam, stay with me," pleaded Michael. He applied pressure to Sam's wound to stop the bleeding.

Tseng killed the assassin and returned to Chen's side.

"Lien." They bowed to her as they greeted her.

"I am glad you have returned, but why are you traveling with so few guards? " Nuygen asked.

"I split them in two. The larger group of guards went with a decoy, and these guards came with me. It seems that my plan has failed." Lien explained. Then she looked down at Sam, whose blood stained the snow red. "Who is this, who saved my life?"

"This is the Griffin, but hurry. We must get him to your home before he dies," Ngo urged, picking Sam up.

He placed Sam back into the coffin, took the wagon's reins, and sped towards Lien's home. Michael sat beside Chen, who was treating Sam's wounds. Sam drifted in and out of consciousness. Her ears were filled with the noise of the wagon and Michael's pleading voice. Finally, Sam closed her eyes, and her spirit drifted into darkness.

"Sam, please don't die. Sam!!"

"Who are you?" asked a voice.

Sam opened her eyes and sat up. The freezing cold and snow were gone; only the warmth of a spring day remained. She felt the grass beneath her and looked into a cloudless blue sky. The pain—it was gone. Sam looked at her side. It was completely healed.

"What in the...?" asked Sam, in complete confusion.

"Ahem, who are you?" re-questioned the voice.

"I'm Sam. Who are you?" Sam looked to her left.

"I am Kin Yom," said a man, sitting in a beige reed chair.

"Where am I?" asked Sam as she walked towards him.

"You have fallen through darkness and into the light." He motioned for her to sit in a chair that appeared out of nowhere.

"In English, please." Sam huffed, and she sat down.

"Minlo is near the border of western China." He answered.

"Am I dead?"

"Yes and no."

"Right." Sam sighed, annoyed at such vague answers. "Well, I can't die, not yet. I must see Cody home first."

"Ah, yes, Prince Michael." He said as if he remembered him.

"How did you know...Is he alright?" Sam asked. She was

wondering just what the hell was going on.

"He's fine, but he mourns for you. He has not left your side since they brought you here." Kin informed her.

"How do you know what's going on?" Sam inquired, none too politely.

"Lien tells her great-grandfather everything." He said most confidently.

"Everything?" worried Sam.

"Yes, Samantha, everything."

"So, what happens now?"

"You must train and enter the black dragon tournament."

"Why?" Sam leaned back into the chair.

"The battle between good and evil rages eternally as Yin and Yang show us. The light and dark are in constant conflict within a circle. Not unlike yourself, really. You see, the Griffin was the head of the Yom clan, and his brother became the Chiou clan. These two families have been in a civil war over control of the western half of China for centuries. However, the Griffin swore that he would return and reclaim his birthright. You have been chosen to fight for the side of good. You will decide the fate of the Yom family and the future of China," lectured Kin.

"Why will they let an outsider decide their fate?" Sam questioned, now sitting up and listening to Kin.

"Because it is their destiny. It is written that this year, the Griffin will return to reclaim his throne." He said.

"So, tell me about this match."

"Ask Master Yom about the match. He will tell you what you need to know. But except no trainer other than Master Sung Li." Kin charged her.

Somewhere in the distance, wind chimes were ringing.

"It is time for you to go." He announced.

"But..." protested Sam.

"Remember, train only under Master Sung Li." He reminded her.

Sam watched as the older man disappeared into nothing.

"I must be dead." She thought.

All of a sudden, Sam felt tired. She wondered why as she fought against the urge to sleep. Soon, Sam fell to the ground and into a deep sleep. It would have been a pleasant, restful sleep, except someone kept calling her name.

"Sam. Sam. Sam!"

Sam woke up. "Will you please shut up? How can I sleep

with you making all that noise? Sam scolded groggily.

"Sam, you're alive!" Michael cheered, and he hugged her tightly.

Now Sam was wide awake, and she coughed as she tried to breathe. "Cody, that's enough." Sam pushed him away. "Of course, I'm alright. Why wouldn't I be?"

"Sam, don't you remember, you died." Michael solemnly stated.

"I What?!" Sam exclaimed in disbelief.

"You've been in a coma for four days," revealed Michael.

Sam looked around the room. The paper and bamboo walls told her she was in a Chinese room...in China.

"Where are we?" She asked, greatly annoyed at the circumstances she kept finding herself in.

"Master Yom's estate, Minlo, China." Michael sat beside her on the bed.

"What are we doing in China?" Sam groaned and fell back onto the bed.

"We were drugged and kidnapped..." began Michael.

"...to fight in the Dragon tournament," completed Sam.

"That's right." Michael nodded. "What's the last thing you remember?"

"Talking to some ancient guy in a green, red dragon painted coat." Sam still could not believe that this wasn't just a bad dream.

"Then you've seen my ancestral grandfather, the original head of our clan." Said a young female voice.

Sam jumped into a guardsman position in front of Michael, ready to attack.

"Sam, relax. It's only Lien." He smiled.

"You're good." Sam complimented her. "I didn't hear you coming."

Lien bowed graciously before Sam. "It is truly a compliment coming from you, Griffin. How do you feel today?"

"I feel...fine. There is no pain." Sam stood, tested her side, and swung her arm. "Even my arms are fine. I am hungry, though."

"Then, a banquet has been prepared for you." Lien escorted them out.

When Sam walked into the dining hall, her jaw dropped in awe. A large table covered with steaming, hot food sat before her. She took a bowl, filled it with chicken and noodles, and sat down.

"Where's the fork?" She asked as she looked over the table.

"Sam, they don't use forks, they use chopsticks." Michael handed her two sticks.

"How do they shish kabob the rice?" Sam asked playfully as she tried to stab a piece of chicken.

Lien smiled, gracefully hiding her laughter behind her elegant sleeves. Michael laughed at Sam and taught her how to eat Chinese food properly.

"Not like that. Here, Sam, like this."

Michael put both sticks in her right hand and laid his hands on her so that she could get used to holding and using chopsticks. Then, he showed her how to scoop the rice, noodles, chicken, and soup into individual bowls instead of dumping them all into one bowl. Once Sam got the hang of using chopsticks, she dove into her meal.

"Sam, you would not believe the medicine here. Most of it comes from herbs and is easy to reproduce." Michael elucidated while Sam ate. "But its effects are much more potent than our own. Their science and technology are also advanced; you should visit their library."

He continued to tell Sam about China and its remarkable differences. Sam was only half listening as she concentrated on what she was eating. She had rice, steamed vegetables, broiled chicken, two different kinds of noodles, soup, sweet and sour dumplings, and egg rolls. Michael watched incredulously.

"Good grief, Sam. I don't think I've ever seen you eat so much." He laughed at her.

"Give me a break. According to you, I haven't eaten in four days." Sam spoke with her mouth full of chicken.

Michael also explained Chinese customs to Sam. She found them to be as insane as other countries, only slightly stricter. Death seemed to be the sentence for any infraction of the rules.

"Why is it that in every country in the world, men are the dominant ones?" Sam complained. "Like cleaning and child rearing is all we can do."

"Sam, please don't start. I merely mentioned it because studying interpersonal relationships and their effect on society is fascinating," commented Michael.

Master Yom's chuckle at their banter became more serious, and he frowned. "But now, young Griffin, I must interrupt your meal for business."

"Yes, the Dragon tournament. He said I must enter and that only Sung Li should teach me." Sam recalled as she sat cross-legged on the floor.

"Who told you this?" questioned Master Yom.

"Kin Yom."

"She met our Ancient ancestor in the dream world," Lien told her father.

"This is wonderful. It means that you truly are the one. When we found out that you were a girl and not a boy, we thought we were done for. A woman has never fought in the tournament, let alone an outsider. But if our great-grandfather approves..." Master Yom considered.

"Who is Sung Li?" asked Sam.

"Only one of the greatest teachers of the martial arts. If you learn what he teaches you, you will be more than a match for Chiou's champion Kung. I will send for him right away. We have very little time to train you. There are only five months left before the tournament."

Chapter 18

Meanwhile, the assassin reported to his master about the Griffin's arrival in China. He entered a long, dark hall lit only by torches. At the far end was a shiny golden throne, where a white-haired man dressed in white robes sat waiting. As the ninja approached the throne, the room became increasingly illuminated. Standing beside this throne are a twenty-four-year-old and another tall, slender man with black hair and a white beard.

"Master Chiou, the Griffin is here. I have seen him," reported the ninja, bowing low.

"So, after eight hundred and fifty-three years, the prophecy has finally come true." Master Chiou stroked his chin in contemplation.

"Do not fear, father. I have trained all my life for this match. I will defeat him and become the greatest shogun ever." Kim boasted proudly as he stood beside his father.

"If the Griffin prophecy comes true, the Chiou clan will forever be destroyed. Kung will fight him."

"Father, do not rob me of my destiny. I am the successor to the Chiou clan." Kim contested and balled his fists.

"I suggest you send for Yung Pham, the shadow warrior," suggested Shing, Chiou's vizier. "He will bring the Griffin here, and they will never know he's gone until it's too late."

"Arrange it," ordered Master Chiou. "I want Griffin here by the end of the month."

Tam Shing bowed and left with the assassin to find Yung Pham.

Sam sighed. Maybe it wouldn't be so bad; just like the knight's game, only the stakes were higher. She had risen to every challenge any boy could ever face and had done better than any boy was ever known to do. Sam was determined to win the Dragon tournament, as well. For two weeks now, Sam has been trained under Sung Li. Never in Sam's life had she been put through such arduous tests. Ropes, water, clay pots, fire, and wooden dummies were used to teach Sam balance, agility, speed, and power.

Day after day, Sam practiced stances, punches, kicks, and blocks for three months. She ran the length of the entire Yom estate, practiced her front and back flips, and dodged swiftly swinging sandbags. Purple and blue bruises now covered the wolf claw scars. At night, Sam tried to teach Michael what she had learned. But he preferred to spend his time studying in the library.

"Master Li, how can I teach him to defend himself if he refuses to learn?" Sam wiped her brow and took a drink of water.

"He doesn't like to fight?" Master Li watched Sam take a drink.

"No."

"He is a wise man. There is more than one way to defeat an enemy. The young prince prefers to use his brains instead of his fists," reasoned Master Li.

"I don't have that luxury. I am his fists." Sam returned to her horse stance training.

"I understand. Maybe he would do better at Tai Chi. It is a form of meditation." Master Li mentioned.

"Meditation?" wondered Sam as she practiced her moves. "How will that help?"

"Trust me." Sung Li smiled. "Now practice the tiger style."

Later that night, as Sam ate her dinner, Sung Li went to talk to Michael. He found him lying under a tree in the garden, looking up into the night sky. Sung Li sat down beside him.

"A beautiful night, is it not?" Master Li asked, breathing in the night air.

"Yes, Master Li. It is," answered Michael softly.

"Young prince, what is wrong? You seem troubled." Master Li looked upon Michael's face.

Michael took a deep breath and let it out slowly. "I'm in love."

"Then why are you so unhappy?" asked Master Li with a knowing smile.

"Because she hates me."

"I don't think Samantha hates you." Master Li chuckled at him.

"What makes you think it's Sam?" Michael was surprised that his feelings were so transparent.

"Because Dafan is also infatuated with her. He hasn't stopped talking about her since she beat him yesterday. He has even told me that he wants to marry her. However, I do not believe Samantha will accept him. Samantha is a remarkable person. She is a disciplined fighter and an eager student."

Master Li sat on the edge of the koi pond and stroked his beard.

"That she is. But she refuses to have anything to do with me, romantically speaking." Michael sighed.

"Young prince, what you and Dafan seem to forget is that she is a Griffin. She is two creatures made one, and they are in constant conflict. She is a woman raised to be a man," began Master Li.

"I know. But..." interrupted Michael as he sat up to face Master Li.

"Put simply, she doesn't believe you are sincere. Remember, she has been raised as a boy. She knows how they think and what their desires are." Master Li continued.

"Sam told me the same thing once. But I don't believe that's true. We're the best of friends; we grew up together. In Spain, we went dancing, and as I held her in my arms, I knew she was the one. I wanted to hold her forever, and when we kissed...I could feel that she wanted me too. But then, it was like she became someone else. We were still friends, like nothing had ever happened, but when I tried to hold her..." explained Michael.

"Sounds like fear..." Master Li thought aloud.

"Fear?" questioned Michael, now confused. Michael stood

up, faced Sung Li, and started to pace. "You don't understand. Sam's not afraid of anything. She once took on ten wolves and fought them to the death. She'll even take on guys ten times her size and ..."

Sam looked out of the window and up at the sky. The moon was a perfect globe as it sat in the sky. Suddenly, the desire to play the violin hit her. So, did the feeling that someone was watching her, she turned.

"Good evening, Griffin." He said, smiling and giving her a low bow.

"Hello, Dafan. Have you got a violin?"

"No, but for you, I will send for one." He told her.

"Never mind, I just had the urge to play." Sam dismissed the thought.

"Griffin, there is something I must ask you," insisted Dafan.

Sam folded her arms as she waited for his question. "What?"

Seeing that Sam was not one to skirt issues, he asked her, point blank," Will you marry me?"

"No," Sam answered without hesitation.

Dafan's countenance dropped. "Why, will you not even

consider it?" He was hurt that she didn't even think it over.

"What would you do with me?" asked Sam curtly. "Love me forever. Give me a job as a palace guard. Make me a queen to rule by your side."

"I would do whatever you wished me to do. Your smallest desire would be my greatest command. I would give up my kingdom before I would let you go," gushed Dafan as he stepped towards her, seeking to hold her in his arms.

"Yeah, right. No thanks. I have a job to do. I must get Prince Michael back to the palace in England before his twenty-fifth birthday, or he forfeits the throne to his brother." Sam lied and walked past him up to her room.

"Then, why did he leave?" asked Dafan as he followed her to her room.

"Manhood quest and all that. You cannot become a man without taking the quest. We would have been back before, but we kind of got sidetracked." Sam explained, and she pulled out a silk nightie dress.

"You are going to bed this early?" Dafan questioned, and he watched her prepare for bed.

"I have to. So, I can get up early and be beaten up again by Master Li. He's even worse than my father." Sam began to undress.

Dafan blushed bright red and turned his back to give Sam some privacy, but continued to watch her undress in the mirror. A fire began to grow from within as he watched her. His eyes followed the curves of her body, from head to foot, and every movement was beauty in motion. Years of physical training had fashioned her into a goddess, Di Vinci's perfect woman in reality. A shudder ran through him as ideas crept into his head. Curiosity chewed at him about the marks on Sam's back.

"Where did you get those marks on your back?" he asked quietly.

"Wolves attacked us on our way to Gatlin's Market in England." She explained as she put on her nightie, and then she remembered. "I was also dragged by a horse in a riding accident."

With Sam now fully dressed, Dafan turned and sat down beside her. "May I?" asked Dafan, reaching out to touch her back.

Sam allowed him to run his fingers over her marks. Dafan slowly moved his fingers over her scars. These marks had been deep and still showed as furrows, but now only the scars remained. Dafan gently followed one groove over her back and up to her shoulders.

"You are very tense, please allow me to show you how to relax." Dafan massaged her shoulders and neck.

Sam had received such neck massages before, but only from her father. So, she thought nothing of it as she relaxed into his grip.

Dafan, feeling less and less tension in her body, very subtly moved his hands from her shoulders to around her waist as he leaned forward to kiss her neck. Sam sensed a change in his mood and the position of his hands; she twisted his wrist backward until he released her. She jumped up from her bed and turned to face him.

"That will be enough of that." Sam warned him, and she pushed him away from her.

"You are no Griffin. You are a tigress to be hunted and tamed. And when I tame you, I will be the most powerful man in all of China." Dafan declared as he prepared for a fight.

"In your dreams, maybe. But if you want to play, I need the practice." quipped Sam; she, too, taking up a fighter's stance.

Dafan tried to roundhouse kick Sam, but she countered with a sweeping ground kick. Back and forth, punches, chops, and kicks were given and countered. However, despite Dafan's superior knowledge of martial arts, he could not defeat Sam. What made Dafan even angrier was that she was not taking him seriously but laughing and taunting him as they fought.

Out in the garden, very loud noises were heard, followed by raised voices and the sounds of breaking furniture.

"What was that?" Michael looked back towards the house.

"Probably, just sibling rivalry. Like you and Sam, Lien and Dafan agree on nothing." chuckled Sung Li as he remembered previous fights between the two when they were younger. "As I was saying, you know there are all kinds of fear. Sam fears dependence."

"Dependence?" repeated Michael, trying to understand what Master Li meant.

"Sam has always been independent. Being raised as a boy, she was taught to be self-reliant. When one is in love, they depend on the love and attention of their partner. They come to rely on their partners as a source of strength. They share joys, sorrows, troubles, and pleasures; they essentially become one. Sam does not wish to rely on anyone for anything. In fact, as she is your guardsman, you are to rely on her. To have any relationship other than this contradicts everything she has ever been taught. Let me ask you, why have you chosen Sam over all of the others that you have met?" Master Li explained.

"Because Sam is my only real friend. Sam likes me, not my title. We can talk about anything, and when we are together, we always have a good time. Anyway, we are exact opposites, like yin and yang. She is a strong and determined fighter and a loyal friend."

"And you are not?" questioned Master Li with a knowing smile.

"I am a scholar. I'm no fighter, and I do not wish to fight if I can avoid it. I am passive and would rather talk than fight." Michael sighed and continued pacing back and forth, thinking about how his father would view him.

"A wise choice," said Master Li.

"But Sam... it's kind of like a shoreline. The power and force of the water are held back by the steadfast sandy beach. A shore without water is a desert. A tide without a beach is an ocean. But together the powerful and the steadfast create a thing of beauty." Michael explained, with love and longing in his voice.

"Well said, but if Sam is the one, then you must give her time. Let nature take its course. As a woman, in time, she may come to agree with you. But she was raised as a boy, and if this mindset overrides her female instincts, then she will never love anyone. She will always be independent. Do you understand?" consoled Master Li.

"Yes, and when we get back to England...Samantha will die, and Sam will be all that remains. She will never love me." Michael stated sadly.

"Here, try this with me." Sung Li stood up. "It is a form of Mediation."

Under a cherry blossom tree, by the moon's light, Sung Li taught Michael Tai Chi.

Sam leaned on the railing and watched them from the balcony. Michael followed Sung Li's feet and arm movements in a delayed rhythm of do what I do. Sung Li's movements reminded Sam of the ballet in Vienna. Then, she heard a yell. Sam stepped to her left and watched as the force of Dafan's jump kick carried him over the balcony. Sam reached over the edge and grabbed his hands.

"Do you still want to play with me, little panda?" Sam teased him.

"Samantha!" Dafan hung helplessly over the edge with his

feet dangling in the air.

Michael looked up and saw Sam holding Dafan over the balcony's edge. He and Sung Li raced over to the balcony. "Sam, what the hell are you doing?!" scolded Michael.

"Just playing," answered Sam, with a whimsical tone.

"Well, put him down, NOW!" Michael ordered angrily.

"By your command," Sam responded by feigning to drop Dafan.

"Sam, don't you dare! You know damn well what I mean!" hollered Michael.

"Alright, Alright." Sam relented. Chuckling with amusement, she grabbed Dafan's other hand.

Suddenly, darkness engulfed them. All the lanterns had mysteriously gone out. Sam froze and cocked her ears, listening for the slightest movement.

"Michael." She thought. Her heart quickened pace, and her muscles tensed in anticipation of a fight. She quickly pulled Dafan up and back onto the balcony. Then she ran downstairs to find Michael.

Michael stood perfectly still beside Master Sung Li and listened. His heart leaped into his throat, and panic ran down his spine. "What's going on?"

"They have come for the Griffin. Now that they know she is here, the Chiou clan will do anything to stop her from participating in the tournament."

"Sam's in danger. We've got to do something," urged Michael, with great concern, as he ran back into the house.

The attack came swiftly and without warning. Sam didn't like not being able to see. But as her eyes adjusted to the dark, she could just make out the moving shadows. Sam took her dagger and ripped the sides of her dressing gown, thus giving her legs a fuller range of motion. Sam's instinct told her to strike behind her, and she did so without hesitation. A ninja lay dead at her feet, a dagger embedded in his chest. The next three attacked simultaneously. Sam knew that they were serious, but she wasn't. She was enjoying her workout when she heard a female voice scream. Afraid of what could happen, Sam pressed harder with her attack to get to Michael.

"Sam!!" Michael shouted when he heard the scream.

Michael's fighting skills were not as sharp as Sam's, and he fought more laboriously. Twice, Sung Li came to his aid and prevented him from being killed.

Maybe Sam was right. Thought Michael. I should learn to defend myself. But a voice deep within him shouted. Never mind that, find Sam! Find Sam, at all costs, find Sam!

Sung Li helped Michael fight his way inside, and Sam fought her way outside. They all met in the grand dining hall.

"Young prince, are you alright?" asked Sam urgently.

"I'm fine, Sam," assured Michael, seeking to see if Sam had sustained any injuries.

"Where's Lien and Dafan?" asked Sung Li.

"I don't know. I haven't seen them." Sam answered with a shrug.

"I heard a female scream; I thought it was you," said Michael, still fearing for Sam. "Sung Li says that it's you they have come for.

"Hah! That's funny." Sam laughed. "When have you ever heard me scream?"

"Sam, go and find them," commanded Michael.

"But..." Then Sam saw the seriousness with which he commanded her.

"No buts, Sam. Just do it." He ordered. "Master Sung will look after me."

Sam turned to Sung Li, and her countenance became very serious. "Swear to me that if anything happens to me, you'll see him home to England."

"Young Griffin, you have my word," vowed Master Li. "I shall guard him with my life."

"Go on, Sam," insisted Michael. Sam left to find Lien and Dafan. And Michael shuddered as a cold and sinking feeling settled into his bones. "Why do I feel like I'll never see her again?"

Sam raced up the stairs and searched each room. Another scream brought Sam back to her room. She opened the door, and the ninja intruders were holding Lien and were about to kill Dafan.

"Stop!" yelled Sam.

"The Griffin, get her!" shouted the ninja leader.

The ninjas dropped Dafan and ran to attack Sam. Sam assumed a tiger's stance. Eight ninjas stood between Sam and Yom's kids, and with a rallying yell, the ninjas attacked. They were fast; Sam had to give them that. By the time her punches got there, they had already moved and struck again.

"*Focus, Sam, Focus.*"

Her heart was racing, and the sound of her breath filled her ears, but Sam pulled herself together and focused her energy. Sensing, not seeing where her enemy was, she struck out instinctively. Sam killed one with a blow to the throat, another with a blow to the heart, and one she broke his neck. With the ninja's attention focused on Sam, Dafan and Lien were now free to fight. Lien took out three of them with blows to the head and legs. Dafan took out two with the tiger's blow. Once all the ninjas were defeated, Sam escorted them downstairs when...

"Where's Sam?" Michael asked urgently, not seeing her as the others descended the stairs.

Lien and Dafan both turned around. There was no one there. Sam was gone.

"But she was right behind us, " Lien answered, confusion, worry, and fear staining her face.

Michael ran through the house looking for Sam, and tears began to well up in his eyes. However, she was nowhere to be found.

"Sam! Sam, where are you?!"

Chapter 19

Sam woke up in prison, the cold stone floor sucking the warmth of her body for itself.

"Ohhh, what happened?" She groaned as she rubbed her sore head and looked around. Bars, straw piles, and stones were all there was to see. Sam went to the bars and looked out. A dungeon of stone stared back at her. "Not again." Sam banged her head against the bars of her cell.

"Please don't do that. It would be a shame to ruin such a pretty head," said a young, comforting male voice.

"Where am I?" Sam demanded. She stood up and tried to see who was talking to her.

"You are a guest of Master Chiou."

"Well then, please convey unto him that these accommodations are not to my liking," joked Sam with indignant anger. "Who are you?"

"I am Yung Pham." He stated. "And you are?"

"My name is Sam."

"Do you know the legend of the Griffin, Sam?" Pham asked

of her.

"Yeah, I've heard it. I still don't believe it, though."

"You should. It's why you're here. Both men saw fulfillment of the prophecy at hand when you arrived, but who knew you were a girl and not a boy. Needless to say, Chiou is no longer worried."

"He should be. Fate may have a weird sense of humor, but it always unfolds as it should," Sam said more confidently than she felt. "I will defeat his champion, and Yom's clan will rule China."

"That will be hard to do, young Griffin, when you are dead. Master Chiou takes no chances when his rule is threatened. Although...to kill such a beautiful young woman would be a terrible shame."

"Would you mind stepping over here where I can see you?" Sam kept scanning the room and trying to figure out where her "companion" might be hiding. "I feel kind of stupid talking to myself."

The voice laughed, and then something moved directly in front of Sam. A grey stone turned around, and two black eyes stared back at Sam. The stone moved forward until it reached Sam's bars. Grey against black, the figure stood out. A man dressed all in grey had been perfectly camouflaged right in front of Sam. Sam smiled, incredibly impressed.

"You're good. You're really good." admired Sam.

The man reached up, drew back his hood, and revealed his face to Sam. Sam was surprised. She had expected an ugly old man, but to her astonishment, the shadow ninja looked no older than she was, and he was very handsome. His hair was short and black. His eyes were slightly pointed and made him look like an elf of Middle-earth. His expression did not change as he stared at Sam. Sam tried to look away but could not. His eyes were soft, inviting, and blue like the ocean in the morning sun. They stood staring at one another until the sounds of a door unlocking invaded their silence. Sam looked up to see who was coming. When she returned her gaze to Pham, he was gone. Sam looked all over the room but could not see him or any movement but that of the two men coming down the stone steps.

He's probably right in front of me. Damn, he's good. Sam thought.

"They will try to steal your fire, Sam. It is imperative that you do not let them," whispered Pham in warning.

"What are they going to do, cut my hair?" She asked in a

low, mocking voice.

"First, they will take your spirit and then your virtue. Be careful, Sam."

"Good to see you up and about, young Griffin," greeted the older man. He stood right in front of Sam, looked her over, and stared her down.

"Sorry, I can't say the same." She said, moving away from the bars. While Pham struck her as one to trust, even though he had kidnapped her, this man, Master Chiou, did not, and she did not want to be anywhere within his reach.

"This is the Great Griffin?" Kim snickered as he looked her over and sized her up. "Nice...dress."

Sam looked down at her clothes. She had forgotten that she was wearing nothing but a nightgown. Kim just stared at her and smiled wickedly. Sam walked slowly and provocatively towards him. She slowly raised her hand and punched him in the eye. Kim wailed in pain as he stepped back from the bars.

"I will destroy you and your entire clan." Sam snarled.

"I don't think so." Master Chiou chuckled as he addressed her. "A few days without food will make you...less aggressive."

"I'm going to kill you, Griffin, but not before I see you bow before me." Kim hissed in anger at being bested. "Your fire will be mine, and I will rule all of China."

"You are not worthy of me," Sam smirked, and then she turned her back on him.

Kim grew very angry and was about to storm into her cell when his father stopped him.

"No." He said, barring the boy's path.

"But father, she has insulted me," growled Kim.

"She is only trying to coax you into fighting her now," reasoned Master Chiou. "If you step inside that cell, you will die."

"Father, I think I handle women." Kim snorted in contempt.

"Do not underestimate the Griffin, no matter what form it may take. Wait. A few days without food will make her weak. Then you can take her and do whatever you wish," his father advised.

"You will kneel before me and beg me to kill you!" hollered Kim.

"I am the Griffin," Sam spoke defiantly, her anger welling within at the thought that anyone would try to take her against her will. "You will watch me as I eat your heart with soy sauce."

"When do I get paid?" Pham interrupted the tension and

drama.

"Ah, Pham. Where are you?" asked Master Chiou, trying to locate the voice. Pham stood up and removed his hood. "You are very good." Master Chiou commented, and he clapped three times.

"I'm the best there is." Pham bowed to him. "That IS why you hired me."

"I have your payment upstairs," assured Master Chiou. "One hundred gold bars for the delivery of one Griffin."

"He will come for her; I have seen her eyes," Pham warned him.

Master Chiou nodded in understanding but seemed otherwise unconcerned. "Come, have dinner with us tonight. Tomorrow, I will send word to the villages to watch for her friend."

Master Chiou escorted Pham upstairs, and Kim followed. The massive wooden door was locked, and Sam was left alone. Sam studied the bars, the floor, and the lock. They were solid and well-built. She would have to trick someone into letting her out. Sam sat on the cold stone floor, crossed her arms, and waited.

"*I hope the young prince is alright.*"

Master Sung was having a hard time trying to convince Michael not to go after Sam. Master Sung followed Michael as he went from room to room, gathering supplies for Sam's rescue.

"Prince Michael, I can't allow you to go after her." Master Sung Li urged as he watched Michael pack.

"Sam is my friend. With or without you, I'm going to find her." Michael feverishly shoved clothes and food into his bag.

Michael shoved money into his pocket, picked up his pack, and left his room. Dafan met him in the hall.

"Michael, please, take this sword with you. It will keep you safe." Dafan bowed as he handed him an ancient sword with Chinese markings.

"I don't...Sam is the...thank you." Michael graciously accepted the sword.

"This sword is called Whisper, the quiet power. It belonged to my great ancestor, who believed that only by whispering would your enemies strain to listen," explained Dafan.

"I will return it to you, I promise." Michael solemnly swore.

"Just...save Sam." Dafan gave him a weak smile.

Michael left Master Yom's house on one of his best horses. He heard hoofbeats behind him as he rode away from the house. Looking behind him, he saw Master Sung Li.

"You don't have to come. You should stay and train Dafan." urged Michael. He knew that someone would have to enter the dragon tournament.

"Tseng will train Dafan. Besides, I swore to the Griffin that I would look after you, and that I must do." Master Li told him seriously.

"Then how shall we proceed?"

"Most likely, Master Chiou has her at his estate. We should ride north to his ancestral home. We must ride fast, the tournament begins in two months, and we must still travel East to Yá an, where the tournament is held," informed Master Li.

Master Sung Li and Michael traveled north for ten days before they came to a small village. They stopped to rest the horses and buy more food. As they walked through town looking for a place to eat, Michael looked around at the people of this village. Some were busy with their trades of selling chickens and vegetables, while others looked over the goods on sale. It reminded him of Gatlin Market, but minus the rowdy sailors. Michael was preoccupied with thoughts of Sam, but all of the townspeople looked at Michael as he passed by them. Michael felt like a fish on dry ground, gasping for air. Asian children laughed and giggled to themselves as they ran past. Michael wondered what games they played here or whether his strange appearance was the cause of their laughter.

As he and Sung sat and ate in an inn, a man dressed in a black mandarin jacket and pants walked into the inn. All eyes were upon him as he sat at a table and ordered chicken, rice, and sake. As the curiosity of the newcomer died down, people returned to talking. Michael instinctively reached for his right ear as a light whisper tickled his ear like a breath of wind. He cocked his head to listen but couldn't make out what was being said.

"What is wrong?" asked Li as he watched the man in black.

"I hear whispering but can't tell what they are saying."

Sung Li turned to Michael with serious eyes. "Close your eyes and shut out all sound except the whispering voices."

Michael did as he was told and closed his eyes. With his mind's eyes, he saw the man in black at a table and Sung Li and himself sitting at another table. The whispering continued, but it grew no louder or clearer for him to understand. Michael saw the man in black get up to leave. As he passed by their table, a blade flashed, and Sung disappeared in a flash of white light. Michael opened his eyes.

"He's going to kill you," said Michael, indicating the man across the way.

Just then, the man in black walked by their table, his hands suspiciously concealed in the sleeves of his jacket. Sung grabbed the man by his wrist before he could pull out his blade and forced him to the ground.

"Don't kill him, yet," said Michael, an idea forming in his head. "He can take us to Master Chiou's."

"How are we today, Griffin? It has been eleven days, are you ready to eat? You must have some strength when my son consummates with you," chuckled Master Chiou smugly, as he looked upon Sam.

Sam sat in the corner of her cell, staring at him defiantly and hugging her knees for warmth. Her eyes had lost their playful luster. They were now sunken and melancholy. Though Sam's face showed no expression, tears dropped uncontrollably from the corners of her eyes. Sam's bright red hair was now long and dull. Her gown was sullied and torn. However, her will to survive was fed and fueled by her hatred of Master Chiou and his son. One of Master Chiou's servants entered the cell and placed food in front of her. Sam didn't move, nor did she take her eyes off Master Chiou. When they left, Sam looked at the food. She wanted to eat it, but she didn't dare. She just moved it to the far side of her cell.

They will try to steal your fire; don't let them. You will bow before me, and I will have your fire.

These words echoed over and over in her mind. Would they drug her food? They might, and she couldn't take the chance. So, she didn't eat. Two days later, Kim came to see her.

"I heard that you're not eating. What's the matter, don't you want to keep up your strength?" He laughed with smug arrogance. "Oh, the silent treatment, how original. You haven't eaten anything in thirteen days. I guess you must be pretty...weak, by now."

Sam didn't say anything as Kim approached her. She knew this was the chance that she had been waiting for.

"Just a little closer, jackass, and I'll show you just how weak I am."

Kim took off his shirt and tossed it aside. He stood over her, grinning in delight. "Time to make your fire mine."

He pinned her to the floor and kissed her wantonly and hungrily. At first, Sam pretended not to respond to his touch at all. But then, she kissed him back, just as hungrily. She put her arms around his neck and back. She broke off, kissing his lips to kiss his neck. Then, she sank her teeth into his neck with all the force her teeth could produce. Kim screamed and grabbed his neck. Kim slapped her across the face and backed away towards the cell door. Sam licked Kim's blood from her lips. With the speed of a viper, she struck out at Kim, grabbing him by the legs. He tried to kick her off, but she rolled out of the way and dashed for the cell door.

"Oh, no you don't." He said, grabbing her hair.

Angrily, Sam turned and punched him in the face. She knocked him to the floor using a forward punch, a back kick, and a sweeping kick. Sam jumped on his back and started pounding his face into the floor. The disturbance had brought the guards, one of whom had gone to get Master Chiou. They dragged Sam from Kim, beating her into submission. Sam curled into a protective ball as hands and feet beat against her back and legs. The wounds that the wolves had given her began to bruise and hurt. With a roar of pain, Sam turned on the guards. Three more guards entered the dungeon with Master

Chiou behind them. Master Chiou watched with impressed anger as Sam managed to kill seven of his ten best guards. Master Chiou stood his ground, daring her to attack him, as Sam rushed towards him with death in her eyes. Sam had Master Chiou within her reach when something stung her leg. Looking down in fear, Sam pulled out a dart. Was it poisoned? As Sam looked at Master Chiou, his image began to blur. The light went from white to grey to black. Sam fell into a deep sleep with the thought, I've failed.

Hours later, Sam awoke. Water dripped into her face from a bucket over her head. Sam tried to get up but found that she was tied down. Somewhere off to her left, she heard a noise that was all too familiar: a whip cracking. Sam turned her head. Master Chiou and one of his servants stood beside a forger's fire with several metal rods sticking out. His servant cracked the whip in practice while Chiou stared into the fire. His servant, seeing that Sam was awake, tapped his master. Master Chiou turned and stared at Sam. His countenance was very calm, but his eyes burned like fire.

This is it. Thought Sam. I'm going to die. I hope Master Sung keeps his promise."

"You have caused my son to lose consciousness. He needed

several stitches to close the gash you put in his head. He will be unable to fight in the tournament. Kung will once again represent the Chiou clan." Master Chiou informed her, his voice filled with contempt.

"Your son should learn to keep his hands to himself. Now that I have stolen your son's fire, I will use it to kill you." Sam definitely pulled at the ropes that bound her.

Master Chiou took a deep breath, smiled wickedly, and walked over to Sam. "If you were an ordinary woman, I would let one of my servants have his way with you. But since you are the Griffin, the man who possesses your fire will rule the world. Therefore, I'm saving you for my son." Master Chiou seductively ran his fingers over her legs and up to her thighs. "I could take you, but you're not worthy of me." He whispered in her ear. "Loc Lou, see that she pays for my son's injuries. Griffin, if my son dies, then so do you."

"If you don't kill me now, it will be the last chance you ever get." Sam hissed.

Master Chiou smiled and then laughed. When Chiou left, Loc began to spin the great wheel. Sam didn't know why they would try this form of torture; it was relaxing, like being rocked at sea. Sam allowed herself to slip into the rhythm of the wheel.

This was kind of fun.

Then CRACK, the whip struck across her stomach. Sam jumped up reflexively, forgetting that she was tied down. Her wrists and ankles grew sore from the friction between them and the ropes. Pain, unbearable, ran screaming through Sam's body as Loc whipped her. Then he stopped.

Sam allowed her body to relax. Every muscle went limp, and she cried in agony. Blood mixed with tears as both fell to the floor. Sam didn't scream. She wouldn't give them the pleasure. The pain in her abdomen and legs was seared with a fire that begged to be released, but Sam forbade herself from screaming. Sam looked to her right and tried to moisten her tongue and throat by swallowing. Sam blinked as she noticed two eyes staring back at her. Pham? The eyes looked sad and almost repentant, and then they disappeared. A change in temperature beside her legs told her that the worst was yet to come.

"How can you be a Griffin without the mark of the Griffin?" asked Loc, smiling widely as he stabbed the hot poker into her side.

Sam let out a horrible yell as the intense heat of the poker burned its way into her flesh, leaving behind it a permanent testimony of its touch. Somewhere in the throne room of his house, Master Chiou smiled as he sat listening to her screams of pain. Outside, night was falling, as a figure rode off into the darkness.

Chapter 20

Michael and Master Sung continued to ride north. Michael tried to keep a fast pace, but the horse kept slowing down. It was walking like Michael felt... tired.

"Dressing as the black assassin was a good idea. But do you think it will really work?" questioned Master Li.

Michael looked back at Sung, whose hands were tied behind his back to give the illusion that he was Michael's prisoner. Michael hoped this plan would work because he had no other.

"It has to. I don't know what else to do," said Michael sadly, hoping Sam was still alive. "But did you really have to kill him?"

"I had too. He would have warned Chiou of our coming if someone had released him. Speaking of which, someone is coming." Sung looked ahead.

Michael quickly pulled the mask over his face, and Sung Li watched as the dust on the horizon drew nearer and nearer. Michael squinted as he tried to make out who was coming. Michael prayed that it was Sam. It wasn't. It was another black assassin.

"Where have you been? Master Chiou is looking for you," the fellow assassin said. You captured Sung, I see. Master Chiou will be pleased. Come, follow me."

The black assassin turned his horse around and headed east. Again, Michael heard whispering as he and Sung rode after the other black assassin. Michael wondered why they trusted this assassin. Where was he leading them anyway? Again, the whispering grew louder but no clearer. Michael stopped his horse and closed his eyes.

He saw himself and Sung following the rider into a field of reeds and tall grass. The rider turned and threw stars at them. Michael was hit in the arm, but Sung managed to dodge them. As Sung started to peruse the rider, about fifty ninjas jumped up from the ground and surrounded them. Michael watched as somebody killed him and Sung. Michael opened his eyes.

"Michael, what is wrong?" Sung asked quietly, not wanting to be overheard.

Michael looked back and only whispered one word. "Ambush."

Sung looked around and then at the black assassin. The black assassin stared at them, wondering why they had stopped.

"Are you sure?" asked Master Li.

"I hear whispering, but it grows no clearer. Just like before," said Michael.

Michael and Master Sung both stopped talking when they heard hoofbeats. The black assassin rode over to them.

"What is wrong with you?" He questioned impatiently.

"Nothing that a blade will not cure." Michael stabbed the assassin.

As the assassin fell from his horse, fifty attacking ninjas cried from the tall grass. Michael cut Sung loose, grabbed the reins of the assassin horse, and rode away at a full gallop. Master Li grabbed his horse's reins and followed him at full speed. Michael rode fast, the tall grass brushing and scratching his legs as he rode by. His heart began to pound beneath his chest, and his pulse raced away uncontrollably.

Hoofbeats, his heart, and the whispering wind were all he could hear. Michael looked behind him; Sung still followed. Ahead, the sun was beginning to set. Michael slowed down and then motioned for Master Sung to stop. Michael jumped onto the horse behind Master Sung and released the other two horses. Giving them both a slap, Michael sent them west.

Then, he and Master Sung rode away to the north.

"Hopefully, they will follow the two horses instead of us," Michael said, remembering all the tricks Sam had taught him.

"Where did you learn such a trick?" asked Master Sung.

"From Sam," said Michael, with fond remembrance.

"Do not worry, we will find her."

Night had fallen, and the horse trod slowly forward. Since they had seen no sign from the ninjas, Michael smiled at his cleverness for remembering Sam's tricks.

"Michael, we must stop and rest this poor horse," urged Master Sung.

"We can't. I have to find Sam." Michael yawned softly, barely awake.

"Even if we find her, you cannot fight Chiou's guards. We must stop." Master Sung pulled the horse to a stop.

"I hadn't planned on fighting his guards, that's why I put on the black assassin's clothes." Michael slid off the horse.

"Well, young Michael, now that they know we are coming, getting into Chiou's will only be the beginning. Getting out will be the problem."

"And I have a solution," said a voice.

Michael crouched in a defensive position and peered into the darkness. Master Sung Li scanned the landscape; his eyes came to rest on a rock.

"Pham? Is that you? Show yourself," requested Master Li.

A boulder stood straight up and turned around. Pham removed his hood, and Michael looked upon a younger version of Sung.

"How are you, Dad?" Pham asked, sincerely happy to see his father in good health.

"Michael, allow me to introduce my son, Yung Pham Li," stated Master Sung Li.

"He's your son?!" exclaimed Michael, pulling his mask off.

"Not all sons will follow in the paths of their fathers. Some must find their own way in life," said Master Sung Li.

"But he's a murderer. He took Sam and gave her Chiou." Michael accused, glaring at Pham.

"I admit that at first, I did it only for money. But now it has become a challenge. To get in, get what I came for, and get out without anyone ever knowing I was there. If you wish to label me, then label me a thief. But I'm no killer." Pham declared, in his defense.

"I'm going to kill you!" cried Michael angrily.

Michael charged at Pham, throwing punches, kicks, and jabs. However, Pham easily blocked them all.

"Michael, you are wasting energy attacking in blind rage." Pham chided teasingly. "I thought my father would teach you better than that."

"Anger is easy to overcome. Anger over a lost love is not so easily bridled." Master Li stated as he groomed the horse and gave it water to drink.

"He's in love? With whom?" questioned Pham.

"Samantha." Master Li watched them fight.

"He's in love with the Griffin?" repeated Pham in disbelief. "You...you are not worthy of her. I watched her defeat Kim, kill seven of Chiou's best men, and she's... she's a warrior, a true samurai."

Michael growled and took another swing at Pham. Tired of playing with Michael, Pham kicked him in the stomach. Michael doubled over in pain.

"Enough, this is unproductive. Pham, where is Sam?" asked Master Li.

"In Chiou's dungeon. He is...punishing her for nearly killing his son. Kim is now out of the tournament. Kung will fight for the Chiou clan," informed Pham.

"What do you mean, punishing her?" asked Michael, still gasping for air, as he tried to regain his feet.

"I mean, she is…rotting away in his dungeons with no food. Punishment for the disgrace of his son." Pham told them with contempt and anger.

Pham saw no reason to tell him about Sam's torture. He knew that Michael would only go and do something stupid.

"Just how had you planned to rescue her anyway, to sneak in while posing as the black assassin? That may get you in, but you'll need my help to get out."

"Why should I trust you?" growled Michael, still wanting to kill Pham.

"What is your plan, Pham?" asked Master Li, undaunted by the boys' animosity.

"To celebrate master Chiou's victory in the Black Dragon tournament, complete with firebombs." Pham smiled.

Meanwhile, back in the dungeons of Chiou.

"Enough, Loc, I told you that I wanted her alive." Master Chiou scolded, looking upon a bloody and unconscious girl.

Master Chiou checked Sam's wounds. Red stripes covered Sam's body, like parallel rivers of red. The smell of burning flesh still stung the nose as Chiou looked at the Griffin brand upon her left hip.

"Untie her, clean her up, and return her to her cell." He ordered.

"Hiy." acknowledged Loc.

Sam was untied and returned to her cell. One of Chiou's maidservants, Kuri, bathed Sam and dressed her wounds. It was then that Shing came down to see Sam. He told Kuri to leave them, and he knelt in front of Sam when she had gone. Two hours later, Master Chiou came looking for his vizier.

"Shing, what are you doing?" He demanded, wondering if his own vizier would be so stupid as to betray him. "Would you take her and steal my throne?"

"No milord, I would never betray you," Shing answered calmly.

"Then what are you doing in there?" asked Master Chiou angrily.

Shing got up and allowed Chiou to see Sam. Master Chiou smiled, impressed with Shing's work; however, its meaning escaped him.

"Why have you tattooed a Griffin on her chest?" Master Chiou questioned.

"Tattooing is a means of torture all its own, especially in her state." Shing grinned with pride. "She has agreed to marry your son and bear him a child."

"Marry my son," considered Master Chiou, thinking most positively of their union. "Not a bad idea."

"After Kung has won the tournament, Kim will marry her. By the new year, he should be able to present his wife and his heir." Shing explained with a smug grin.

"Excellent. Then my rule over China will be established forever," approved Master Chiou. Now, hurry; we must leave for the tournament."

Michael was angry. This was taking longer than it should, and he still didn't trust Pham.

"What's taking him so long?" asked Michael as he paced back and forth.

"Have patience, he will return." Sung Li patiently tended the campfire.

"How do we know that he will not betray us to Chiou?" growled Michael.

"Because, despite what you think of me, I do not wish to see her marry Kim," said a voice from the shadows.

"Marry Kim?" echoed Michael, incredulity painting his face.

"Once Kung has won the tournament, Chiou will marry Griffin to his son, Kim. By the Chinese New Year, he plans to present Sam as his wife and their child as his heir. The Chiou clan's rule of all western China will be established…forever." Pham revealed.

"Is everything ready then, Pham?" asked Master Li.

"Yes, Father, all my firebombs are in place. Michael, you have one hour to find her and get out before my firebombs go off. Try not to be late," instructed Pham.

With the moon as the only witness, Pham distracted the guards while Michael slipped inside. Dressed as the black assassin and walking like he belonged there, no one stopped to challenge his presence.

Maybe Sam was right about body language. Perhaps she wouldn't have stopped me that night if I had walked more confidently.

Michael found his way down to the cellar and searched the dungeons. He found Sam sitting unconscious with her arms changed to the wall.

"What are you doing here?" asked a voice behind him.

"Master Chiou sent me to relieve you...he wishes to see you right away." Michael lied, most convincingly.

"Why?" questioned the guard.

"Something about Pham's betrayal." He said, hoping that the guard would buy it.

"I knew he couldn't be trusted," growled the guard. "Never trust a man who works only for money."

"Don't we all?" Michael chuckled.

"There's a difference," insisted the guard. "I am loyal to my master."

The guard turned to leave. With his back facing him, Michael struck the guard from behind. He bound, gagged, and threw him into the cell next to Sam's. Michael took the keys, opened Sam's cell, and unchained her from the wall. Then he took his extra clothes out of his pack and dressed Sam. Tears came to Michael's eyes as he looked over the bruises, gashes, and stripes of dried red blood from her beating.

"Come on, Sam." He whispered to her. "It's time to go." Michael gently lifted Sam into his arms and carried her upstairs.

"How is she?" asked Pham, appearing out of nowhere.

Michael jumped, nearly dropping Sam. "Good grief, I really wish you wouldn't sneak up on me like that," chided Michael in a loud whisper.

"Did you find her?" asked Master Li, also appearing out of thin air.

"What is it with your family?" scolded Michael. "Don't you guys ever make any noise?"

Master Li just smiled at Michael as he checked Sam's wounds.

"This is not good. Michael, you must get her to a doctor. Take the southeast trail, in a day and a half, you should catch up to Master Yom's clan. We must get her to the tournament."

"She can't fight in her condition," Michael complained.

"She must. We need her to overthrow the Chious," insisted Master Li.

"Well, isn't this a touching scene?" said another voice, interrupting.

The Li's and Michael looked behind them; Shing and twenty guardsmen stood in their way.

"Although, Pham, I'm a little disappointed that you would betray us," chastened Shing.

"The evil of the Chiou clan is at an end," stated Master Li.

"Go now, Michael, we will hold them off." Pham smiled, relishing the fact that he would get to avenge Sam's honor.

"But how can two fight two hundred?" questioned Michael, concerned about the lives of his new friends.

Just then, the first of Pham's firebombs went off. KABOOM!!!

"You mean one hundred and eighty-six." Pham chuckled with a sly grin.

"Good luck...and thanks." Michael turned and carried Sam out of the house.

"Kill them all! Do not let them escape!" hissed Shing.

Under the cover of confusion, the night, and exploding firebombs, Michael lifted Sam into the saddle, mounted the horse behind her, and rode away at full speed.

Chapter 21

The day of the Black Dragon Tournament was dark and cloudy. A cool breeze lightly blew across the arena as giant torches lit up the tournament platform where the fights would occur. Master Chiou, Kim, and Kung had arrived this morning and had taken their seats as the dominant clan. Kung, the reigning champion, would fight only one fight today, that of the winning contender. Twenty-five top fighters from the north, south, east, and west had also come, seeking a chance to defeat Kung and become the dominant clan.

"Today is the day of the Black Dragon Tournament. The one fighter who defeats all twenty-four of his opponents will face Kung, the champion dragon fighter. The first match will be Kin Jin Lee vs. The Raven," stated the announcer.

Five hours later, Master Yom's clan finally arrived.

They had stopped to seek a doctor for Sam. Sam's wounds had been cleaned and wrapped. Sam slept as they carried her to the arena.

"This will not do. She is still asleep." Dafan complained.

"Her body needs time to recover." Lien was still worried that Sam's wounds would keep her from fighting.

"She has had two weeks!" He yelled impatiently as he paced back and forth.

"Maybe we should starve you to death, torture your ass, and see how fast you recover!" shouted Lien.

"That is enough, you two. Master Li, Sam fights next."

It must be now," urged Master Yom, worry covering his face, as the future of his country hinged on an unconscious young girl.

"Give her this. I guarantee you that it will wake her up, " he assured them, handing Michael a bottle of liquid.

"What is it?" Michael asked as he poured the liquid down her throat.

"Red Lilly Saki." Sung Li answered with a grin.

"Saki! Are you out of your mind?!" Michael took the bottle from Sam's lips.

Just then, Sam's eyes popped open. She sat bolt upright and yelled. "Whoa, that's good stuff."

"Sam, are you alright?" Michael helped her to sit up.

"Sure." She said with a smile. Hiccup. "Why wouldn't I be?

Can I have some more of that?" Sam reached out for the bottle, but Michael pulled it out of her hands.

"Why didn't you give her that before now?" exclaimed Dafan.

"Her body was not yet ready for it," said Master Li.

"The next fight will be Dou Jung vs. the Griffin."

A deep and silent hush fell over the assembly as they awaited the appearance of the legendary Griffin.

"Come on, Griffin, time for you to fly." Dafan took Sam's hand and pulled her up.

Michael helped Sam to stand up. However, he could tell Sam was in no mood for a fight. He knew he had to make her mad, like when she had fought the wolves.

"Sam, please forgive me," sighed Michael with regret.

"For what?" She asked.

Michael struck her with a backhand, as hard as he could, across her face. Sam just licked the blood from her lip, stared at him, and smiled.

"Oh, come on. I know you can do better than that." She taunted.

While Sam faced Michael, Dafan kicked her in the back. Sam grimaced at the pain in her back and turned to face Dafan.

Then Lien kicked her in the back of her legs, causing Sam to fall to her knees. Sam growled in pain as every fiber of her being screamed for this game to stop. Michael fell to his knees and looked Sam in the face.

"Sam, I want to go home." He whispered. Sam looked at Michael, not believing him. After all, it was his fault that they had been in Austria in the first place. "I mean it. It's time to go home." However, this time, his voice was serious and assertive.

"As you wish, sire."

Sam smiled, stood up, and walked onto the platform as Master Yom's family took their places. Sam wore a black loose-fitting Cheongsam tied with a red sash. A giant griffin was embroidered on the back of her shirt. Sam's hair had been washed and cut. Once again, it held a bright red luster. Michael smiled as he overheard some other girls talk about what a handsome boy Sam was.

"Well, well, it would seem that the Griffin has made it after all." Master Chiou commented unhappily. "Remind me to kill Shing when we get home."

What he didn't know was that Shing was already dead. His sword-severed body lay among the others as their blood flowed and mixed upon the ground. The bodies of dead guardsmen and servants lay everywhere; some died by fists, some by swords, but most by firebombs. The Chiou palace was in cinder-ashen ruins, and the family nameplate had fallen from above the door. The large and grand name of the Chiou clan now lay broken in the street. The domicile of the great warlord was no more.

"Good, finally, a challenge." Kung smiled, and he looked at Sam as she entered the platform.

"She is no challenge. She's a woman." Kim stated spitefully as he touched the stitches in his head.

"She beat you," laughed Kung.

Kim growled and ground his teeth at Kung. But there was nothing that he could do, nothing that his father would allow him to do. All he could do was sit and endure the humiliation.

"Enough, I want to see this." Master Chiou held his hand up for both of them to be silent.

Michael looked up into the sky and prayed. Please help her to survive.

Michael also wondered what his father and brother were doing. He imagined how the other knights would enjoy watching Sam fight. He could see them betting on Sam or against her and drinking large mugs of ale. Michael chuckled and returned his attention to the present. Sam and Dou Jung bowed to the judges and then to each other.

"Begin."

Dou Jung struck first, trying to forward-kick Sam. She blocked it and gave a jab to the face. This blow was stopped, and a back kick to the stomach was delivered. Sam growled in pain as she fell to the floor. The whelps from her beating tingled with very sharp and unpleasant sensations.

I must remain calm and focused. Sam thought as she stood up. Above all, I must not be beaten.

She stood, turned, and stared at her opponent. Sam stood perfectly still. Dou Jung was unsure of her new stance, but he rushed at her with a forward kick. Sam turned sideways, avoided the blow, and sent Dou to the floor with a back kick. Before he could get up, Sam delivered another body blow. The judge called for a separation, and Sam was given a full point. Sam smiled; she was beginning to like this. Angered by his stupidity, Dou Jung attacked Sam with everything at once; Blow after blow of punches, kicks, and chops were delivered until he had scored a full point. Sam limped back to her side of the ring.

"Resume."

This time, Sam didn't wait for Dou to come to her. She attacked him from below with a sweeping ground kick. Once Dou had fallen, she finished him with a blow to the head. Dou lay unconscious beneath Sam. Sam stood; the judge took her hand and declared her the winner. Michael could feel the crowd's mixed emotions. Some were happy, believing the Chiou's rule at an end. Others, like Master Chiou, feared an end to their rule. Sam staggered off the platform. She spied three girls in the front row cheering for her; to them, she bowed and gave them a wink.

"Sam, stop that," warned Michael as he helped her down the stairs and back to their seats.

Sam only stared at Michael playfully. "Jealous?"

For the next two days, the fights continued. Sam enjoyed fighting in the tournament, and it reminded her of home. In fact, she took great pleasure in knowing that the techniques that Master Li had taught her improved her fighting skills tenfold.

"*If only my father could see me now.*" Sam beamed.

Michael shook his head as he watched Sam again become the confident, skillful, and swaggeringly playful man she used to be. Opponent after opponent, Sam used every lesson she had learned to make them mad and lose their focus, making it easier for her to defeat them. Every once in a while, Michael would sit on the edge of his seat as an opponent beat Sam into a defensive posture, only to sigh with great relief when she beat them.

Sam, your playing around is going to get you killed. Michael muttered under his breath.

After each fight, Michael would wipe his sweaty brow and thank God that Sam was still alive. But then his worst fear was yet to come.

"The final match of the Black Dragon tournament will be fought between Kung, reigning champion of the Chiou clan, and his challenger, the Griffin."

"Sam, this is your last fight. Are you O.K.?" asked Michael.

"Piece of cake," said Sam, full of confidence. "This is just like the knights' game back home."

"Have you seen Kung?" Michael worried about Sam's arrogance. "Look up, he's sitting on Master Chiou's right."

"Oh, boy." Sam stared at him in disbelief. "He's a gorilla."

"Sam, before you go..."

"Go? I'm only going over there. You make it sound like I'm going to die."

"Sam, I'm serious!"

"You're depressing." Sam jested, giving Michael a gentle slap.

"I give up..." Michael threw his hands up in defeat.

"Good, then wish me luck. I'll be right back." She winked at him.

"Yeah, but in how many pieces?" worried Michael.

"Young prince, your faith in me is overwhelming," chuckled Sam.

"It's just that you're the best friend I've ever had, and I don't want to spend the return trip home sitting beside a pine box for company." Michael stared at Sam as if trying to burn her image into his memory.

Off in the distance, a deep-sounding gong was rung.

"I'll see you later, young prince." She turned and went to face her last opponent.

"Swear it," insisted Michael earnestly.

"I swear." Sam gently smiled. "I'll be back, don't worry."

Sam strolled towards the platform stairs. Sam looked all around her at the spectators of this sport. Somehow, there was a feeling of...something she couldn't yet put her finger on. Sam looked up at Kung. Kung was a giant man; he stood about 6 feet 2 inches. His arms and legs were like pumpkins end on end.

His head and face were clean-shaven, except for the one long braid of hair that went down his back. Sam watched as Kung warmed up and flung his hair like a whip. Sam's stomach felt uneasy, so she took a deep breath.

"Is there anything wrong, young Griffin?" Master Yom asked of her.

"You mean besides the fact that I have to fight Kung?" Sam jested, but then she got serious. "I feel like I'm being watched by...by someone...I mean, besides the spectators here."

"You are. All of China awaits the outcome of this fight. You will determine whether we will live in freedom or die in slavery." Master Yom informed her.

"Oh, good, no pressure," quipped Sam.

"Do not worry." Master Yom comforted her. "The spirit of the Griffin is within you."

"I'd prefer a crossbow and some arrows." Sam rubbed the goosebumps on her arms.

"Fighters, take your places," called the announcer.

Sam hurried to take her place on the platform. Her heart was pounding as she bowed to the judges, and she swallowed hard as she bowed to Kung. Her knees felt weak and unstable as she moved into her starting stance.

"Stop shaking, little Griffin, it will all be over soon." Kung laughed.

Sam looked at her hands and arms; they were still. But she was still nervous. Can he smell my fear?

"Begin."

Kung rushed at Sam. Sam didn't think; she just reacted. Sam front-flipped into the air and landed behind Kung as he stood up.

"Very good; I thought you'd try to duck to avoid me.

I've been watching you. You always attack from beneath." Kung turned to face Sam once more.

"Like the lion in the grass. Would you like to see my eagle spearing fish?" Sam mocked him.

To Michael, the match looked like a sparrow attacking an elephant. Sam tried everything she knew, but nothing seemed to faze him. Sam, on the other hand, was slowing down. Not only was she getting tired, but the blows that had hit her were causing her great pain.

One blow to her right leg was causing her to limp. One blow to her stomach knocked the wind out of her. Another slap across the face had caused her wolf scars to start bleeding again. Michael winced at each blow as if they had been given to him. However, the crowds cheered, as this was the most suspenseful and thrilling fight. None had ever taken as many blows from Kung and still wanted to get up. Kung stood in his corner, grinning wildly at his assured victory, and waited for Sam to get up.

Finally, Sam stood up. Her muscles ached, and her bones cracked as she straightened her shoulders. She glared at Kung and motioned for him to come to her. Kung only laughed as he crossed the platform to where she was. Sam didn't wait for him to arrive. She faked a sweeping kick and roundhouse kicked Kung in the head. Sam faked a forward Jab and delivered a front kick to the head. As Kung shook off these kicks, Sam kicked Kung in the left knee as hard as she could, forcing it backward. You could hear the bones cracking as Kung roared in pain and fell to his side.

"There, now we are even." Sam declared, standing above him.

Michael looked up at Master Chiou; his frown replaced his smile. Michael could only imagine what he must be thinking. Master Chiou looked worried about the outcome of this match as his control over western China slowly slipped away. Michael returned his attention to the match.

"O God, Sam, no." breathed Michael, in panic shock.

Somehow, Kung had pinned Sam to the floor. He was about to deliver the final blow when a memory hit Michael like a lightning bolt.

"Nedder, Sam! Nedder!" Michael screamed, praying that Sam could hear him above the din of the cheering crowd.

Sam moved her knees up as far as she could, hiding the position of her fingers. As Kung's fist flew towards her, Sam thrust her forefingers up Kung's backside as far as they would go. Reflexively, Kung jumped up, giving Sam enough room to place her knees beneath him. Then, using all her strength in one great thrust, Sam hurled Kung over her head and onto the floor. As she scrambled to get up before he did, Sam noticed he was near the ring's edge. Sam ran straight at Kung and, with a front kick, forced him out of the ring. Kung hit the ground with a loud thud. The force of his head hitting the ground cracked his skull open, and Kung bled to death. Sam landed on the very edge of the ring, straining every muscle in her legs to keep her balance. Michael held his breath.

"Come on, Sam. Just one step back." He prayed.

Michael shouted and cheered in exuberance with the assembly as Sam took two steps back from the edge and bowed to her fallen opponent. The judge took her hand and declared her the winner.

"The Griffin, new champion of the Black Dragon Tournament."

The roar of the cheering crowd was deafening. Master Yom's family, Sung Li, and Michael ascended the stairs and stood by Sam. Sam looked around as the entire audience bowed before them.

"What are they doing?" asked Sam, still trying to catch her breath.

"Acknowledging the Yom clan as the new head clan of the Western tribes and the new Shogun under the emperor." Michael was elated that the Western tribes were now free. But then he looked at Sam. "Are you alright?"

Sam looked around the entire assembly. There were ever so many more people here than at the knights' game. This time, she fought to save a country instead of fighting for a position. The match was over, and she had won. But instead of feeling like this was the end, she felt that, somehow, this was only the beginning.

"Yeah, I'm fine. Nothing that more of that Red Lilly Saki won't cure." She smiled weakly.

"Forget it, Sam. It's bed rest for you," ordered Michael.

"Yes, doctor."

Chapter 22

Later that night, fireworks flew into heaven, filling the skies with dazzling color and light. The sky was filled with the brilliance of blue, reds, yellows, and gold. The night was warm, and the moon was full, casting glorious light upon the land as China celebrated the end of the Chiou's rule. There was music of high flutes, low drums, and the funny twangs of the Pipas. The food was a vast array of everything China had to offer. Rice, noodles, chicken, fish, soups, fruits, and wines of all kinds lay spread upon the tables.

Firecrackers snapped at the feet of a dancing dragon, and songs mainly about the Griffin filled the air. Michael sat beside Sam at a banquet in her honor at Master Yom's house. Michael noticed Sam's sad and melancholy eyes as she watched the proceedings. Though joyous, this wasn't the playful Sam that Michael had known.

"What's wrong, Sam?" He whispered in her ear.

"Nothing." She lied. "What could be wrong? I'm the best fighter in the whole world. I just saved over 100,000 people from a long and terrible rule of the Chiou clan, and now they are throwing the biggest party I've ever seen, in my honor. What could possibly be wrong?"

"That's what I want to know."

Sam just smiled, waved him off, and drained her cup of tea.

In the morning, Sam awoke to the sun in her eyes. The night had been warm, so she left the windows open. Now, the sun and the birds were telling her to get up. Sam sat up and let out a yell. The pain in her back, shoulders, and legs was unbearable. Sam's continued groans of pain brought Michael and Master Li running.

"Sam, what's wrong?" Michael rushed to her side and checked her wounds. "Are you O.K.?"

Sam only answered Michael with groans of pain every time she moved.

"They are just simple aches and pains from the tournament. Your adrenaline level has finally returned to normal, and now your body is feeling the effects. Take a hot bath and get a massage," suggested Master Li as he left. "You will be fine."

While Sam lay relaxing in a tub of hot water, Michael told her about all the preparations for their departure.

"Master Yom has bought for us a ship, a vessel small enough for a two-man crew but big enough to see us all the way home, provided good weather favors us. The ship is being loaded right now. So, as soon as you are able, we will leave for home." He reported happily.

"How long have we been away?" Sam asked as she stared at the ceiling. "It feels so long ago that I've almost forgotten what my home looks like."

"Well, given today's date and accounting for the calendar differences between the east and west, I'd say that it's been about three years," calculated Michael.

"My god! My dad's going to kill me." Sam groaned in fear of judgmental retribution from her father. "How did we get so far from home anyway?"

"Well, I took your advice and wrote it down. So, let's see. We were mauled by wolves, shanghaied by pirates, chased out of Spain by Spanish soldiers, chased out of Austria by Alex and Jacob, and then drugged and kidnapped by Yom's servants for the dragon tournament," recounted Michael. "We'll both have plenty of stories to tell when we get home. What an adventure, huh?"

Sam sat only half listening to what he said. She was

thinking about what her father would say when they returned. He would be furious, of course, but when he saw the man Sam had made of Prince Michael, how could he complain? Then, he would probably ask where her child was. Michael kept talking, but Sam wasn't listening anymore. She was daydreaming...

**

"Sam, you mean to tell me that you went all the way to China and back and didn't bring back a son to train and one day replace you as Captain of the guards?" scolded Sam's father.

"Dad, I was kinda busy keeping us both alive to be worried about bringing back a son." Sam retorted under her father's damning gaze. "Besides, I'm still too young to get married and have kids. Anyway, what if he doesn't share our views about me being a guardsman and wants me to stay home to raise his kids and cook him dinner?"

"If he cannot accept your role as a guardsman, then you will have to kill him. A secret between you and a dead man..." reminded her father.

"...remains a secret. But dad,..." Sam finished.

"Sam, promise me that you will take a year off and have at least one child. Swear it." Her father demanded of her.

**

"Sam...Sam...are you listening to me?" called Michael.

"I'm sorry, Cody. I was just thinking about my father. Hand me a towel, would you? I think I'm starting to prune." Sam pointed to the towels on the table.

"Well, I'll go see how things are coming." Michael handed her the towel and then turned to leave. "See you later, Sam."

Sam thought about Michael as the father of her son. "*He's strong and clever; he knows my secret and has sworn not to tell. If I had two children by him, one would be a guardsman, and the other one would be an heir to the throne. What am I saying? he's the king's son. I can't have children with him. God, what problems that would create? One brother is a king, and the other is a guardsman, and if the two ever found out about each other, there could be a war over the throne that could split all of England apart. No, I will have to find another mate.* "

Sam dried off and got dressed in a man's two-piece Hanfu of black and red, and then she went to find out about their new ship.

Sam's preoccupation with the Dragon Tournament didn't give her much time to admire the scenery of China. As she and Michael sailed away, she could see the majestic mountains that seemed to reach right into heaven. The sea air was crisp and cool, and the wind was high as they sailed into the South China Sea.

"Alright, navigator, which way do we go?" Sam stood at the helm.

"Starboard, we want to go west. And I suggest that we keep as close to shore as possible. We don't want to get lost at open sea." Michael looked over the maps that Master Yom had given him.

"Lost? TwoStar, how could we possibly get lost?" joked Sam.

Michael laughed. He hadn't been called TwoStar since they had served on Captain William's pirate ship. Day became night, and Michael took his turn at the helm as Sam roasted fish in the galley. Michael stared out over the sea and inhaled the sea air. It was a beautiful night. A yell broke his serene thoughts.

"Hey Cody! How do you like your fish, rare, medium, or well done?!" hollered Sam.

"Well done, please, Sam. I'm tired of Sushi."

Michael sat and thought about Sam cooking for him as his wife. Then he remembered that he was a prince. He had servants to cook for him, do his laundry, and raise his children. After all, he hardly ever got to see his mother unless she came to see him, or he wanted to talk to her. Teachers and scholars had brought him up. So that would leave Sam with a lot of free time for other things. He focused his thoughts on one memory of the distant past, and although it seemed like a hundred years ago, he still enjoyed the idea of holding Sam in his arms.

**

"Cody, we shouldn't do this." Sam pleaded as Michael lovingly kissed her neck.

"Yes, we should."

Michael kissed her lips, which tasted like blueberries. He kissed her neck and shoulders. He leaned forward, gently forcing Sam onto her back. He opened her shirt and tenderly kissed her breasts, gently caressing her abdomen and waist. Lower and lower, he let his hands wander. And then...

**

"Cody, what the hell are you doing?" shouted Sam.

Michael jolted back to the present and looked up at Sam. Sam walked over to him and took the helm.

"Will you watch what you are doing, or you'll have us going around in circles. Are we still on course?" rebuked Sam.

Michael looked up at the stars and over the horizon at the land on his right. "Yes." He said sheepishly, letting his gaze fall from the heavens to the floor.

"What were you daydreaming about anyway?" Sam gave him a small punch. "You looked like you were having fun?"

"I was." He grinned from ear to ear.

"Well, go and eat. I'll watch the helm," instructed Sam.

Michael did as he was told. What made you think she would ever let you love her? If anything, she would be on top. A smile returned to Michael's face as he thought about it. I could live with that.

In the following weeks, good weather favored them as they sailed the Straits of Kartimata through the Philippines and up into the Bay of Bengal. Here in Puri, India, Sam and Michael stopped to stretch their legs, replace supplies, and look around. The bizarre markets of India reminded Sam of Gatlin's market. They had everything from hand-woven rugs to exotic spices. Sam and Michael spent the day wandering around, looking at the merchant's wares and the strange people from different vistas, and watching a snake charmer amaze the audience with his command of things serpentine.

Michael mainly bought water. It was a sweltering day, and he could taste the dust of the streets in his mouth. In this hot sun, he was beginning to tan like Sam. Michael stood watching Sam try on a hat. He liked that they looked well together as he looked into the mirror. Michael turned around when he heard someone beckoning him. A woman, thinly dressed in silks with a black veil, stood in a doorway, enticing Michael to see her.

"Well, aren't you going to see what she wants?" Sam smirked mischievously.

"I know what she wants, but she's not my type." He chuckled.

"Oh, and what is your type, cherry boy?"

"Amazons." He winked at her with a broad grin.

Sam elbowed him and rolled her eyes. Shouts and a disturbance turned Sam's attention down the street; two huge and outraged men were chasing a small boy. The small boy ran straight at Sam and hid behind her. She looked down at him, and he looked up at her. The fear in his eyes asked for her help. The two men stood before Sam, yelling at her and the little boy.

"What are they saying?" asked Sam, keeping the small boy behind her and away from the angry men.

"I'm not sure. Arabic is not my forte. But I think they are

saying that you should teach your son not to steal and that you should pay for what he stole?" Michael interpreted.

"They think he's my son?" exclaimed Sam.

"Well, he came to you."

"How much?" Sam asked. She would pay anything to get these two foul-smelling men out of her face.

"Twelve Rupees." Michael clarified.

"Twelve, you tell them that if they are lying, I'll cut their hearts out and feed them to them," threatened Sam.

Michael made peace with the two men, and they left. Sam took the boy in her arms and examined what he had stolen.

"Bread? They made all that fuss over bread?" charged Sam. She questioned the mindset of these people to make such a big fuss over such a little thing.

"Theft in this country is punishable by death," Michael informed her. He looked the skinny, dirty child over.

"So it is in England, but they get a trial first," reminded Sam.

"Sam, here, depending on what you steal and how many times you're caught, they will either cut off your hands or kill you outright. No trial, no appeals," said Michael, seriously.

Sam looked at the child. The frail little boy looked no older than eight or nine years old. His hair was black, curly, and dirty. He looked like he hadn't eaten in days, yet his little eyes sparkled with life. A memory in Sam's mind of Michael at that age flashed in her mind.

"What's his name?" Sam asked Michael.

Michael asked him his name and then gave Sam her answer. "He says his name is Razi."

"Ask Razi if he would like to join us for dinner." Sam smiled.

The boy shook his head yes as soon as Michael translated. Sam and Michael rented a room at a local hotel and ordered everything that room service had. Sam watched as Razi dove into his meal.

"Where are his parents?" asked Sam.

"Most likely, he doesn't have any. At least those who are willing to acknowledge him. In these countries, it is not uncommon to have a child out of wedlock or too many children to afford to feed, so they turn them onto the streets to fend for themselves." Michael explained as he ate.

"Then he will stay with us. He can teach me Arabic, and I can teach him to survive, " Sam declared.

"Sam!" Michael was shocked by this out-of-the-blue

decision.

Michael began to say that she couldn't do that; it was a child and not a stray dog. Or that they were on their way home, and this was an unnecessary stop. However, the look in Sam's eyes told him that it was more than that. Was it motherly instincts or because the boy reminded him of how scrawny and afraid he used to be? Whatever the reason, Michael couldn't say no.

After dinner, Sam bathed the boy. Michael smiled as he watched Sam, a mother, with her child. He wondered if he would be a good father if he could ever marry Sam, and if not, what kind of princess would his father betroth him to. Sam dried Razi, dressed him, and combed his hair like Michael's. Michael laughed. The boy asked Sam a question.

"What did he say?" She asked.

"He wants to be told a story," revealed Michael.

"You tell us one." Sam sat Razi in her lap.

Sam sat on the bed with Razi in her arms as Michael acted out stories in Arabic. Sam laughed as she watched Michael make all kinds of hand and body gestures. The gentle snoring of Razi and Sam told Michael he could stop telling stories now. So, he blew out the candle and lay down beside them.

The next three months were the happiest for Michael and Sam. Razi and Sam spent their mornings training. Sam finally had a willing and eager student to learn all the combat skills she had to teach. Michael, on the other hand, insisted that the ability to read and write would benefit him much more in the long run.

Late in the afternoon, as the red sunset in the evening sky, Razi took them into the jungles. He taught them Arabic and all about India. Sam sat, listening to all the jungle animals, and then remembered her mother and their walks in the English woods.

"We're being watched," announced Sam.

Razi also listened to the rustling of the wind. He and Michael jumped when a flock of birds took flight. Michael looked around for Sam, but she was gone.

"Sam? Sam?" Michael wondered just where she had gone.

Just then, a giant tiger leaped out of the trees. Michael turned to run, but Razi held his arm.

"No. Don't run. Stay perfectly still." He urged.

The tiger roared and flashed its claws. Suddenly, it pounced at Michael and Razi.

"Sam!!" Michael shouted, and he grabbed Razi, hiding the boy behind him.

Just when Michael thought the tiger would have them, something knocked the tiger out of the way and onto the ground. Michael opened his eyes and watched as Sam wrestled the tiger. Sam held and wiggled out of the hold of the tiger. Soon, both were on their hind feet, each pushing against the other. All the time, Sam stared into the tiger's eyes. Then the tiger stopped roaring, it stopped pushing against Sam, and it too just stared into Sam's eyes. Suddenly, the tiger walked away and disappeared into the jungle.

"Are you guys alright?" asked Sam as she dusted herself off and watched the tiger retreat.

"Sam, you never cease to amaze me." Michael sighed with a smile and great relief.

"That was incredible!" gushed Razi. "Now you are a tiger."

"Actually," laughed Michael. "She's a griffin."

As Sam tucked Razi into bed in the evenings, Michael would write down the day's adventures in his journal. Looking up from his journal, Michael watched Sam sing Razi to sleep.

"Go to sleep, my little lamb. Sail to dreamland, my little

Sam. Lay down your head and close your eyes..." She sang.

"Sam, someday you are going to make a great mother." Michael praised.

"I've been thinking, maybe we should take him with us," suggested Sam. "When he grows up, he can replace me as Captain of the king's guards."

"Don't you want to marry and have children of your own?" asked Michael, saddened by Sam's revelation.

"I never used to think about it before," said Sam thoughtfully. "Father had my entire life planned. When I turned thirty, I was to take a year's vacation and have a child to continue the family tradition..."

"That's only five years off."

"I know. Besides, it will take us about a year to return to England. I could have the child now without worrying about finding a mate. I've got a feeling I will be too busy for such things when we get back." Sam feared the future. She knew what awaited her. "Anyway, this child fits the bill. He doesn't want to be here, and I need an heir. What could be better?"

Allowing me to sire your son. Michael thought.

Chapter 23

In the morning, shouting voices awoke Sam from her sleep. She looked around for Razi, but he was gone.

"Razi!" She called out.

"Sam, what's wrong?" Michael asked with great concern as he scrambled to his feet.

"Razi's gone," Sam informed him with fear in her eyes.

Sam jumped out of bed, got dressed, and ran downstairs. Michael followed. Dread overwhelmed Sam like a black wave as she looked up and down the streets for Razi.

"Razi! O, God, No."

A large crowd was streaming down the street. Michael inquired of the watchers what was happening.

"They are going to behead a thief." A basket merchant told him.

"Razi." Michael pushed his way through the throng of people. "Excuse me. I'm sorry." Michael continued to fight his way forward. "Sam, where are you?!"

Michael looked around for that familiar tuft of red hair and finally saw it heading straight for the chopping block.

"Razi! Razi!" Sam shouted at the top of her lungs. Sam pushed people out of her way, caring nothing for the angry shouts behind her. *Damn these people. Damn, this heat.* "Out of my way. Get out of my way! "Razi! Get out of my way!! Razi!" Sam stopped dead in her tracks when she saw that it was indeed Razi they would behead. "Razi! No!" Sam shouted at the top of her lungs. "Stop! Wait!"

The guards completely ignored Sam. Time seemed to stand still as Sam rushed forward, trying to reach the chopping block. Razi was made to kneel as the executioner raised his ax. Razi smiled at Sam as he watched her try to reach him. Then he closed his eyes.

"NOOOO!!!"

For Sam, everything went black as Razi's head rolled around on the platform, leaving a trail of crimson behind it. Michael fell to his knees as he knelt beside Sam's fallen body. It was too late. Michael picked up Sam, carried her back to the hotel, and laid her on the bed. Then he went to ask for Razi's body.

When Michael returned, he heard weeping. He opened

the door to his room and found Sam sitting in a corner, hugging her knees and crying. Michael had never known Sam to cry. In fact, he couldn't remember a time that Sam had ever cried at all, in her whole life. To see her like this now tore his heart in two. Michael walked over to her, sat beside her, and held her in his arms. Sam cried until Michael's shirt was soaked with tears. Michael searched for something to say but could think of nothing. He let his head rest on Sam's as she cried in his arms.

"It's alright, Sam. It's alright." He tried his best to comfort her.

"I should have been able to save him." She whispered.

"You tried," confirmed Michael. "He knows that. He saw you coming for him."

"I never should have let him out of my sight."

"Sam, he was never really ours. For three months, he was an orphan who allowed us to prove that we would indeed make good parents. Wherever he is now, he isn't hungry, he isn't in pain, and there is plenty of jungle for him to play." Michael spoke softly.

Sam gave Michael a weak smile and wiped her eyes with his sleeve. "What was he accused of stealing this time?" Sam's voice was choked with tears.

"Nothing." Sam looked up at him. "He was accused of making a fool out of the sultan's guards. Razi was protecting a group of child thieves, just as he used to be, from the cruel brutality of the guards. He saved the children, and they all escaped, but the guards beheaded him for his insolence.

"Oh, Razi. I failed you." Sam wept; her tears wouldn't stop falling.

"No, you didn't, Sam. You taught him well. Now, I understand what you've tried to teach me all these years." Michael realized. "And when I become king, I will defend my people as Razi defended his friends."

Day turned to night, but the air remained hot and heavy. Neither Sam nor Michael moved from the corner of their room. As Michael held Sam in his arms, he realized that he loved her with all his heart and that letting Sam go would be as painful as losing Razi.

"Sam, will you marry me?" Michael asked her quietly.

"What will they do with his body?" Sam asked as if she had not heard him.

"At sunset, they will send his soul skyward by burning his body."

"Sunset was an hour ago." Sam slowly got up. "There's no reason to stay here now. So, we should leave."

"Sam." Michael grabbed her wrist and gently pulled her to her knees. Sam stared at Michael. His eyes were black, serious, and sad, a sadness that Sam had never seen before, nothing like the sad pity he had for himself as a child. "Sam, I love you with all my heart," Michael confessed sincerely. "Please say that you will marry me."

Sam looked at Michael and smiled. She remembered a scarecrow of a boy becoming a man and steering a pirate ship true to its course, coming to rescue her on a flaming wagon and saving her life, and their duets in the parks of Vienna. She ran her fingers through his thick black hair. They had been together for so long that she could hardly imagine being without him.

"On one condition." She said.

"Name it." Michael was thrilled that she had not said no.

"When we get back home, you keep your word to me and tell no one that I am a girl or that I am your wife, " Sam ordered. Promise?"

"If becoming my captain of the guard means more to you than becoming my wife. I promise." Michael sighed heavily but nodded.

"To my father, it means everything," said Sam, steadfast in her convictions. "Tradition, honor, and our duty to the king and his country are our first priority. Everything else is second."

Sam leaned forward and touched her forehead to Michael's. Michael wrapped his arm around Sam's waist and kissed her lips. Tears fell as Sam kissed Michael. Then she fell into his arms and started to weep again.

"Oh, Sam." Michael braced himself for her second wave of tears.

Michael looked out at the night and could think of nothing else to do but sing to her.

"Go to sleep, my little Sam. Sail to dreamland, my little Sam. Lay down your head and close your eyes. Let go of all your questions, ask no more whys." He sang.

For the first time in her life, Sam felt perfectly safe in his arms, so warm and strong, like her father's. Sam cried herself to sleep as she sat listening to Michael sing. Michael rocked Sam in his arms as he sang. Then, in the wee hours of the morning, he, too, drifted off to sleep.

In the morning, Sam got up and stretched. She looked at Michael, who was asleep on the floor. The only traces of the little boy she knew were when he slept with his knees curled up to his chest.

"I really said I would marry him, didn't I? Are you thinking about backing out? I could, but I have no reason to. What about because he's the king's son? What about your destiny of becoming a guardsman, something you can't do if you're his wife? What about he's four years your junior? What about that he's a good kid? What about he saved my life more than once? What about he knows all my faults and still says he loves me? What about that he intends to keep his promise to me, knowing that when we get home, things will return to how they were before we started this adventure."

Sam shook her head. She had never doubted anything that she had ever done. She either did it or she didn't, but somehow, the thought of marriage filled her with maybes. Sam knelt and gently woke Michael.

"Cody, it's time to go." She gently pushed against his shoulder.

"Good morning, Sam." Michael stretched. "Will you do me a favor?"

"Name it."

"Call me, Michael."

"The minute I say I do," assured Sam.

"Then you still agree to marry me?" He asked, seeking to verify that she had not forgotten and that she wouldn't back out.

"Yes. A promise is a promise. You have kept yours to me, and I will keep mine to you."

"What's wrong, Sam? You don't seem as confident or as arrogant as you used to be." He reached out and stroked her hair.

"I'm not. I used to be so sure of my place in the world." She confessed with uncertainty. "But now, I'm not so sure where I belong."

"You belong by my side. Whether as my guardsman or my wife, you belong with me." Michael declared.

Sam smiled and gave him a playful push. "Now don't you go all mushy on me."

As she stood, she reached down and helped Michael to stand. Michael stretched and then left to settle their bill as Sam quickly packed. They went to load up their tiny ship, but it was gone.

"Damn, it! I don't believe this country!" Sam growled in anger. "First, take my son, and now they take my boat!"

"Looks like we'll have to journey west on camels." Michael

looked around for the nearest camel dealer.

Michael bought five camels and enough supplies for four months. Sam packed the food and water onto four camels, and they shared the fifth. Crossing the Indian jungle into Pakistan was a challenge, as they tried to keep the camels under control when the tigers roared. Other than that, their trip to Pakistan was uneventful. It was even pleasant, with the tall, thick trees shading out the sun and the mild breezes providing cool relief.

"Sam, you are uncommonly quiet. So much so that I can feel it. Are you alright?" questioned Michael.

"Yes. I was just thinking about Razi."

"Well, according to this map, we should be in Pakistan by tomorrow night."

"Good. I never want to see this country again," Sam growled, annoyed by her unhappy memories.

Sometime after crossing the border into Pakistan, Michael and Sam stopped for the night. As Sam set up the tents and tied up the camels for the night, Michael inquired about a place and a person to marry them. Michael then entered the tent, blowing on his hands.

"I've got good news, Sam. They had a religious festival

yesterday, and the holy man is still here. He has agreed to marry us. Tonight, if you want to."

Michael looked at Sam, the frown on his face matching hers. He could feel Sam's broken heart and knew only time would mend it. Still, to see Sam this way was unnerving. She seemed lost and no longer sure of herself. The cocky, swaggering, confident young woman he had come to love was no longer there. He went to her side and took her in his arms as if trying to give her back the strength she had given him.

"I'll be alright," promised Sam. "I just need to get children off my mind."

"That's not going to be easy, Sam," warned Michael. "The holy man isn't...that...tall."

"What?" Sam was confused. "Why?"

Sam understood when they showed up to be married. The holy man was only four feet eight inches tall. So, Michael and Sam were married on their knees. Two other couples, three sheep, and a yak were their only witnesses. A lonely wolf howled his approval as Michael placed a ring on Sam's finger. A kiss was shared as the couples clapped and the sheep bleated. Michael escorted Sam back to their tent and shut the flap to keep out the cold winds. Michael sat beside Sam as she stared at the ring around her finger.

"Is it too tight?" He asked. "I didn't know your size."

"No, it's just so...strange," inferred Sam.

"Now, what's my name?" He quizzed her, a mischievous smile on his face.

Sam looked at him and laughed. Michael smiled. It was good to hear her laugh again.

"Michael, but I still say you look like a Cody."

"Try to get some sleep, Sam." He gave her a quick peck. "We still have a long ride ahead of us."

"Michael," Sam called.

"Yes, dear," teased Michael.

"You call me that again...and so help me...." Sam threatened, punching him.

"How about Princess Samantha?" He laughed and tried to grab her hands to keep her from punching him again.

"No!" She punched him in the shoulder again. "Seriously, I have a favor to ask."

"For you, Sam, anything." He beamed.

"As long as we are headed that way, can we stop in Tor?"

"Your mother's ancestral home?" remembered Michael. "Of course, it would be very interesting to see the land of your mother; the land of the warrior women."

"Michael." Sam laughed and shook her head.

"Good night, Sam." Michael lay down to sleep.

"Good night...Michael," said Sam softly as she did the same.

The sun beat mercilessly down upon them as they crossed the desert sands. Their clothes were heavy with perspiration, and their tongues were as dry as the desert. Their camels trudged westward slowly and steadfastly, seemingly unbothered by the heat. Michael and Sam's only relief was their water and the setting sun. But the night held its own dangers as they huddled together for warmth.

"I thought that deserts were supposed to be hot as hell during the day and cool at night," complained Sam, edging closer and closer to Michael. "So how come we are freezing to death?"

"Technically, deserts can reach one hundred and fifty degrees during the day and fall to about fifty below at night," informed Michael.

"Fifty below, maybe we should ask the camels if they would like to join us." Sam chuckled, and her teeth chattered with cold.

"Sam, stop that. You get any closer, you'll be inside me," joked Michael.

"Good idea, where's my knife?" She snickered as she pretended to look for her dirk.

"Sam. Here, lie with your back to me..." Michael moved over and made more room for her under the blankets.

"Next time, get more than four blankets," griped Sam, thankfully pulling them closer and closer to her body.

"Yes, Your Highness." Michael agreed in mock obedience.

"Michael, call me that again and you'll sleep with the camels."

"At least, they don't hog all the blankets." He retorted.

Sleep fell upon Michael and Sam like highwaymen. Outside, the wind howled as it crossed the desert sands, leaving Michael and Sam marooned in the storm of sand. Although its voice went on unheard, other voices filled Sam's head.

**

"Samantha 'Redshot' Bowman, you are hereby accused of deceit, treason, for disobeying a direct order to return to the castle, the attempted murder of Alex and Jacob Tanner, and the seduction and kidnapping of the king's son. How do you

plead?"

Sam looked all around her. She was in a courtroom. To her left and right were rows and rows of people whose faces she could not see because of the light that engulfed her. She could barely make out the judge's stand before her. Alex and Jacob stood in red guardsman uniforms, just to her left and right; neither smiled nor said a word. Sam turned her attention back to the judge.

"Not guilty. I have done my duty as a royal guardsman. I've protected him all my life. I raised him into the man that he is and..." avowed Sam.

"And were you doing your duty when he saved your life from wolves, the chopping block of Spain, or the dungeons of Chiou in China? Putting his life in danger to save yours is not the duty of a true guardsman. Nor are you truly a man, but a woman. Was it not your plan all along to get inside the king's household and seduce his youngest son?" charged the judge.

"No!" Sam was shocked by the accusations against her.

"Then why did you agree to marry him?" accused the judge.

"I don't know; my feelings for him are hard to explain. We've been friends since the day he was born. He's trusted me all his life, and now I trust him with mine. Besides, he said he *loves me, and I believe him," revealed Sam.*

"He loves you. Sam, you should know better than that. Boys will say anything to get a girl to like them. Take her away," ordered the judge, with no mercy in his eyes.

Alex and Jacob each grabbed an arm and dragged her from the stand. They carried her from the courtroom down a long, dark hall. All around her was darkness and whispering voices. Some soft and some shouting, voices of people she knew, but their faces remained unseen.

"Let go of me!" She hollered.

Suddenly, Sam's father appeared before her. He was shaking his head as she went by. He made no effort to help her or even defend her.

"Father, help me." Pleaded Sam.

"I tried, Sam. But you broke your word to me when you told Prince Michael that you were a girl. Not only that, but you had the audacity to marry him. What the hell were you thinking?" rebuked her father. "I'm sorry, Sam. It's out of my hands now. I should have known that a girl would never be Captain of the King's Royal Guards."

"No! Father! Please! Father!"

Sam struggled against Alex and Jacob as they dragged her

away toward the chopping block. Jacob tied her hands behind her back. Alex pushed her down, making her kneel before the executioner. Then Sam heard laughter, and she looked up.

"I told you that you would bow before me, before I killed you," taunted a familiar voice.

"Kim," realized Sam, her eyes wide in fear and Dread.

"That's right. You took my house, my honor, and my life. So now, I'm going to take yours." Kim gleefully laughed as he raised the ax over his head.

"You can't even save yourself," said another voice, full of sadness. "So how could you ever save me?"

Sam looked to her left and saw Razi. He was kneeling at a chopping block. His eyes were sorrowful, just like Michael's had been that night.

"Razi, I'm sorry. I tried, but I couldn't get to you. I tried! I swear!" Sam hollered.

"Say goodbye, Griffin." Kim gleefully brought the ax down. "Time for you to fly."

Sam's spirit jumped from her body as the ax fell upon her head. Sam's body jerked.

**

"Ow! Sam," Michael complained as Sam's violent struggle

awakened him.

Sam breathed in short breaths, and her heart was racing as she looked around her for the courtroom and chopping block, but only the walls of a tent stared back at her. Sweat dotted her forehead as she looked at Michael, who was rubbing his chin and licking his bottom lip; it was bleeding.

"I'm sorry. Are you O.K.?" She asked as she tried to slow down her breathing.

"Yeah, but... what's wrong?" questioned Michael. "You look scared. Were you having a nightmare?"

Sam took the sleeve of her shirt and licked it. She dabbed his lip with it, softly wiping away the blood.

"Nothing a full pardon couldn't cure." She joked, still uneasy about the dream.

Michael gave her a questioning look. As Sam gazed into his eyes, she felt a longing desire from deep within her. She didn't know why, but something seemed to pull her towards him as she leaned forward and kissed him. A gentle kiss that grew more passionate as Michael kissed her back.

"What were you dreaming about?" asked Michael as he kissed her neck.

"That I was on trial for everything that we've done." Sam

held him close to her.

"Were you innocent or guilty?" He asked, letting her go as she lay back down to sleep.

"I was sentenced to death by beheading, and Kim was the executioner." She sighed as she looked up at him.

Michael leaned down and kissed her tear-stained cheek. He gently caressed her cheek and her lips with his. Sitting on his knees, he opened Sam's shirt. The tattoo of the griffin stared back at him. Michael burst out laughing.

"I forgot you had that." He said, pointing to her tattoo.

"What?" asked Sam, sitting up on her elbows.

"That tattoo. Boy, he really did a great job," admired Michael. Using his middle and forefinger, Michael softly caressed the colorful lines on her chest and abdomen. See, his head is here in the middle of your chest. His wings reach out to your arms, and..."

Sam chuckled under his touch. "Michael, that tickles."

"...and the wingtips touch your shoulders. His front paws end at your hips and his tail..." Sam felt a bizarre sensation as Michael followed the griffin's tail down the front of her stomach. Michael looked at Sam and smiled. "Oh, Sam. You should see where his tale ends."

"Stop that." She ordered, and she pulled his face back up to her own. Sam lovingly kissed Michael's lips. He wrapped his arms around her waist and kissed her wings. "My father once told me that making love was like riding a horse." She was enjoying his attention.

"Did he say anything about riding griffins?" Michael chuckled and gently forced Sam onto her back.

"No." She gasped under his weight.

"Well, then... let's see how well you can fly." He said, undoing his pants.

The strangest and most exotic sensations swept over Sam and made her head swim as Michael entered her. As Michael drove himself deeper, a storm of emotions more powerful than any storm at sea overpowered even her most pious of restraints. She arched under his touch and gladly received him as they became one in rhythm, movement, and body.

A thunderous rumble drifted under the sands. Sam awoke to sounds like cannons rolling across the sands. She raised her head and cocked an ear.

"Ow! Sam. If you want to do it again, all you have to do is ask." Michael chuckled and rubbed his chin.

"Shush, do you hear that...quiet rumbling?" Sam strained to listen.

"It's my stomach," joked Michael. "I'm hungry."

"I don't think so." Sam kissed him and jumped up. "Stay here, I'll be right back."

"You'd best put some clothes on then."

Sam put on her shirt and pants and went outside. The bright, radiant sun streamed down into her face, so she raised her hand to block it out and scanned the horizon.

I must be going nuts. She thought. *Is that an elephant?*

Sam watched as a caravan of elephants, camels, merchants, musicians, and others marched across the sand. Michael, now dressed, stood by Sam's side.

"It's a caravan and it's moving west. We should join it." Sam told him as she started shoving their stuff into a bag.

"I kinda like traveling alone." He kissed her neck, and he wrapped his arms around her waist.

"Enough play." Sam pushed him away. "It's time to go. Pack up."

"Yes, dear," smiled Michael.

Sam jumped onto his back and laughed as she pushed him into the sand. "Toad."

Michael jumped up and chased her into the tent.

Chapter 24

"So where are you two young ones headed?" asked their host.

Michael looked at their host, who had allowed them to ride his elephant with him. It was like having a Chinese coach on top of an elephant. The thin white cotton sheets gave excellent protection from the sun. The man was a tall Middle Easterner with a large handlebar mustache, a long, black beard, and a white turban on his head.

"Tor, Egypt," stated Michael.

"Really, and why do you go there?" He asked.

"It's my ancestral home," Sam said. She enjoyed the view of the rolling sands from the top of an elephant.

"With such red hair, little one, I never would have guessed." He chuckled at her.

She ran her fingers through her hair, which again had grown long. It now reached just past her shoulders. She reached down for her dagger, cut off a piece of her sleeve to make a ribbon, and tied her hair in a French ponytail.

For the next three weeks, the sun remained unkind. However, Michael and Sam didn't notice. Their new company was far more interesting. The merchants had told them tales at the fireside of their adventures in traveling and trading. When Sam asked about the western borders of China and the Yom clan, she liked what she heard. The Yom clan had opened the western borders to travelers and traders to bring more money into the western communities. So far, business has been good for both sides.

Sam's legs grew tired and weak as she walked beside her camel. Lately, riding anything has made her sick. Michael walked behind her, allowing her to stop when she needed to.

"Sam, you don't look well?" He commented, extremely worried about her health. Sam stopped, bent over, and threw up. "Oh, Sam, not again."

Michael stood beside her and held the camels. He wondered what was wrong with her. It seemed that she had been sick every morning for the past couple of days. Then, all of a sudden, he understood.

"Sam, are you...?"

"Yes." She answered, the pain in her sides subsiding

enough for her to stand and walk on.

Michael followed behind her. "Are you sure?" He pressed, not wanting to be wrong.

"Yes, I've seen it enough times in the women back home." She affirmed.

"I'm going to be a father." Michael beamed. "What do you think we should name him or her?"

"You chose. Just do me a favor."

"Anything." He promised.

"Say we can stay in Tor until the child is born." Sam requested, still holding her sides to alleviate the pain.

"But that will be another year." His eyes widen at Sam's request. After all, she's the one who wanted to go home. "We could be home by then."

"I know, that's my point. My father spent his whole life preparing me for the Captain of the Guards; nothing must prevent me from becoming one. After he dies, I promise to name my child as successor and publicly become your wife. Until then, please grant my request," pleaded Sam.

"Done, but Sam, the child remains with me. He will become heir to the throne. Besides, your father planned for you to have your child at thirty. In five years, we will go anywhere you wish, and I will give you another heir, alright." Michael offered a compromise.

"Done., agreed Sam.

Michael hugged Sam, then they trotted off to catch up with the caravan.

Chapter 25

An inhuman scream of such pain sent chills up Michael's spine. It sounded like Sam was being tortured again. Outside, Michael chewed on his fingernails as he paced back and forth. Inside, Sam and two midwives labored to bring her child into the world.

"Push...harder." The midwife instructed Sam.

Another scream sent Michael to the door, but it was blocked by a very large and strong black man with an earring in one ear. Although he had no hair on his head or chest, his presence still sent a powerful message.

"Sit down, little friend. She will be fine." He assured Michael. "You will only be in the way."

Michael knew he was right but he was far too nervous to sit down. So, he just paced back and forth as he chewed on his fingers. Michael looked up into the sky. The sun was setting in the western sky, splashing orange, pink, and violet throughout the clouds. The hot, humid air did help Michael's impatience. It only made him sweat and worry. Two hours later, a baby's cry told him his wait was over. He rushed to the door. Again, his way was blocked.

"Not until they say you can enter." The guard told him yet again.

"Oh, come on!" begged Michael, anxious with impatience. His nerves were on end, and his body was about to explode from curiosity and excitement. Michael turned to go sit down, but then one of the midwives came out. Michael raced over to her. "How is she?"

"She is fine." The midwife smiled joyfully.

"Is it a boy or a girl?"

"A boy. A healthy baby boy."

"Can I go see her now?" He asked impatiently.

"Of course," allowed the midwife.

The second midwife came out, and the three of them left. Michael went inside to see Sam. Seven lamps dispelled the darkness as Michael walked over to Sam. In her arms was a baby boy who cooed with happiness.

"Are you OK?" He asked, kissing her forehead.

"Yes, but I think I'd rather be in the dungeons of Chiou than do that again." Sam sighed, glad that the ordeal was over.

"Aww, he's so beaut,ful." Michael uttered amazement.

"He looks just like his father," Sam stated proudly.

"May I hold him?"

"Of course."

Sam handed their new son over to his father. Michael sat on a stool and held his son. An overwhelming feeling of awe at the miracle of life he held in his arms overshadowed him. The boy was white like him and had black hair, but he had blue eyes like his mother. Michael smiled at his baby son. He had little hands, little feet, and a little nose that wrinkled cutely as his little mouth yawned. Michael held his son close to him and rocked him.

Sam smiled at Michael. He was meant to be a father. "So, have you decided what to name him?" She asked as she rested.

"Oh." Michael gasped as his mind went blank. "Yeah, I was supposed to think up a name." He had been so worried about her that he forgot to think of one. "I don't know."

"Well, you've had all day to pick one." Sam chastised.

"Then you name him."

"Oh no, I gave birth to him, you name him."

"How about William?" suggested Michael.

"Are you stupid?!" Sam shouted, glaring at him.

"I'm Sorry. I forgot about the pirates," Michael apologized

with a chuckle. How about George?"

"No."

"Edward."

"No."

"Sam, I thought you were going to let me name him." Michael objected with mirth.

"I will, so long as you choose a name worthy of my son," disputed Sam with a smirk.

"Your son? Oh, I've got it. Kevin Alexander." Michael beamed with pride.

"No." Sam groaned and rolled her eyes with annoyance.

"Yes, it's perfect. Kevin Alexander Rowland," declared Michael.

"Fine, have it your way," relented Sam.

Michael smiled at his new son and gently rocked him in his arms. As Sam rested, Michael sang to him. A sharp cry woke Sam up. Sitting bolt upright, she watched Michael walk back and forth, trying to soothe the crying child. Sam yawned and stretched.

"Sounds like he's hungry, " she observed. Bring him here." Michael walked over to her, and Sam took off her shirt. Sam took Kevin in her arms. "Yeah, he was hungry," chuckled Sam as she watched her son feed. Then she heard Michael laughing at her. "What are you laughing at?"

"Your griffin tattoo," laughed Michael. "I just can't get over it."

"Well, just don't tell anybody about it," ordered Sam.

"I won't." He promised. "And I always keep my promises." Michael kissed Sam's forehead.

In the morning, Michael packed up for the trip home as Sam fed Kevin.

"Sam! Come here," Michael called out. He was more than a little worried about the group of people approaching him.

Sam got dressed and wrapped Kevin up. "What's wrong?"

Sam came outside and stood by Michael with Kevin in her arms, wrapped in a white blanket. She was surprised to see the number of people standing before her. She was even more surprised when they all bowed before her.

"Who are they?" asked Michael.

"They are from my mother's tribe," gasped Sam in awe.

"How can you tell?" asked Michael.

"That one over there," Sam pointed. "I remember seeing him in one of my mother's drawings."

"Relatives, come to see the new baby?" Michael asked, hoping they were not enemies.

"Possibly. Take Kevin, and I'll find out." Sam stepped forward. As Sam walked towards the chief priest, he stood. "You're...Sanyu, right?" questioned Sam, pulling his name out of a long-gone memory. The man nodded. "What's going on? What do you want?"

"We have come for the child," Sanyu informed her.

"What do you mean?" Sam didn't like where this was going.

"You are the only child of Princess Karimah, daughter of King Obayana, ruler of our tribe. He has no son to inherit his throne, so his great-grandson will rule. He has sent us for the child," declared Sanyu.

"No," challenged Sam, her hands instinctively curling into fists, but they remained at her sides. "He's my son and he is going home with me to England."

"He is your son. He was born here, so he will remain here." Sanyu was unmoved by Sam's declaration.

"Over my dead body," Sam threatened with a growl.

"A white man took away your mother, and you have been brought home to us by one. You are home now, and a son has been born to you. He is kind of pale to be one of us, but the sun will ripen him. And when his time has come, he will take his place as king," expounded Sanyu.

"You're right. One day, he will be king," agreed Sam, not wavering, and not taking her eyes off Sanyu. She didn't trust him at all. "But he will be king of England."

The chief priest realized that this approach would not work, so he changed his tactics. "Then come and see, King Obayana. Your grandfather will be pleased to see you, " he invited Sanyu with a warm smile.

"What's wrong, Sam?" asked Michael, standing beside her.

"Grandfather wants my son because he has no heir either. So, we've been "invited" to his house, so that he can see his great-grandson." Sam told him, fearing that she shouldn't have requested this stop.

"If we're invited, what's with all the spears?" asked Michael with concern.

"To make sure that we accept."

Michael, Sam, and Kevin were escorted to a massive, grand adobe temple. Torches burned brightly, lighting the steps ascending to the courtyard. Sam and Michael were escorted through the yard and to the king's throne room; before them sat a huge black man with three scars on his left cheek and a crown of gold upon his head.

Sanyu told Sam and Michael to wait here. He walked towards the king, bowed, and whispered in his ear.

"That is your grandfather?" asked Michael, in awe.

"I guess so, I've never met him," replied Sam, just as stunned.

"I didn't know you were a princess," smiled Michael.

"Neither did I," said Sam, wondering what else she didn't know.

"Come forward, Granddaughter. Let me look upon you and my great-grandson," ordered King Obayana.

Sam swallowed. She had never shown fear before, and she would not now. Boldly, with her son in her arms, she stepped forward and approached her grandfather.

"Hello, grandfather." Sam greeted him and forced a smile.

"You are beautiful. A credit to your mother, except for that ugly red hair." The king said with a disapproving smile. "Inherited from your father, no doubt. Where did you get those scars on your cheek?"

"Wolves attacked us," answered Sam, retrieving a memory that seemed ages ago.

"I received mine from a panther, the day I became a man." Her grandfather crowed with pride. "I see that you have also inherited your mother's sense of adventure."

"Adventure, dear Grandfather, is my life." Sam smiled proudly.

"Who is the boy beside you?" He asked, finally acknowledging Michael's presence.

"My husband, Prince Michael Rowland of England, son and heir to the throne of England." Sam introduced him.

"Good, if you had married any less than a king or his son, I would have killed the boy where he stood." King Obayana threatened. "Come forward, boy, and be recognized."

Michael showed no signs of weakness as he stepped forward. Sam had trained him, loved him, and bore him a son. She was a warrior and a princess; no husband of hers should have weak knees. Michael smiled as he bowed before his host.

"Your majesty, we appreciate the opportunity to enjoy your hospitality." He spoke most diplomatically.

"You are welcome here, son-in-law," obliged King Obayana. "Treat my granddaughter well, or I will curse your tribe forever."

"Yes, sir." Michael nodded politely. He did not really

believe in curses.

"Samantha, what an awful name. May I hold my great-grandson?" King Obayana requested, no longer wishing to dwell upon Michael.

Sam looked over at Michael. He nodded, so Sam handed the baby over to her grandfather. The king smiled as he held his great-grandson. Then he nodded to his guards, and the four of them took hold of Sam and Michael. Angered by her grandfather's conduct, Sam kicked, punched, and hip-tossed her grandfather's guards until all four guards lay unconscious at her feet. Michael just smiled with pride.

"That's my Sam."

"Impressive." King Obayana congratulated her. "If you were a man, I'd make you my head guardsman."

"I am a head guardsman! I am his head guardsman! Now, give me back my son! We have had enough of your hospitality." Sam's eyes burned with anger.

"If you want my great-grandson, you will have to fight for him; otherwise, he stays here and becomes my heir," declared King Obayana.

"He is my son, and he will go wherever I go! But since you want to play games, name your challenge. And when I win, we will leave," asserted Sam.

"Spoken like a true warrior, except our women do not fight. It is a man's job to protect his woman. Your "husband" will fight for you and the child." announced King Obayana.

"Name your game," Michael responded sternly.

"Michael, you don't have to do this." whispered Sam.

"Yes, I do. Everyone has been telling me that I am not worthy of you, and maybe they're right. But now is my chance to prove it." He said, with a determination that Sam had never seen before. "I will not let people push me around anymore."

"You don't have to prove anything. I know the kind of man you are."

"Yes, I do. That's why we started this journey: to prove to my father that I am worthy to take his place as king. Ironic, isn't it, that I must prove it to your father as well." remarked Michael with a grin.

"And if you lose?" Sam worried.

"I won't. I was taught by the best." He smiled brightly at her.

Sam rolled her eyes. "Good luck, then."

Michael returned his attention to the king, stood full of confidence, and smiled. "I will accept any challenge, your majesty." He declared.

"You will compete with Oto in three tests of manhood: strength, speed, and endurance. The first challenge is a wrestling match. You will wrestle Oto. The second challenge is a test of endurance. You will swim the Nile. And third is a foot race between you and Oto. The winner, two of three games, will claim Samantha and her child as his. Understood?" King Obayana reported.

"Yes." Michael nodded. "When do we begin?"

"The tests will begin tomorrow morning at dawn. In the meantime, we will celebrate my granddaughter's return." smiled King Obayana.

King Obayana kept the child with him, and Sam and Michael were escorted to the feast. Foods the likes that Michael had never seen adorned the tables. Baobab fruit was cut in half and used as bowls. A thick white paste that looked like rice but tasted nothing like it sat before him— monkey, wild boar, and zebra, roasted on spits. A strange concoction of drink was set before him. It was a milk of some kind. But since there were no cows or goats that he had seen, he didn't want to know where it came from.

Michael looked over at Sam, wondering how she was

doing. Sam seemed to be upset. Servants waited on her, as his servants had done back home. However, she was used to doing things for herself, and their service to her only annoyed her. Sam tried talking to them in their language. Her mother had probably taught her, but it was evident that she had forgotten a lot of it. Michael couldn't help but laugh as he watched her. However, coming here had been a good idea, and it was re-educating Sam about who she was and where she had come from. But Sam's only concern was for her son, Kevin.

As the king's granddaughter, Sam was given clothing befitting a queen. She was also given a headdress full of the colors of birds' feathers. Michael tried to hide his laughter as Sam argued with her servants about wearing the hat. Every time she sat it on the table, her maidservant would pick it up and replace it on her head. Meanwhile, people chatted in a language that Michael had never studied. As Michael ate, he was poked and prodded by curious children. They spoke to each other and giggled as they pointed at him. Had they never seen a white man before?

When night fell, the entertainment began. Sam and Michael sat and watched as a huge bonfire was set. Then the drums started to beat; the high tones of the bongos joined their low, thunderous rhythms. Voices, numbering hundreds or more, chanted and sang to the gods of the earth and fire. Young men with painted skins and masks danced to the low rhythm of the drums. The women circled the fire, dancing and chanting to ward off evil spirits. Then Sam saw him. Oto was the mightiest of their warriors. He was big and strong and dark as the night. He danced with the others and symbolically vanquished all his enemies.

Sam found it hard not to be fascinated. Here was the embodiment of all the stories she had been told as a child. Staring into the fire, she remembered her mother. Her mother used to dance in such a fashion, but she had been too young to understand why. Sam remembered that her father had enjoyed watching her mother dance, though he never believed in evil spirits, just leprechauns. Late into the night, the feasting and dancing ended. Sam and Michael were separated and escorted to King Obayana's adobe. Two guards stood outside their doors. Sam, however, was not one to be caged. Sam silently slipped up to her guard. Sam pounced on him and struck him unconscious. Propping him up in his guard position, she left him to guard an empty room as she went to see Michael.

"Michael." came a soft whisper.

"Sam," called Michael softly as he got off his bed to greet her. "How did you get here?"

"Michael, really? What kind of guardsman would I be if I couldn't always get to you?"

Michael's room was dark and full of shadows. Sam's features were hidden, half in shadow and half in light. This candlelight showed Michael that Sam's face had been painted. Lines resembling a panther's claw covered her face. She looked more catlike than human, and the wolf scars only complemented her new look. He smiled at her and shook his head.

"What happened to my guard?" He whispered.

"He's...napping? Now listen carefully, do you remember your Judo and Ti Chi?" She asked.

"Yes." He answered as they both sat on his bed.

"Good, then the first challenge is no problem. As for swimming the Nile, be careful. It has crocodiles." She warned.

"Crocodiles?" He nearly screamed.

"Shhh, don't worry. Take this dagger. If you are attacked, go for his eyes. Or push you dagger up through his throat to close his mouth. O.K.?" instructed Sam.

"Yes, but Sam..." Michael frowned with worry.

"Shush, I've got to get back, before my guard wakes up." She stood up to leave and then smiled at him. "Good luck, Michael." Then she slipped away into the night.

"Sam... Sam." He wanted to ask her more. He waited for a response and got none. She was gone. He ambled back over to his cot of furs and climbed onto the bed. He was tired, and if he was going to have a prayer in beating Oto. He needed to sleep. He fell asleep, waiting for dawn and wishing for Sam's reassuring touch.

Chapter 26

Michael awoke when he heard a baby's cry. "Kevin?"

Michael went to the door and peeked around. A beautiful day stared back at him, as did two guards with long, sharp spears. Michael was fed and escorted to the fighting ring.

"You must pin your opponent to win." Sanyu declared. "Is that clear?" Both fighters signal their understanding.

"Then begin," ordered King Obayana.

Drums played deep, hollow tones as Michael faced Oto. Oto was six foot one and looked to be about two hundred pounds. Michael wondered if he really had a chance.

"The size of your opponent does not matter. You can use his body weight against him." Michael remembered the words of Master Li.

Michael hoped he could remember what Master Li had taught him, and Oto charged at him. Michael moved a little to his right and hip-tossed Oto onto the ground.

"Well done, Michael! You can beat him, just concentrate!" Sam shouted encouragement.

Michael wanted to look for Sam, but he knew he had better keep his eyes on Oto. Oto quickly got up and tried to take Michael's feet out from under him. However, Michael front flipped up and over Oto. Oto turned and growled at him. Michael didn't move but stayed in his tiger's stance. Oto tried to clothesline Michael, but he ducked and pushed Oto into the crowd of cheering onlookers.

As they continued fighting, Michael noticed that Oto was wasting a lot of energy and growing tired. Michael soon saw the opportunity to pin Oto. Oto stood in a wide stance, which left plenty of room between his legs. Michael slid under his legs and grabbed him by the ankles. Then, using his legs, he forced Oto to bend backward and pinned him to the ground. Sam cheered as Michael stood victoriously. Reluctant to declare him the winner, the King took no notice of Michael and just announced the next challenge.

"Take them to the river." He ordered.

The King's guards pushed both men toward the river, and the entire village followed behind them. An ivory horn sounded, signaling the beginning of the race. People stood on the shores and watched the two men enter the water.

"Begin!" shouted the King.

Oto was off like a fish. Michael paced himself and swam with a steady rhythm. The water was refreshingly cold in this heat. Michael found it to be a refreshing relief. However, he was not out for a swim; he had to win this race, or he would never see his wife and child again. The Nile was vast and would take them a while to cross. Ten minutes later, Michael had caught up to Oto, who was beginning to tire. But soon, they both had other problems. Crocodiles had come out for lunch. Both men swam faster, trying to outswim the crocks, but to no avail. Michael didn't hear the crocodiles snapping at his feet because his heart was beating so fast. He didn't hear Sam shouting instructions because of the water splashing in his ears. Michael's heart was full of fear as he tried to think of what Sam would do.

"You don't have the strength to fight head-on, so you have to move faster. Use your brain." He remembered.

Snap! A crock had caught a hold of Michael's leg just below the knee. Pain ripped through his leg as he screamed and was dragged under the water. Water filled his ears, and a sense of failure filled his heart as he struggled to escape. Michael quickly grabbed his dagger and stabbed it in the eye. The crock let go and began swishing his tail violently. A second crock tried to swallow Michael's head, but Michael stabbed at its tongue with his dagger, cutting it in two. Michael swam under the third crock and stabbed it through its chin, thrusting the blade as far as his dagger would go. The crocodile's blood mixed with his as both spilled into the water.

Sam ran to the river's edge and tried to save Michael, but the King ordered her to be restrained. Sam struggled and fought with the guardsmen, defeating three, hurting two, and biting one's ear. But her grandfather will not let her help him.

"Samantha!!" shouted King Obayana. "He must do this alone."

Sam stormed over to her grandfather and looked him dead in the eye. "If he dies, so do you." She swore.

King Obayana merely laughed at her fiery spirit. Then he returned his attention to the waters. Sam stood on the shore, praying. Fear gripped her like an invisible hand, squeezing, trying to crush the life out of her. "*Come on, Michael. God, please don't let him die.*" She watched as Oto climbed onto the shore first. The King smiled, and the village cheered Oto's accomplishment. Sam looked out over the water and saw no sign of Michael.

"Michael!" She screamed.

Up through the water came Michael, wet and covered in blood. Sam went to help him to shore, but King's guards prevented her from helping him. Sam growled at them with hatred but thanked God that Michael was still alive. Michael lay huffing and puffing in the sand on the shore; his leg was still bleeding, and his dagger was gone. Michael was carried to the medicine man. The footrace was delayed for a week, thus giving Michael time to heal.

Later that night, Sam came to see Michael, but this time, he did not get up to greet her.

"Hi, Sam." He brightened as she appeared.

"Hi, how are you?" She asked, looking at his leg and the strange concoction of healing herbs on it.

"I've been better." He said with a smile, just glad to see Sam again. "How is Kevin?"

"He's fine. Grandfather is treating him like a king. But I only get to see him at feeding time. Grandfather has grown really attached to Kevin. By the way, his name has been changed to Akin." reported Sam.

"Akin?" exclaimed Michael. "What does that mean?"

"It means hero. Michael, do you think that you will be able to race by the end of the week?" Sam asked, in all seriousness.

"No, not like this." He answered truthfully. "But I'll have to. I don't want to lose you."

"Michael, look at me. There is nothing you can't do..." Sam began.

"But first, you must try, " Michael said with a smile, remembering the words Sam had told him a thousand times.

Michael sat up, hugged Sam, and kissed her lips. "Don't worry, Sam. I won't let you down. I promise."

The flap of the tent was brushed aside, and a guard entered.

"Samantha, your son cries for you." stated a guard.

"When he cries, he's my son." chuckled Sam to Michael.

Sam kissed Michael one last time and then left with the guard. Michael lay there wondering about Sam, his son, and the race. Then, someone called his name.

**

Michael, Michael, wake up, you sleepy head," called a voice.

Michael looked up. Sam was smiling as she stood over him. He stood up and hugged her.

"I'm so glad to see you, Michael," whispered Sam in his ear.

Then he realized that his leg was no longer in pain. He

looked down and saw that his leg was as good as new. Then he saw the short, green grass beneath his feet. He looked up into a cloudless blue sky and wondered where on earth he was. Then he felt Sam's hand leading him away.

"Who cares where we are, so long as Sam is here." thought Michael.

Sam led him to a majestic-looking house. It was three stories tall and at least twelve hundred feet across. Its windows and doors were grand and clear as glass. The lawn was endless, and the grass was plush. Trees dotted the landscape, providing just enough shade from the brightly shining sun. As Sam drew Michael closer to the house, two children, a fifteen-year-old boy and a four-year-old girl, came out to greet them.

"Hello, father. Good to see you home." smiled his son.

"Welcome home papa." chirped the little girl, hugging his legs.

"Did your diplomatic meeting go well?" asked Sam.

"Yes, it did." He answered, picking up his daughter and giving her a hug.

Just then, the wind picked up, and the skies turned dark. Michael looked at Sam; her simple gown of blue had turned into a ninja suit of black with a griffin on the chest. Lightning struck Sam, and she fell to her knees. She was showered in light as the lightning consumed her body. Sam screamed, twisted, and growled as the glowing light transformed her hands and legs into paws, and she sprouted wings from her shoulders. Sam's face grew twisted and contorted, as her face became a lioness' with an eagle's beak. Sam let out a great roar when the transformation was completed and spread her wings.

Suddenly, another shout was heard. Michael watched as twenty men with spears and nets chased and captured Sam. Sam roared and roared, but she was helpless against them. They also took Kevin and his sister prisoner. Then a giant man about ten feet tall with three heads, confidant, and swaggering, walked up to Michael.

"King Obayana." feared Michael.

"Son of England, you have been given a throne, a wife and two children which you have not earned. You must prove yourself worthy to have them. Do so and they will remain yours. If not, they become mine." said one head.

"You cannot treat me like this! I am Prince Michael Rowland, son of the King of England!" shouted Michael in defiance.

"Son-in-law, you are not a man. You will wrestle with life,

outswim the sea, and run a race with the wind. Begin." said another head.

Michael was punched in the stomach and face by an invisible force. "What the hell is this?" asked Michael, holding his stomach in pain.

"Life is unknown and full of surprises." answered the third head.

"How can I fight, what I can't see?"

"How will you know you, unless you try?"

The voice was not the giant's voice, but Sung Li's, as it rang clearly in his head. Michael stood up and faced off against he knew not what. Straining to listen for the sounds of an attack, Michael scanned the land but saw nothing.

Suddenly, something punched him in his right hip. Michael swung violently at nothing. Each time he swung and missed; he grimaced in pain as he was hit. Finally, Michael focused his mind and put all he had into one punch. Something yelled in agony as Michael rubbed his sore fist. Lightning cracked, thunder rumbled, and a flash flood of water washed Michael away.

Water filled Michael's ears and nose as he swam against the current. Michael realized that he couldn't fight the current and turned, allowing it to carry him wherever it dared. Suddenly, Michael found himself running on dry land, the wind against his back. Michael ran and ran for all that he was worth. Fields of green changed to white fields of snow and then to endless sand. The sand flowed beneath his feet, pulling him down into the earth. A lion's roar was the last thing he heard as his head was pulled beneath the sand.

"Too bad little prince, you have been found unworthy. Now your wife and children are mine."

"No! Sam! Kevin! No!" He shouted.

**

Michael woke up with a jolt. "Sam!"

The animal hides on the wall told him that he was still in the medicine man's hut. The brushing aside of a flap drew Michael's eyes to the door.

"It is time for the race. Come with me." ordered the guard.

Michael winced in pain as he got off the bed. He looked at his leg. It was still bandaged. He sighed and followed the guard. Although the sun was setting, the heat was still unbearable. He shielded his eyes from the sun. Torches lit the starting line, and people lined both sides of the racecourse. Michael saw Sam standing beside her grandfather, with Kevin in her arms. The King stood up and spoke.

"This is the final test. Torches outline the path you will take. You will run to the sun's temple and return. Do not stray from the path. The first one back wins my granddaughter's hand in marriage and will take my place as King when I step down. Ready. Begin."

Both Michael and Oto took off running as fast as they could. Oto outdistanced Michael as Michael began limping.

I have to win this race. Michael pleaded with himself. I have to.

Michael's heart froze with fear when he heard a lion's roar. Sam? No, he had forgotten that they had lions in Africa. Hopefully, they wouldn't come after him. Still, it was wise to keep to the path. The sun said goodbye with one last ray as it sank below the horizon. The wind blew lightly across the torches, threatening to blow them out. Even the call of the wild birds seemed to be laughing at him.

All of nature seems to be against me. He thought in despair. A shadow ran past Michael. He watched it flee by. Damn. Oto can't be that fast.

Michael pushed the pain out of his mind and ran mindlessly forward. The sun god's temple was magnificent by firelight; the gold bricks reflected the light of the torches. Its construction was a perfect trapezoid. Many stone steps lead to the temple's door, which faced the east. No doubt to capture the morning's first rays. Another lion's roar brought his mind back to the present.

"Sam."

Michael took off running as hard as he could. He ran so hard that only the sound of his heartbeat filled his ears. A heart beating so fast, it felt like it would explode inside his chest. Just when he thought he could run no more, that his legs would collapse beneath him and fail, he ran into Oto. Both men fell to the ground.

"You are cheating," accused Oto, and he pushed Michael off of him.

"No, I just didn't see you." Michael offered his hand to help Oto up.

A hand that was soundly refused as it was slapped away. "No, of course not, I'm only bigger than you and stronger. When I win this race, Samantha will be my wife, and I will be King of this land," claimed Oto.

"But she is already married to me." Michael retorted, not backing down.

"And who are you…boy. You are not a man of our tribe, and you have no marks of bravery upon your hairless, white chest." charged Oto disgustedly.

"Say what you want. Sam has accepted me and bore me a son. She loves me and that's all that matters." Michael stared Oto down, completely unafraid.

As Michael stared unwaveringly at Oto, he realized that he wasn't backing down and he wasn't afraid. Sam had always told him, "*If you don't stand up to Prince Mark, he's always going to beat you up because you let him.*" He was facing Oto like he should have faced his brother.

"What matters little boy, is the respect and honor of your name among your tribe. And that will be mine when I beat you." Oto pointed a finger in Michael's face.

"Well," smiled Michael. "I've already beaten you in a fair fight and when I win this race, I will be a king among your people as well as mine. Besides, if I'm as insignificant as you say, what honor, respect, or glory is there for you in such an easily won match as this? Who will honor your name, when any man or any child could outrun a cripple?"

Michael slowly walked away, leaving Oto to think about this, and then he took off running. Oto thought about this as he watched Michael's back get further away, and then he realized he had to chase after him. He soon caught up to Michael and ran with him stride for stride.

"That was sneaky and unfair," Oto growled.

"It was a valid question," Michael stated plainly. "I just have no time to wait around for your answer."

"Your woman will be mine." snarled Oto. He reached out and pushed Michael off the path and into the underbrush.

Michael swore as he fell to the ground. Michael wasted no time in getting up and chasing Oto down. The cheer of onlookers drew Michael's attention, signaling that the end of the race was near. He looked up and saw Sam cheering for him and his son Kevin in King Obayana's arms. The thought of losing Sam stirred up an anger within him like he had never felt before. For him to fail Sam, someone who had never failed him, was unacceptable. Michael looked forward and saw the finish line. He also saw Oto's back. Michael put his head down and ran straightforwardly with all his might.

When Michael awoke, he noticed he was back in the medicine man's hut. Michael sat up on his elbows and looked around the room. Sam sat on a stool, holding their son and smiling at him. He lay back down to rest. He didn't need to ask if he had won. If he hadn't, Sam wouldn't be here now.

Sam rode with Kevin, now two years old, sitting in her lap. Michael rode beside her as he led the pack mules.

"We should reach Niger by the end of the week. There, we can get a ship going north. In six months, we should be home," informed Michael. "God, I can't wait to get home and see my father. It's been, what, about six or seven years."

"Have you become the man you wanted to be since we left home?" Sam asked him seriously.

"I was thinking the same thing myself just now. However, I don't believe that it was anything that I did that made me a man, but how I felt about myself," reported Michael.

"So, how do you feel?" She asked.

"Good, remarkable. When I left home, I was afraid. I had no faith in me, and neither did anyone else."

"And now?" She queried.

"Now, I feel like I can do anything. I have become as independent as you are. I think I was using the wrong yardstick to measure myself against. Being able to ride, to fight, and make love to women doesn't necessarily make you a man. After all, you were a better man than I was, and you are a woman. So, now I know that it is confidence and self-worth, how you think of yourself that makes you a man. I am no longer the boy I was because I have stopped thinking of myself as one," said Michael with pride.

"I think, therefore I am. Is that it?" snickered Sam.

"Something like that." Michael smiled.

"Blue, big blue." Kevin pointed up at the sky.

Sam looked down at Kevin, riding nicely and unafraid in her lap. He's going to be a warrior, just like his mother. "Yes, Kevin the sky is blue," Sam responded, giving him a kiss on his shiny black hair.

Chapter 27

A week later, Sam, Michael, and Kevin sailed over the high seas. Since then, Sam had reclaimed her male persona. Sam had again cut her hair short. She got dressed in black pants, black boots, and a dark blue shirt that was two sizes too big. Sam removed her wedding ring from her finger and placed it on a silver chain around her neck. Now, her shirt covered more than her chest. Michael didn't like the thought of Sam becoming Kevin's uncle, but he relented. After all, a promise was a promise.

Michael smiled as he watched Sam explain how ships sail over the ocean to Kevin. Kevin liked running and rolling around on the decks as the ship tossed up and down against the waves. Sam's reflexes had become even faster now that she was a mother. Twice, these reflexes saved little Kevin from going overboard. Moreover, the Captain insisted that Sam keep the child out of the way of his men as they worked.

"Uncle Sam, look fish." Kevin pointed into the sea.

"Those are dolphins," explained Sam. "Sailors believe that

if dolphins sail with you, that you will have good luck throughout your journey."

Kevin spent his days with his Uncle Sam, playing games to strengthen his coordination. In the evenings, Michael told his son stories and taught him to count in Spanish, French, and Chinese.

"Guess what, daddy." Kevin prompted as he sat on his bunk and let his legs dangle over the edge.

"What?" Michael leaned forward in his chair to hear his son better.

"Guess."

"You want to be a guardsman just like your Uncle Sam when you grow up."

"No, I'm a sailor." Kevin laughed with childish glee.

"That will thrill, Sam." Michael laughed and closed the book he had been reading to his son.

"Daddy?"

"Yes, Kevin."

"Why so sad?" Kevin copied his father's frown.

"Because I miss your mother." Michael sighed, wondering if they would ever tell Kevin the truth.

"Where is she?" Kevin looked around as if to find her.

"I left your mother in Tor," Michael told him.

"Why?" asked Kevin, in childish wonder. "Did you forget to bring her?"

"Because she didn't want to come back with me." chuckled Michael at his son's logic.

"Why?" asked Kevin, with inquiring eyes.

"Time for you to go to sleep young man." Michael changed the subject.

"Nooo," Kevin whined.

"Yes." Michael insisted firmly as he tucked his son into his bunk.

"Sing to me." His son requested of him.

"Tell you what; I'll get your Uncle Sam to sing you to sleep. He sings much better than I do. O.K.," suggested Michael with a warm smile.

"O.K." Kevin smiled and snuggled down into his sheets.

Sam came down to see Michael and say good night to Kevin.

"Hi, Sam," greeted Michael with a smile.

"Good evening, Cody." Sam acknowledged him with a nod.

"Are we back to that again?" Michael frowned.

"It's safer this way, and you know it."

"Where is your ring?" He studied her naked finger.

"Around my neck."

Sam took it out and showed it to him. Michael just looked at her, trying to find some trace of the woman he loved. But only his guardsman stared back at him.

"Will you sing Kevin to sleep?" asked Michael. "Then I would like to talk to you."

"As you wish. OK. Kevin, are you ready to set sail with Capt. Sandman?" smiled Sam.

Sam tucked Kevin in, and she sang to him. The little boy fell asleep with the rolling of the sea and his mother's soothing voice. Sam kissed him good night and then joined Michael on deck.

"OK, Cody. What is it?" asked Sam as she joined him by the railing.

Michael looked out over the sea. A thousand stars shined down, dotting the water with light. The crescent moon sliced its way through the night sky as it rose. The wind blew heartily into the sails, moving the ship steadfastly along. Michael brushed his hair out of his eyes and turned to Sam.

"Are you ever going to tell him the truth?" Michael asked

sadly.

"Someday. When his grandfather dies, as I promised. I will tell everyone the truth. Until then..." Sam assured him.

"Until then..." He continued.

"Until then, stop looking so sad. We're going home, and you have a son to introduce to your father." She nudged him.

"Yeah, you're right. I just wish..." He said, looking out over the sea.

"What?" pressed Sam.

"That I could introduce his mother as well." He stared into her eyes.

"Now, none of that or people will think you queer," warned Sam, gently pushing Michael away from her. "You'll just have to take a lot of cold baths."

"Or run away from home more often." He chuckled.

"Ahoy, French ship off the port bow." The watchman called from the crow's nest.

Michael and Sam looked to their left and scanned the horizon. Sure enough, there was a French gallon coming at them. A puff of smoke told Sam that they were being fired upon. The ship's company ran to their battle stations and prepared for a fight. At the Captain's orders, cannons were loaded, ports were opened, and rounds were fired.

"Go and stay with Kevin," Sam ordered.

"What are you going to do?" Michael asked warily.

"I'm Redshot, remember. They'll need a good gunner." Sam smiled brightly.

As he had feared, the gleam in Sam's eyes grew brighter.

"Alright, Sam just don't make Kevin an orphan." consented Michael.

"Don't worry, Cody, what could go wrong?" Sam laughed, and she turned to leave.

"Sam, Need I remind you what happened the last time you said that." laughed Michael. "Just be careful."

Michael went below decks, wrapped Kevin in his blankets, and held him in his lap, in a corner, as the ship lurched and rolled from being fired upon.

"What's wrong, daddy?" Kevin asked, more curious than afraid.

"We are under attack, but don't you fear—everything will be alright," Michael assured his son.

"Where's Uncle Sam?" wondered Kevin.

"He's helping to defend this ship. So, we can get home safely."

"Can I go too?" He asked, full of adventure.

"No. War is not a game." Michael frowned at his son's fondness for fighting.

For two hours, shots were exchanged between the two ships. Michael struggled to keep Kevin and himself from being crushed as the ship rocked violently against the barrage. Shouting voices called for course changes, gunpowder and balls for the cannons, and trimmer sails. Michael told Kevin stories about his Uncle Sam in order to take his mind off the fight outside. In time, cheering voices alerted Michael that the war was over, and all was well. At dinnertime, Michael and Kevin listened as the sailors talked about the battle and Sam.

"You should have seen Sam. He was a magnificent shot. He took out their sails and made their haul look like Swiss cheese. He even had the gall to blow their Captain's hat right off his head." Praised one sailor.

"I did not, Ohjoe. Stop telling tales." Sam laughed with great joviality. "That was the first mate's hat."

"And then, when they tried to board us, Sam gutted them and pushed them all into the sea. Instead of them taking us, we took them. You should see all the gold and silver they were carrying. They must have looted a lot of ships and were heading home with their haul. And now it is ours. All hail Redshot, best gunner's mate in all the seven seas. Hip Hip..." Crowed another sailor.

"Hurrah. Hip Hip Hurrah. Hip Hip Hurrah." All the sailors cheered and raised their glasses in Sam's honor.

Sam just grinned and thanked them for their praise. Kevin beamed at the fact that his uncle was such a great hero. Kevin talked about nothing else as Michael tried to return him to bed.

"Bash, Bash, Bash. I fight too." Kevin beamed.

"Yes, your Uncle Sam is my head guardsman. It is his job to watch over you and teach you to fight. Now go to sleep." Michael tried to wrestle his son back into bed.

"No. Not sleepy." Kevin whined, wanting to stay up and play.

"Yes, you are. Now go to sleep, Kevin," ordered Michael.

"Do as your father says, little one," Sam said as she entered the room. "So, you can grow up as big and strong as he is."

"Aye, Aye, sir." Kevin crowed and climbed back into bed.

"He's going to be a wild one, isn't he Sam?" feared Michael.

"Sure will." Sam beamed with pride.

"Sam, promise me one thing; that you'll teach him defensive fighting only. I don't what him growing up like..."

Michael complained.

"...Like a barbarian, like his mother. Who enjoys getting into fights, showing off her skills, and taking pleasure in the defeat of a worthy opponent." Sam crowed with mock bravado.

"Something like that." Michael chuckled at Sam's display.

"I promise." Then Sam's smile fell from her face. "I also have some bad news."

"What is it?" He asked, disturbed by Sam's change in countenance.

"We are at war," Sam reported.

"With whom?" He was astonished by the news.

"France, that's why they attacked us; they must have thought we were carrying goods to England."

"What happened?" Michael sighed heavily as he sat down to listen to Sam's report.

"I'm not sure. The captain and first mate are in the brig. From what they told me, a war broke out between England and France about four years ago. We were still in China at the time. However, Prince Mark and my father had pushed French troops back to Gatlin's Market and have staged their own attack against the French. I don't know who started it and neither do they, but my money is on your brother." enlightened

Sam.

"I don't care who started it we have to stop it." Michael declared.

"How?" Sam asked. She knew he didn't have a plan.

"I don't know."

Chapter 28

As Michael and Sam returned to the castle, they saw a terrible sight: empty, beaten-down, and destroyed homes. Sam listened to the still, quiet air—no laughter, no music, no animals, no sounds of life at all.

"What happened here?" Sam wondered aloud. "My father would never allow such destruction."

They hurried their pace towards the castle. Then Sam stopped.

"What's wrong Sam?" Michael took Kevin in his arms.

"Where's the guard? My father always posted a gate guard. Let's see if we can't enter through the kitchens," suggested Sam, thinking a frontal approach was unwise.

Sam quietly opened the kitchen door, surveyed the room, and then let Michael and Kevin in.

"Soup smells good," said Kevin.

"Shhh." encouraged Sam. "I hear voices. Hide."

"Ooohhh. I hate him. I really hate him." came a female's voice.

From her hiding place, Sam could see the two kitchen maids. Sam remembered both of them. They used to work under the kitchen Matron. Sam couldn't remember her name, but she'd have a fit if she saw these two now. Both maids were tall and skinny, their hair poorly kept and their manner dirty. Sam had seen men who had been dead for three days, who looked better than these two.

"Don't let him hear you say that, or it will be the dungeons for you," said one as she stirred the soup.

"Better the dungeons than his bed." Said the other while cutting the bread.

"I wish Prince Michael would return." She stopped stirring the soup and collected a chicken for cooking.

"He's dead. Prince Mark said so." Said the other, now cutting cheese for the bread.

"And you believe him." The other scoffed, ripping the feathers off the chicken.

"Why else would the prince stay gone for so long?" She wondered as she placed the bread and the cheese on a tray.

"I bet Prince Mark had his brother murdered, so he could keep the throne." Reasoned the other one, still violently mistreating the chicken.

Suddenly, both maids fell silent as heavy footsteps trodden down the stairs. Both hurried about their work, trying to look too busy to talk.

"Alright you wenches hurry up with the King's meal!" ordered the male voice.

Sam gasped. It was Jacob. How different he looked. Her father insisted that all guardsmen be clean-shaven, well-dressed, and well-mannered. Jacob looked drunk, shabby, and cruel. Where was her father? Why wasn't he here?

"How is his majesty today?" Asked one of the maids with genuine kindness and concern. "Will he be getting better?"

"No. He won't. In fact, the doctor says that it won't be long now. Then Prince Mark will be King, and I will be his captain of the guard." Jacob sneered at them both. "Now hurry and get this food upstairs."

When Jacob and the two kitchen maids had left, Sam and Michael came out of hiding.

"So, it seems that my brother is ruling in my father's stead." feared Michael.

"And his war is ruining the country. I wonder where my father is. He would not let this happen." Sam assured fiercely.

"First, we find my brother. It is time that I become the man that my father wanted me to be." Michael declared.

Going up the stairs and into the main hall was easy. Everyone was partying in the main dining hall. All the guards were drunk; nobles who never really liked the King sat eating, drinking, and talking to Prince Mark. Wenches that Sam had never seen before sat in the lap of Prince Mark as he drank wine and laughed about the war.

"How would you like to be queen, my dear?" Prince Mark asked with great merriment.

"I don't think I would want her for my wife." Prince Michael said, stepping into the great hall.

Glasses dropped, people stared, and the laughter stopped. Jacob stood and drew his sword.

"Now, Jacob, that's no way to treat my brother." Prince Mark stood up and walked over to stand in front of his brother. "Well, what a man you have become, Michael." taunted Prince Mark as he looked his brother over. "Sam, what took you so long to train him? Although you were always a slow learner when it came to fighting, weren't you, Michael? So, don't tell me you've come to take the throne from me."

"Yes." Prince Michael answered, finally standing up to his

brother.

"Fight me then," challenged Prince Mark.

"Gladly." Prince Michael drew his sword.

Suddenly, without warning, Jacob attacked. Sam rushed to defend Prince Michael, but he told Sam...

"No, Sam. Watch the boy." He ordered.

Sam and Kevin watched as Prince Michael fought Jacob. Jacob thrust his sword at Michael's head. Michael used his sword to block the blow. Jacob swung his blade left, then right, and then left again. Trying to drive Prince Michael back, but each blow was blocked and returned. Sam watched proudly as Prince Michael was finally the man the King had charged her to make of him. Prince Michael knocked Jacob's sword from his hands with one tremendous blow. Jacob stood defenseless against him. That's when Prince Mark attacked.

"Prince Michael behind you!" Sam shouted in warning.

Prince Michael turned in time to block his brother's blow. "In the back Mark? You never did play fair."

Jacob turned, grabbed a dagger, and was about to stab Prince Michael in the back when a dagger struck him in the neck. Jacob turned, looked at Sam, and fell dead upon the table.

"You used to cringe in fear when you saw me." Prince Mark

tried to kick his brother in the stomach.

"I was smaller than you and I had no reason to fight you." Prince Michael blocked his brother's blow to his head. "I didn't care about me, and I didn't care about our people."

"And now you do?" Prince Mark scoffed, trying to strike at his brother's feet.

"Yes. You see, for twenty-three years, I let you get away with it. Now you kill our father, you neglect the land, you mistreat the people, and I won't stand for it anymore." Prince Michael declared.

With that, Prince Michael knocked Prince Mark's sword out of his hands and hit his brother with a solid left punch. Prince Mark fell to the floor and lay at his brother's mercy.

"You must kill him, you know that," Sam told him quietly.

"I will not kill my own brother." Prince Michael stared at his brother with contempt.

"He'll kill you at the first chance he gets," reminded Sam.

"No, he won't," Michael assured her. "Not if I will banish him."

"Banishment won't stop him. It will only leave him an enemy to the throne."

"Sam's right, little brother. Are you man enough to kill me

and take the throne?" Prince Mark challenged smugly. Prince Michael hesitated. "I didn't think so. Kill them." Prince Mark ordered his guards.

Twenty guardsmen flew at them. Prince Michael killed the first two easily, but a third was coming fast.

"Stay right here," Sam told Kevin, and she flew into the fray.

Sam and Prince Michael made short work of the guardsmen who were drunk and without practice.

"Daddy!"

Hearing her son's cry, Sam turned and glared at Prince Mark. He was smiling smugly and holding a dagger at Prince Kevin's throat.

"So, whose son is he?" Prince Mark held the little prince tightly.

"He's my son." Sam seethed with anger like the sun rising upon the Earth.

"I know you Sam. You'll say anything to protect the throne." Prince Mark grinned evilly, so sure that he did know Sam. "So that means he's your son. Isn't he little brother?"

"I said he's my son," Sam growled at Prince Mark and stepped closer. "And I mean he's my son."

"Stay back Sam or the boy dies, whoever's son he is." threatened Prince Mark.

"Hurt my son, and no law on earth will keep you from my sword," Sam growled with fury.

"Mark." Prince Michael called, his voice steady and solemn.

"What little brother?" Prince Mark turned his attention back to his brother.

"I'm king now," said Prince Michael. "And that's my son."

Sam blinked as a dagger embedded itself into Prince Mark's brain. Sam rushed forward and grabbed Prince Kevin.

"Are you alright, young prince?" Sam hugged him tightly.

"Yes, uncle. I was not scared." Prince Kevin replied with a smile.

"You weren't?" Prince Michael walked up to him.

"No. Sam was here." Prince Kevin beamed.

"And I will always be here," promised Sam. "I swear. I will never let anything happen to you, ever."

"Well now, how would you like to meet your grandfather?" Prince Michael asked, taking Kevin from Sam.

"Sure," agreed Kevin.

"Well then, I guess I'll go and clean house." Sam stood and

blinked back her tears. "I should see just how many rats are left in the castle."

"Your majesty, your son, Prince Michael, has returned," the King's advisor reported.

Upon hearing the good news, a look of surprise and happiness spread across the King's face. With the help of his nursemaids, the King sat up in bed. A whisper of a man stared back at Michael as he entered the room. His strong chest had sunken into his body, his face was full of age and worry, and his eyes were dark and stared blankly into nothingness. This man was not the bold and boisterous man Michael had left behind. What had happened to him?

"My son, where are you?" asked an old, raspy voice.

"I am here, Father." Prince Michael answered. He came and stood beside his father's bed.

"Michael, I thought you were dead. Alex and Jacob lost you in Austria, and then you just disappeared. What happened to you?"

"We were kidnapped and ended up in a Dragon's tournament in China. Then we tried to make our way home and ended up in a sandstorm, there was a contest for your grandson's life, and then..." reported Prince Michael.

"My grandson...?" The King asked, in confusion and joy.

"Father, allow me to introduce to you your grandson, Kevin Alexander." Michael smiled with pride.

A young boy with black hair and bright blue eyes stepped out from behind his father.

"Say hello to your grandfather, Kevin," instructed Michael as he lifted his son into his father's arms.

"Hello," smiled Kevin.

"This is your son. He looks just like you. Who is his mother?" inquired the King.

"She is...was a princess of Tor," Michael revealed.

"Sam's mother was from Tor," said the King, holding his grandson on his lap.

"You knew Sam's mother?" Michael questioned his father.

"Yes, she saved our lives. Thomas and I found ourselves traveling through Tor after coming from a diplomatic meeting in India. The King took offense at our being there. Sam's mother intervened on our behalf.

When we returned home, she came with us. Two years later, Sam was born. "I take it that the young lady did not wish to come with you," the king explained.

"No, she chose to stay in Tor. But tell me what happened to Sam's father, and what about this war?"

Michael sat and listened to his father explain about the war. Indeed, Prince Mark had started it when he insulted the honor of the French consulate. The King was willing to forget the incident if Mark agreed to marry his daughter, an alliance of good faith, but Prince Mark sealed England's fate when he said that he would rather die than marry her.

"After the war began, I took ill. I knew Mark would not stop the war. So, I named Thomas my successor. Prince Mark challenged him and, with the help of Jacob, killed him. Please tell Sam I'm sorry, but I was powerless to stop Mark. So, for four years, the war has gone on. But now that you are alive, you can marry the princess and stop this war," enlightened the King.

"But father, I'm already married," protested Prince Michael.

"And she is in Tor, a thousand leagues from here. This war must be stopped. Please, my son, end this war," pleaded the King.

The King started coughing, and his breathing became shallower and more labored. The doctor took Kevin and handed him back to Michael. The nurses attended to the King as he lay down to sleep. The doctor escorted Michael out into the hall. Michael held Kevin in his arms as the doctor explained that the King was dying and that it was only a matter of time. Emerson, one of the King's advisers, suggested that Michael be crowned immediately.

"Sire, I urge you; the coronation must take place immediately." Emerson urged him. "Give your father peace of mind."

"With his health so poor, I thought that you would have crowned my brother king."

"Sire, your father knew better than that. He prayed that you would return before he had to crown your brother...and you have."

"When?" asked Michael.

"This afternoon. The priest, clergy, and nobles were already assembled. We were to crown your brother this morning." Emerson explained.

"Where is Sam?" Michael asked as they walked the hall to the coronation room.

"Well, after killing everyone else in the house, not loyal to your father. He has taken control of your Army and Navy. He sent the Navy to deal with the French ships in three patrols. The 27th and 84th infantry divisions have been left behind for the castle's defense. The 42nd and 22nd divisions are in Gatlin Market. The 14th division and 18th are at Loren and Toad Lake in case the French get through." Emerson reported.

"He doesn't waste time, does he?" Michael was in awe at the speed with which Sam had replaced her murdered father. "Emerson, as soon as I have been crowned king, prepare for my wedding to Princess Dominique."

"Yes, sire." Emerson smiled brightly. "Welcome home, sire."

Chapter 29

Sam stood just behind Prince Michael on his left as he was crowned king. Her cunning and serious eyes scanned the crowd for any more people unhappy with the new king, potential betrayers to the crown. Once he had been crowned, he stood and turned to the audience.

"At the death of my father, I have been crowned King." King Michael declared. "Sam Bowman, stand before me and kneel."

Sam did so.

"Sam Bowman, you have guarded me all my life. I have never had a more loyal subject or better friend. As I take my place as king, you shall take your place as head of my Royal Guardsmen," professed King Michael.

"Thank you, Sire. I shall try my best to be the man my father was." Sam promised.

"My lords, my ladies, my people, hear me. My brother has committed many wrongs against you, and I intend to correct them." King Michael announced. Then he looked down at Sam and whispered into her ear. "Sam, I must speak to you alone."

The assembly rose, bowed to King Michael, and left. King Michael escorted Sam to a side chamber and locked the door.

"Sam, my father's dying wish was for me to end this war. I can do so without further bloodshed." King Michael informed her.

"You're going to marry her, aren't you?" Sam lowered her eyes.

"I won't if you declare yourself a girl and my wife." Michael insisted. "Then I won't be able to."

"I can't." Sam sighed, with tears in her eyes.

"And I can't let this war go on when I can stop it," Michael said solemnly. "Too many people have died already."

"Then let me stop it." Sam requested, with fire in her eyes. "Let me win this war for you."

"And how long will it take you, Sam?" Michael questioned her sternly. "My people, your father, and our friends have died for four years when they didn't need to. Will you let it go on for another four years?"

"Then you have no choice. You must marry her." Sam sadly said as she turned away from him. "Even if I told the truth, the war would continue because the King of France will only take an alliance as succor. Marry her and end the war."

"Sam, you know I love you and always will." King Michael whispered. He turned her chin towards him and looked deep into her eyes.

Sam allowed him one last gentle kiss before she pulled away. "Stop that, before someone sees us."

Two nights later, after all the burials, Sam and her guardsmen, still loyal to her father, celebrated the end of the war, the king's return home, and Sam's promotion. The bonfire burned brightly, chasing the darkness away from the cheerful group. Nearby, a deer and a boar roasted on an open spit while the beer flowed like a river.

Sam was glad to be home among the men she had known since childhood. She helped train them, she had fought beside them, and now she was their Captain. She had fulfilled her father's dream. And yet, as happy as she should have been, she couldn't help wondering about Michael.

What was to happen now? Sam looked towards the castle in doubt and dismay. Then, a big slap on the back returned her conscience to the present. Timothy was one of the last guardsmen she helped train before she left. He was strong, bold, and cheerful as he handed Sam another drink. Among the singing and telling of old times, they asked where Sam and the king had been all these years.

"Where the hell have you two been for so long?" Timothy asked, holding a mug of ale.

"Ask me where didn't we go. We were only supposed to go to the Swinton School. However, while we were in Gatlin's Market, Captain William of the Shark's Eye shanghaied us. We were to sail to France, but were shipwrecked in Spain..."

Sam told them all about their adventures, leaving out a lot of details and, of course, embellishing others. The full moon rose, ever steady on its journey across the sky. The men enjoyed the food, the beer, and Sam's tall tales. But the night had been far spent, and the bonfire had gone out. So, one by one, the guardsmen staggered home and into their waiting beds. Sam looked towards the palace. She wanted to see her old room so badly. Would things be as she left them? But try as she might, her feet wouldn't move. The butterflies in her stomach and the dread of meeting King Michael or Queen Dominique prevented her from going to the castle.

Instead, Sam turned and headed for the churchyard. Through the darkness of night, a full moon guided her steps.

As she entered the churchyard, a flood of memories swept into her mind. Echoes of sermons, laughing children, crying mothers, and the church bell ringing filled her ears. Shadows of angles and crosses seemed to follow Sam as she searched for her father's grave. Sam didn't stop until she had finally found his final resting place.

Sam tried unsuccessfully to control the tears that fell from her eyes as she looked upon a father whom she would see no more. Like chains, thick and strong, Sam's guilt and regret weighed her spirit down.

"Hello, Father, I'm sorry I was gone for so long. I'm sorry that I wasn't here to stop Prince Mark. I'm sorry that you never got to see your grandson...."

Time passed seconds...minutes...an hour. The breezes of a warm summer's night softly blew around her and kindly escorted leaves around the graveyard. A chorus of crickets and other night creatures sang while Sam's memories and regrets encouraged her tears.

Sam heard footfalls, but she ignored them as she wept. Gentle hands grasped her shoulders, gently pulling her off her knees and into his arms. Sam cried into his shoulders.

"I thought I might find you here," said Michael softly. "I'm truly sorry about your father."

"If I had known that I would never see him again, I swear I never would have left." Sam cried as her empty soul froze her entire body.

"It's all my fault, Sam. I never should have left. It was a foolish venture..." Michael tried to comfort her.

"No, you needed to leave. You would not be the man you are now if you had not." Sam wiped her tears away with her sleeve. Sam broke his embrace and turned towards her father's grave. "Father raised me to take his place someday, and now the day has come."

"Come on, Sam, let's go," urged Michael.

"Go where?" Sam laughed in despair.

"Home, back to your old room and your old life. It's what you wanted, right?" inquired Michael.

"I can't." Sam sighed heavily. "Why do you think I came here?"

"Sam, I know this must be difficult for you, but I had no other choice."

Sam stood with her back to Michael. "What a life... I'm a woman, raised to be a man, married to a man who has now taken another wife." Sam reasoned at the absurdity of it all.

"What did you tell them about Kevin's mother?"

"That she died in Damietta. Which is sort of true, you became Samuel again when we left there. Don't worry, whatever happens, Kevin is my heir." Michael stood beside her and ran his fingers through her hair.

"Please don't do that." Sam pushed his hand away.

Michael smiled, and then he frowned. "What will happen to us? I can't imagine what our lives are going to be like now. I've got two wives. One wife I can't touch, and the other won't let me touch her. I don't even think she likes me."

"So, tell me about Dominique," Sam requested. "How does Dominique feel about all this?"

"Most likely, she feels betrayed." He answered her.

"Betrayed?" scoffed Sam.

"Her father has married her off to a complete stranger in a strange land. She is far away from home and misses her friends and family. She feels alone." Michael explained, feeling sympathy for her. "In fact, I want you to become her protector and friend. Be to her what you were to me."

"You have got to be kidding." Sam protested, and she turned to face Michael.

"Please, Sam," urged Michael earnestly. "This is not her

fault, and now this is to be her home. I want her to feel comfortable here."

Michael waited for her answer as Sam wrestled with the idea. Sam paced up and down. Part of her said no, babysitting your husband's wife is a bad idea. You might come to like her. The other half of her said he was right. It's not her fault she's in the middle of your strange and twisted lives. You should do your best to make her feel welcome. Sam looked at Michael.

"Alright. Alright, just stop looking at me like that," relented Sam.

"Thank you, Sam." Michael smiled at her.

"But what do I do with her?" asked Sam. "What do I say?"

"Sam, just be her friend and lend her an ear."

"And a husband and a son," joked Sam.

"Sam, you are so weird." Michael smiled, and he hugged her.

Chapter 30

Sam arose with the sun. She stood out on the roof and looked out over the world. A horizon splashed with orange showed Sam the East. Sam took a deep breath of the morning air. A flood of memories from her youth filled her mind and soul. Then, the realization of a father no longer with her brought her forward in time. Sam looked down at the practice field. Two boys seemed to be having a disagreement. Sam watched them fight it out until the older chased the younger one inside. It was time for the Captain to begin training her guards.

Sam leaped off the roof and landed in the hay below. It felt good to be home. She brushed herself off and headed for the practice field. Sam felt hopeless at the sight of all the work before her. A war of four years had left the practice field abandoned and in decay. Sam shook her head, rolled up her sleeves, and began rebuilding the practice field. However, she decided to add a few new surprises from the East to her training field.

The sound of hammering woke Michael up. He yawned, stretched, and walked over to the window. The sun blinded him with its brilliance. Michael groaned. Looking below, he saw someone he didn't know working in the practice field. All of a sudden, it came to him. Sam. He smiled to himself. Then he remembered Dominique, and he frowned.

"What am I going to do with two wives?"

Later that afternoon, Sam assembled all the young men ages ten and up. She was disappointed as she looked them over. They were the scraggliest bunch of dogs you ever saw—unkempt, undisciplined, and unruly. Turning them into elite guardsmen would be an enormous challenge. However, Sam was in the mood for a challenge—anything to take her mind off Michael and her son Kevin.

"Alright, gentlemen, today is a new day. The war is over, and your fathers have earned their rest. You scruffy mutts have been chosen to become royal guardsmen. To protect the king and the royal family, even at the cost of your own lives, is our sworn duty and privilege. When I finish with you, you will be one of the world's best-trained and most disciplined guards. But for now, you must begin with discipline and obedience...."

Sam lectured sternly.

Sam began with stretching exercises, and then she made them run around the castle yard. Michael laughed as he watched Sam drill his new guards. She was so like her father that it was hard to believe she was Kevin's mother. Kevin. Michael went down the hall to check on his son. He opened the door to Kevin's room and found him playing with his toys on the floor. Kneeling, Michael took his son in his arms and hugged him.

"Do you like your new room?" Michael asked his son.

"Yes, daddy," said Kevin, paying more attention to his toys than his father.

"Did you know that this used to be my room when I was your age?" Michael asked. Kevin shook his head, no. "What do you say we greet your new mother?"

Kevin shook his head no. "I want to play with Sam."

"You can't play with Sam right now. He is busy training new guardsmen. But when you're old enough, then you can train with him. Would you like that?" said Michael.

Kevin shook his head yes.

"For now, let's go greet Dominique, and then we'll get breakfast. O..K?"

Kevin thought about it, then shook his head yes. "O.K., Daddy."

Michael and Kevin walked down the hall to Dominique's room. Michael knocked. A small French voice said Come in. Her voice was so unlike Sam's, which was strong and sure. It was more like his own voice when he was a boy. Michael felt sorry for Dominique as he and Kevin entered her room. Dominique was sitting on her bed and staring out the window at the beginning of a new day. When she looked over and saw the king, she bowed. Michael motioned for her to rise. Kevin jumped onto her bed. Dominique looked at him and walked over to the window. Kevin looked at her sadly, hurt at being ignored. Michael walked over to Dominique and placed a hand on her shoulder.

"Dominique..." He began.

Dominique moved away from Michael. "Please, don't touch me." She requested softly.

"Dominique, I know this must be difficult for you, but..." He continued speaking to her in French.

Dominique wasn't listening to him. She was watching his son Kevin. Kevin had made his way over to her bookshelf and began pulling books off the shelf. He sat on the floor with a pile of books around him and began to read them. He couldn't read the words, so he made up his own, but the fact that he liked books impressed her.

"...and if you ever need anyone to talk to..."

"What is his name?" She asked King Michael.

Michael looked at Kevin. "I'm sorry, this is my son Kevin."

"How old is he?"

"Quatre...Four years old."

"What happened to his mother?"

"She's... she's...dead." He lied as he cleared his throat.

"Je suis désolé." Dominique said softly. "I'm sorry."

"Kevin, be sure you put her books back. O.K.?" His father reminded him.

"O.K.," Kevin promised, running his fingers across pages of words he couldn't yet understand.

"He's very smart," commented Dominique.

Michael nodded a yes.

Dominique picked Kevin up and sat him in a chair. Kevin listened as Dominique read to him. Michael walked over to the window. Although he couldn't see the practice field from here, he could still hear Sam drilling them. Michael sighed as he kneaded his brow.

"Two wives?"

Time passed, as it always does, and the castle settled into a routine. Under King Michael's reign, the land and its people began to recover. Even young Prince Kevin grew fast and strong. However, there were still some things that he was afraid of.

Thunder roared, and lightning flashed. The wind howled as it blew the rain in through Kevin's window. Kevin pulled the covers over his head, trying to shut out the storm's noise. A colossal lightning crackle sent Kevin running to his Uncle Sam's room. Sam was sitting on her bed, playing a tune on her violin. She stopped when Kevin ran in and jumped on her bed.

"Afraid of the storm, young prince?" Sam asked, and she tucked him into her bed.

"I'm not afraid of the storm," declared Prince Kevin, but his voice was trembling. "But it's so loud."

"Well, let's see if I can't play louder than the storm." Sam offered.

Sam put away her violin, picked up her lute, and began to play. Sam played a Spanish love song for him. As Kevin listened, he no longer noticed the storm. His fear drifted away on strong chords and quiet melodies.

"Uncle Sam?" Prince Kevin yawned sleepily.

"Yes, young prince," answered Sam.

"Will you teach me to shoot and to fence?" He asked.

"I don't see why not. You're what, seven now? I was playing daggers and darts with my father when I was seven." Sam gave him a soft smile. "In the morning, I'll ask your father if it's OK."

"Will you teach me to play the lute like you?" He asked as he closed his eyes.

"Ask your father to teach you. It was he who taught me." Sam remembered days long gone into the past. "He also taught me that there is more to life than fighting, so don't be so eager to start leaning. OK."

"OK." Prince Kevin nodded.

Kevin lay listening to Sam play the lute, and soon, he was fast asleep. Sam carefully placed her lute in its case and closed it. Unlike her clothes and books, she took good care of her violin, lute, and weapons. She placed her lute in the corner and her violin on the bookshelf, then prepared for bed. Sam made her bed on the floor while Kevin slept in her bed.

In the morning, Dominique told Michael that Kevin was gone. Michael went to Sam's room with Dominique right behind him. Quietly, Michael opened the door to her room. Michael stifled a laugh as he saw Sam lying on the floor and Kevin asleep in her bed. Dominique stepped into the room and went to check on Kevin. Michael held out his arm and stopped her from stepping on Sam. Dominique looked down at her feet.

"Why is he sleeping on the floor?" questioned Queen Dominique, who found it a bizarre practice.

"Because he is a guardsman and the most loyal friend I've ever known. He used to do the same for me when I was a boy. That seems so long ago, now." King Michael mused.

Michael stood, watching Sam as she slept. A great emptiness welled up within him at the sight of her. It had been eight years since he had last held Sam in his arms. He missed her touch and her companionship. They were no longer friends. Now, they were just a King and his guardsman. A scream snapped his attention to the bed. Sam was holding a dagger to the queen's throat. Damn, she's fast. I didn't even see her move.

"Touch him and you die," threatened Sam.

"Sam! Stop!" Michael shouted as he rushed forward to stop Sam from killing Queen Dominique. "It's only

Dominique."

Sam let her go and looked at her. Then she fell to one knee and bowed her head. "Your majesty, I am so sorry," Sam apologized. "Please forgive me; I did not know it was you."

"You're quick," said Queen Dominique as she rubbed her sore and tender throat.

"As I told you," King Michael smiled, "he is one of the best guardsmen that has ever lived."

Chapter 31

Winter turned into spring, spring into summer, and summer into fall, and eleven years passed in a blink. For eleven years, Sam trained the royal guards. They were no longer dirty little boys but clean-shaven and well-mannered young men. She had created strong and loyal guardsmen by using mind and body techniques from the East. Sam beamed with pride as she watched them practice their sword skills. Her father would have been proud. These men obeyed without question and counted it a joy to give their lives for their King. Sam was so impressed with Timothy's loyalty and fighting skills that she named him her second in command.

Prince Kevin was now fifteen years old. He was a tall and strong young man. Sam had pounded him into a sleek, fast, and vigorous young tiger. King Michael ensured young Kevin's mind was as sharp as his sword skills. And though Prince Kevin was more than adept in his academic studies, he still favored the subjects he studied with Sam.

Cheers and shouts of encouragement from the King's

guardsmen urged two runners towards the finish line. Prince Kevin raced against Sam, running as fast as he could. Whenever he raced Sam, it seemed that no matter how fast he ran, he always saw Sam's back. However, today was different. Today, he saw Sam's face as he looked back. Kevin jumped for joy as he crossed the line first. He received a lot of pats of congratulations and a lot of adulation from the other guardsmen. Sam smiled as she caught her breath. Her son had finally beaten her.

"Congratulations, young prince." Sam conceded. "You finally beat me."

"Yeah, and it only took me fifteen years to do it." Prince Kevin laughed.

"Fifteen, that's right, you'll be fifteen within a week. God, how time flies." Sam smiled at him. "You can ride, fight, shoot, and outrun me...What do you need a guardsman for?"

"Come on, Uncle Sam." Prince Kevin beamed, full of pride that he had finally beaten Sam. "Who taught me everything I know?"

"I thought I did," interjected Queen Dominique as she gracefully walked towards them.

"Your majesty."

Sam and all the guardsmen bowed before Queen Dominique.

"Oh, Kevin, look at you," sighed Queen Dominique, completely disappointed by Prince Kevin's appearance. "You need to wash up before your lessons. Go on."

"Yes, mother," acknowledged Prince Kevin.

Kevin kissed Dominique's right cheek and hurried off to wash up. Queen Dominique faced Sam and motioned for her to rise.

"He greatly admires you, Sam," Dominique told her.

"And I admire him, Your Majesty," replied Sam warmly. "He is a strong young man with a sharp mind. He will make an excellent King someday."

The day turned into dusk, and Sam stretched her aching body as she returned to her room. Voices wafted up from the main floor, and Sam could hear Kevin and Michael laughing. She went to the stairs' railing and looked down into the main hall. Below, Michael and Dominique were playing a game of chess, and Kevin was telling them both about the day he had had with Sam.

A strange and twisted gnawing ate away at Sam as she

watched another woman be a wife and mother to her husband and son. Eleven years of memories flashed before her. King Michael and Queen Dominique were always in front, with Prince Kevin by their side. Sam followed them on their diplomatic functions, royal balls, and public audiences with his subjects. Sam was always in the background, watching over them. This she had done for Michael and his brother in the past; this is what she had been raised to do. So then, why did she feel so bad?

A singular memory of a patient lute teacher crossed her mind, bringing the memories of duets in a Vienna park at sunset. Memories of their walks, talks, and snowball fights flooded her soul. Longing and loneliness suddenly filled her with a disturbing sorrow.

I never used to feel like this. But this is what my life would have been like. The young prince, now King, married to a princess, and me guarding his family. It's not your fault that your life is this way.

Sam walked away and returned to her room. With aching bones and a tired body, sleep came easily, but peaceful dreams did not.

Late at night, well after sunset, Michael liked to write in his journal about the day's events. This journal, Michael had kept even before Kevin had been born. He had hoped to give it to Kevin someday to explain all the questions he had about his mother. However, since Kevin had no other desires except to be with his Uncle Sam, who was his mother, Michael saw no reason to give him the book. So, Michael kept it for himself as a family record, recording all of Kevin and Sam's achievements and his thoughts and desires.

It was such an evening when Queen Dominique came to see him.

"Michael, mon cher, we must decide on preparations for our son's birthday party," she said as she entered his room. He will be fifteen in two days, and…"

Michael quickly closed his book and turned to face his wife, hiding the book behind his back.

"…and what are you hiding?" She questioned with a smile.

"Nothing… It's just my journal. I had hoped to give it to Kevin someday." Michael answered.

"May I see it?" She asked.

"No! Ah, no. I don't like for anyone to read what I write. It's all very…personal." Michael said, trying his best to keep his book away from her.

Dominique tried to snatch it from Michael, but he was quicker. She pursued him and the book. It became a game between them, a game of keep away; only Michael was serious. He couldn't let her read that book. Queen Dominique chased Michael around his room, both laughing as they dodged one another. Memories of such games between him and Sam emerged from their long-dormant sleep.

Slightly distracted by these memories, Dominique finally tackled Michael on his bed. Michael threw the book under the bed and clutched Dominique in his arms to keep her from getting to it. Dominique stopped laughing long enough to look into Michael's eyes; they were bright and playful. Dominique could feel Michael's heart beating as their breathing became synchronized. A long-denied desire caused Michael to kiss Dominique. A kiss that Dominique did not refuse became a more passionate kiss between them.

Michael rolled over on her and softly kissed her neck and chest. Dominique took off Michael's shirt and caressed his back. She had never intended for this to happen. Dominique had no wish to be involved with a man whose only reason for marrying her was to stop a war. However, she had denied herself for eleven years, and feeling him so near her now...

"Oh, Sam," Michael whispered.

The name of Sam hit Dominique like ice water. She pushed Michael off her with great force.

"Who is Sam?!" She demanded as she stood up.

Michael rolled his eyes. "Oh no, here we go. What do I tell her, the truth? "Well, ah..." He began.

Dominique's eyes widened as she jumped to the only person she knew with that name.

"Not Sam, not your guardsman." She exclaimed in disgust.

"No! Well... It's not what you think," said Michael, desperately trying to think of what he could tell her.

After all, what could he say? It was with Sam, but not as she was thinking.

"No wonder you won't let me read your diary. You and Sam? My god, that is disgusting. You know, I always thought you two were a little too close. Just what do you do when you go on your evening walks? No, wait, on second thought, I don't want to know." Dominique concluded, her French accent growing heavier as she stormed out of the room.

"Dominique, it's not like that at all. Sam and I grew up together; we played chess by the lake, as we did when we were kids. We're just...best friends." Michael insisted as he followed after her.

"Well, actually, we're married. But I can't tell you that either. But maybe it's better this way. She thinks I'm queer and wants nothing to do with me. Nah".

"Dominique, wait, let me explain," pleaded Michael.

Michael followed Dominique. And Dominque tried her best to stay away from him. Minutes later, Prince Kevin came looking for his father.

"Father, Father?" He called out.

He scanned the room for his father, and his eyes fell upon his father's book. Kevin walked in and picked it up. The book was in good condition and had the words Michael's Journey in silver letters on the front. Kevin opened the book and read the inscription.

"To my son Kevin, in answer to your questions about your mother."

About Dominique? Kevin thought. Kevin took the book to his room and began to read it. A great grin spread across his face as he began to read. Sam is Samantha. I don't believe it. He laughed.

Sam sat out on the roof as she used to when she was younger. She enjoyed the full, gusting fall wind as it blew over her shoulders and through her hair. The darkness of the clouds in the evening sky warned her that a thunderstorm was coming. The wind grew colder as she watched the moon climb its way into the sky. Voices below drew her attention to the ground; she saw Dominique and Michael in the gardens. Whatever they were discussing, it was obvious that Dominique was upset.

Suddenly, a voice calling for Uncle Sam drew her attention inside. She climbed off the roof and jumped back inside through her room window. Prince Kevin stood waiting for her with a great smile spread across his face.

"Hello...mother." He greeted her.

Sam shook her head as she prepared for his questions. Then, she walked over to her bed, sat down, and motioned for him to join her.

"Did he tell you?" She asked.

"No, I read it in his journal." Prince Kevin took a seat beside her.

"Do you understand everything that's happened...and why? Do you have any questions?" She asked as she wondered how Prince Kevin had gotten hold of the book.

"Just three. Do you really have a griffin tattoo with a tail that..." He began to ask.

"Yes," interrupted Sam, slightly embarrassed, as she remembered Michael's fascination with it.

"Did you really kiss other women to prove you were a boy?" He asked, grinning from ear to ear.

Sam laughed. "Yes. Yes, I did. But that was so long ago now that it seems like a lifetime away."

Then Kevin's smile was replaced by a frown as he asked his third question.

"Why was becoming a guardsman more important to you than me?"

Sam's frown matched his. "Kevin, you are more important to me than anything. But I had to become Captain of the guardsmen to continue my father's tradition. It was a matter of great importance to my father. No matter what, I had to become Captain of the King's guardsmen. I promised him. Neither your father nor I knew there would be a war. I didn't know he would have to marry Her Majesty Queen Dominique to stop it. After that, how could we tell anyone the truth? In time, it just became easier to forget our relationship. But never believe that I would forget you or that you are unimportant to me. I would give my life for you." Sam explained sincerely.

"They told me that you were dead. I cried for a long time because I knew that Dominique was not my mother. Then I guess I grew used to her, because I forgot that she wasn't my real mother. At least now, I know why I've been so attached to you all my life." Kevin sighed, a smile creeping upon his face.

"You are not angry that I was never there for you?" asked Sam.

"Never there for me. Sam...mother, I can't remember a day in my life when you weren't with me. You always protected me; you took me riding and taught me to play the violin; you taught me almost everything I know," gushed Kevin.

"But I was never your mother." Sam sighed, regrettably.

"As my Uncle, in sword training, you mothered me enough," smiled Kevin. "Besides, I thought Dominique was my mother. Who needs two?"

"Speaking of which, what is up between them? I saw them arguing in the courtyard."

"Dominique thinks father is a catamite." Prince Kevin informed her.

"What?!" Sam laughed. "How did she...what makes her think that?"

"Well, from my understanding, she and father were making love, and he called your name."

"Oh, my god." Sam snickered, covering her mouth.

"And she doesn't know that you are a woman, so..." Prince Kevin laughed.

"So, she thinks he's gay." Sam held her sides with the pain of laughter. "Why wouldn't she believe that Sam is another woman?"

"Because father spends more time with you than with any woman in the palace. Right now, I think she would prefer if you were a woman," laughed Prince Kevin.

Thunder rumbled in the distance, and lightning flashed; Sam and Prince Kevin stopped laughing. The wind blew into Sam's room, causing her to shudder. Prince Kevin looked around his mother's room as she stood up to close the window. Her room was in no better condition than his. Several pairs of clothing lay across her bed. Books lay open and scattered on the table. Her chain mail and armor lay in a pile on the floor. Only her weapons lay neatly stacked on the weapons rack. I guess I do take after my mother in more ways than one. He stood up, took a dagger off the shelf, and stabbed playfully at the air.

"He still loves you, Sam. You should read what he writes

about you in his journal." Prince Kevin told her.

"Speaking of which, where is it?" inquired Sam with great seriousness. "Dominique mustn't ever get it."

"In my room on the bookshelf, hidden behind my schoolbooks," assured Prince Kevin.

"What if she cleans your room?"

"She never cleans my room. We have servants for that." Prince Kevin said with certainty.

"Hmm." Sam still didn't want to take any chances.

"Well, come on; let's see what culinary treats the cook has for us," urged Prince Kevin.

Sam and Kevin left her room. Kevin ran ahead towards the kitchen, and Sam headed downstairs towards the dining room. Sam passed Dominique on her way up. She was not in a good mood. Dominique gave Sam a wide berth with a disgusted sneer as they passed each other. Sam just smiled at her and bowed before her like she always did. Dominique just walked down the hall towards her room, but she didn't want to see anything that reminded her of Michael at this time. So, she went to her son's room with an invitation to join her for dinner.

"Kevin? Kevin?" Dominique called.

Hearing no reply, Dominique went in and looked around

his room. As usual, it was a mess. Books lay on his dresser and bed, clothes were all over the floor, his practice armor lay on his dresser, and his school papers were all around.

How can this child be so sloppy, yet his father is so meticulously clean? Dominique wondered.

Dominique began to tidy his room a little. She put his clothes in the laundry bag, his school papers on his dresser, his practice armor on its stand, and his books on his bookcase.

"I give him good books, and this is how he treats them."

While she neatly restacked his books, one book, hidden behind several others, caught her eye: Michael's Journey. Dominique took the book and flipped through the pages.

"To my son Kevin, in answer to your questions about your mother. Sam?!" exclaimed Queen Dominique, in total shock and surprise.

Anger welled up inside Dominique as she read Michael's book. Then Dominique left Kevin's room, taking the book with her.

Chapter 32

Sam, Kevin, and Michael sat in the great hall with eight of Michael's senior guardsmen. They enjoyed a full roaring fire as they ate dinner and drank ale. Prince Kevin reached out to pour himself a mug, but Sam forbade him.

"None for you yet, young Prince." Sam moved the ale jug far from him. "You're still too young."

"I am not. I've seen other boys younger than me drink." Prince Kevin protested.

"Sam, He'll be fifteen in two days. Besides, I was about his age when I had my first ale." King Michael reminded Sam.

"And you were always sick. Young prince, your father was nothing of the man you see before you now," teased Sam.

"Oh, stop 'mothering' me, uncle." Kevin gave her a knowing wink.

Sam threw back her head and laughed. "Alright, go ahead." She consented.

Sam passed him a glass and filled it half full. Kevin looked at his father and then around the table. The guardsmen only encouraged him with nodding heads. He lifted his glass and drained it dry. The guardsmen cheered.

"Well done, young prince," commented Sam. "How do you feel?"

"I feel...fine." He said, curious why he was being asked such a question.

"Definitely nothing like your father." Sam chuckled, and she looked at King Michael.

"Kevin, did you know that your Uncle Sam can outdrink anybody?" King Michael silently challenged Sam's last jest.

"Yes, he fills their glasses to the top but only half fills his. They get drunk faster, and he wins." Prince Kevin revealed.

"Squealer," taunted Sam.

"So that's how you do it," Timothy exclaimed, and he filled her glass to the top. "OK. You and me right now. First one to drain their glass wins twenty-five shillings and a week's vacation from practice."

"Deal." Sam accepted the challenge with a grin. "Sire, if you please."

"Begin." King Michael stated with an amused chuckle.

As Timothy and Sam rushed to drain their glasses, a great shout came from upstairs. A scream so angry and shrill that

Sam and Timothy choked on their ale and coughed for air as they dropped their glasses to the table.

"Sounds like Dominique is still angry with me." King Michael sighed.

"Sounds like her majesty has found out the truth." Sam feared.

All heads turned towards the stairs as another screech was heard about murdering someone. Dominique came down the stairs carrying Michael's sword.

"YOU!" Dominique glared at Michael as she approached the table. "You lying son of a..."

Michael stood up and faced Dominique. "Dominique! What's wrong? Put down the sword and we'll talk about it," offered Michael.

"You menteur!" She shouted. "You liar! You told me she was dead!"

Dominique swung at Michael. Michael ducked and ran. Dominique chased him around the table. As Michael passed by her, Sam stepped in front of Dominique and blocked her way.

"Out of my way!" Dominique shouted at her.

"I cannot allow you to harm his majesty." Sam stared her down.

Dominique slapped Sam across the face with the back of her left hand.

"Dominique!" scolded Michael, surprised by her actions.

Sam stroked her sore, wolf-scarred cheek but did not raise a hand against Dominique.

"Your Majesty, please, lay down your sword, and I will gladly explain everything," Sam said sternly.

"Don't talk to me, Great Griffin. You have lied all your life. So why should I believe what you say?" Queen Dominique charged.

Dominique pushed Sam out of the way and continued to chase Michael. Michael grabbed a sword from one of his stunned guardsmen and ran out the door into the rain. Timothy and the other guardsmen followed. Someone had to stop them.

"Sam, do something," Kevin begged his mother.

"I will, young prince, but I cannot lay hands upon the Queen." Sam reminded him.

"Sam, you are her equal. You are the granddaughter of a King. You can fight her for the throne and my father." Prince Kevin told her, hoping Sam would do something to stop this. "He did for you."

"They don't know that." She said, filled with fear about how all this would end.

"Maybe it's time that they did," stated Kevin flatly, and he left.

Sam sighed and followed Kevin as he ran out into the pouring rain. Thunder roared, and lightning ripped through the sky; Sam and Kevin watched Michael dodge or block each of Dominique's blows. Michael was extremely skillful with a sword; Sam had taught him to be so. However, Michael never pressed his attack. He only defended himself from her blows but gave none of his own. Sam squared her shoulders, walked over to them, and stood between them.

"Your majesties, please," Sam begged. The rain splattered her eyes and caused her to blink. "All this can be explained."

"HA!" growled Dominique.

With a sneer, Dominique thrust her sword at Michael. Sam grabbed the blade, preventing it from entering Michael's chest. Dominique yanked the sword back from Sam, the blade's edge slicing Sam's skin. Sam grimaced in pain as her hand began to bleed. The falling rain washed the blood to the ground as Sam took a cloth from her pocket and wrapped her hand. Dominique stood looking at Sam. The rain may have clouded her vision, but its coldness only intensified her hurt and angry heart.

"You're no woman, you are an abomination." Dominique accused, with her heavy French accent.

"Your majesty, I can explain," said Sam, calmly.

"Why should I believe you?!" Queen Dominique shouted. "Would you tell me the truth?!"

"I think you know the truth." Sam stared at Queen Dominique.

"I want to hear it from your own lips." Queen Dominique's eyes burned with hatred. "Swear to me that you will tell me the truth."

"I swear it," Sam vowed. "On my father's grave."

"You are a woman?" Queen Dominique questioned her.

"Yes," Sam answered. *"This is not how I wanted it to be."*

"You are married to Michael even now?" Queen Dominique charged her like a judge.

"Yes," Sam answered. *"I didn't want the truth to come out like this."*

"And you are Kevin's true mother?" Queen Dominique stood against her. Thunder roaring and rain falling.

"Yes," Sam confirmed. *"And that is the end of it. Now, it all comes crashing down."*

The guardsmen stared at her in disbelief. Could this be true? Of course, it was. She had sworn to tell the truth on her father's grave. None of them knew what to say. They could only stand and watch as the truth unfolded.

"And did you or did you not make love with Michael, on your own father's grave, during the witching hours?" Queen Dominique questions with intensified anger.

"No!" Sam was utterly shocked by the question.

"Liar!!" Dominique screamed and swung her sword at Sam.

Sam jumped out of Dominique's reach, her sword just missing Sam's throat. "What the hell did you write in that book anyway?" Sam asked Michael.

Dominique turned her attention back to Michael. "And you, how long have you been carrying on with this woman behind my back?! How could you marry me, knowing full well that you were wedded to her?!"

"I only married you to stop the war. We both know that was the only reason that I married you." Michael explained sadly. He hadn't wanted her to find out this way. After all, she had done nothing wrong. "And neither Sam nor I have 'carried on' since the day I married you." He professed. "I swear it. I'm sorry. This is not how I wanted you to find out."

"I do not believe you! For eleven years, you've been married to two women! Tell me the truth, Michael, do you still love her?!" Queen Dominique demanded.

Michael looked at Sam, who was dripping wet. Her hand was still bleeding as the rain fell, and her bright strawberry hair clung to her head, standing out against the dark, black night.

"Yes." King Michael confessed with a small smile.

"God, damn you!" Dominique screamed furiously.

Dominique lunged at Michael. Sam pushed him down and out of the way of her sword. Michael fell on his left shoulder and lost his sword in the mud and rain. Sam stepped in front of him and faced Dominique, unwavering and sorry. Timothy helped Michael up, and the guardsmen stood around him, protecting him from another attack.

"Your majesty, please give me the sword, and we'll talk," Sam said evenly.

Dominique looked Sam dead in the eyes. "As for you, there can only be one Queen of England."

Dominique thrust her sword at Sam, and Sam easily sidestepped the blow. Dominique turned and continued the attack, her anger growing with each missed swing.

Kevin stood in distress as he watched his mothers fight. *Why won't Sam defend herself? She could easily defeat Dominique.*

"Mother, stop this before you hurt someone!" Kevin cried out desperately.

"Don't you dare call me mother! She is your mother! But you knew that already, didn't you?" Dominique screamed, pointing the sword at him. "How long have you known?!"

"I only found out today." He said with a heavy heart.

"Did you ever plan to tell me?!" shouted Queen Dominique.

"No. Not really." Kevin felt slightly ashamed. "Everyone seemed happy with the arrangement. Sam carries on her family tradition. Father is king and has an heir. The war is over, and you seemed happy with father. What good reason would there have been to tell you?"

"Damn you, Bloody Englishmen!" Queen Dominique ranted.

Lightning flashed as Dominique looked at Sam with blood-red eyes. Dominique cried in wrath and anger as she swung her sword at Sam. Hatred, betrayal, and loneliness rushed through Dominique like a hurricane.

She lost all she was when she married and moved to England. Her whole marriage was a farce and a lie. She had nothing left to give or to lose; to kill Sam would be her only reward. Dominique raised her sword for another blow. She meant to kill Sam, and Sam knew it, but she still refused to raise a hand against her. *Never raise your hand against the royal family, even if it means your death.* A rule so ingrained in her that Sam didn't even think to draw her sword.

"Your majesty." Timothy looked at King Michael. "Is Sam really a woman?"

"Yes. Thomas' family tradition demanded that the first-born son replace him as Captain of my guards. Unfortunately, Sam was born a girl, and her mother died before a son was ever born. Thomas made a son of his daughter, and she has fulfilled her family tradition..." King Michael explained, wishing all of this had never happened or at least had gone better.

"I cannot believe Sam is a woman. I have never found a better fighter or a friend, " Timothy praised.

"Sam was raised as a boy all her life. She truly believes she is a man." King Michael said

"If she is Kevin's mother, surely she can no longer believe that?" scoffed Timothy.

"Sam's greatest strength is that she has always been able to quickly adjust to the changes in her life." King Michael told him.

A great flash of lightning drew Michael's attention back to the duel. Sam was still dodging Dominique's blade. Kevin, still watching and filled with fear, finally decided to put a stop to this. He grabbed Dominique from behind and tried to make her drop her sword. While they struggled, Dominique used her free hand to punch Kevin in his groin. Kevin let her go. Dominique thrust her sword at Kevin's back. Sam pushed Kevin out of the way and took the blow. Lightning flashed as Dominique's sword entered Sam's body. Cold, firm steel against hot, soft flesh, Sam shuddered as she remembered a long-forgotten memory of Lien. Sam laughed as Dominique pulled her blade from her body.

"Oh...not again." Sam laughed as she fell to the ground, clutching her stomach.

"Mother, No!" Kevin cried.

"Sam! Dominique, this has gone too far. Stop it, now!!" Michael shouted.

"Not yet, it hasn't. Not until she is dead," hissed Queen Dominique.

Dominique raised her sword above her head for the final blow. Sam lay helpless before her, clutching her bleeding abdomen. Tears fell from her eyes as the thought of never seeing Kevin grow up passed before her eyes. Blood mixed with rain as both fell to the ground. The sky flashed. Sam looked into heaven as the rain fell into her eyes.

"Sorry, Dad."

"SAM!!" Kevin screamed.

"Young Prince, no." Timothy grabbed Kevin by the arm.

Timothy and another guardsman held Kevin, preventing him from going to Sam's side. They were not about to let Kevin throw away the life that his mother had given hers to protect.

Suddenly, a lightning bolt lashed out from heaven. Attracted by the steel of the sword, lightning surged through Dominique, levitating her off the ground. Dominique screamed in agony as every fiber of her being burned with fire from within. Then, as quickly as it had started, it had ended. Dominique's lifeless body fell to the ground. The stench of burning flesh invaded the night air. Steam arose from her body as the cool rain dropped upon her.

Kevin and the guardsmen stood in speechless awe as they looked upon her. Michael held Sam in his arms and tried to stop the bleeding. Curious about what had just happened, Kevin moved closer to Dominique's fried body.

"Kevin, don't touch her," ordered Michael. Kevin looked at his father in surprise. "Take a blanket and cover her body. But don't touch her until the rain stops. I don't want anyone else to get struck by lightning, so keep your swords sheathed. After the storm, we will bury her with my father in the family tomb, unless her family requests her body. Ben, go get a doctor." King Michael commanded.

"Yes, sire." They acknowledged, and they ran off to obey him.

"George, send a message to her family, tell them she is dead. Tell them she died by a lightning strike, but do NOT tell them about Sam. Understood." King Michael tasked him.

"Yes, sire." He acknowledged with a bow.

Kevin went to his mother's side and knelt beside her. Tears and rain ran down his face and onto Sam's shirt.

"You saved my life," Kevin whispered in pain and sadness.

"Such is my duty...young prince." Sam gasped softly.

"Please, mother, call me Kevin." He insisted.

"Sam has always lived by the rules. That's why she would not defend herself against Dominique. To raise your hand against the royal family, even in defense of your own life, is unforgivable." King Michael explained to his son.

"That's stupid," growled Prince Kevin.

"That's the law," said King Michael.

"Then I'll change it."

Sam coughed, and blood spilled from her lips. "Little Kevin...So like... your father." She whispered.

"Please don't die, Sam." Prince Kevin begged.

Sam smiled as she looked at her son's face. Then she turned to face Michael, tears flowing from the corners of her eyes.

"I love you."

Her lips formed the words, but no sound came with them. Michael ever so gently lifted Sam into his arms.

"I love you, too, Sam." He whispered.

Kevin followed behind his father as Michael carried Sam's body inside.

Chapter 33

Church bells rang throughout the kingdom, announcing the birth of a baby girl to the king and his new queen. It had been more than two years since Queen Dominique's death, and Sam was no longer the Captain of the guards. Timothy, son of Alexander, had been named her successor.

Michael walked into his wife's room as the doctor left. A great smile spread across his face as he saw Samantha holding his baby girl. He kissed Sam's forehead as he lifted his new daughter into his arms. He laughed as he pulled back the blankets, revealing a little girl with a few strands of red hair.

"A redhead, like her mother." King Michael proudly commented. "What will you name her?"

"Tracy, it's Gaelic for the strong defender. And she will become Captain of the King's Guards, like her mother."

About the Author

Tracy Carol Taylor is a freelance writer, poet, children's e-book author, and young adult novelist. She holds a degree in English and Liberal Arts from Northern Virginia Community College and a degree in English from George Mason University.

Tracy Taylor served in the United States Army for four years. She currently lives in Arlington, VA, with her family. She enjoys reading, writing, and watching movies.

Other novels include:

Adventure Books:

The Journey

Children's Books:

Small Fry Tales

The Brave Little Bottle

Christian Books:

60 Christian Traits

Basics of Christianity

Parody of Parables.

Dental Books:

Toothache at Big Mouth Bend

Cavities of the Caribbean

Tale of Two Teeth

Poetry Book:

Wondering Ardor

The Journey